A case of mis

Annie opened the door and was stunned to find herself staring into the brilliant green gaze of Lucky Logan, bail jumper at large. "You owe me a pair of handcuffs, Lucky. But don't worry, I've got a spare. Step in while I get them."

"I'm not Lucky, Ms. Ryan." The man before her wore a well-cut gray suit. The sleeves of his shirt protruded an exact quarter-inch from the sleeves of his jacket. He didn't have a hair out of place.

Annie's puzzlement grew. Apart from the clothes, he looked just like Lucky. His voice was the same as she remembered. He could sell anything to any woman with those dark-honey tones.

Whatever con game he was playing, she wasn't buying. "Yeah, that would be your evil twin brother, right?" she retorted.

Moving quickly, she grabbed her spare handcuffs and locked one around his tanned wrist. The other she attached to the drainpipe.

Logan sighed, not struggling. "Actually, he is," he said wearily. From a pocket, he pulled out a flat wallet and flipped it open. "Matthew Logan, Federal Bureau of Investigation."

Dear Harlequin Intrigue Reader,

Harlequin Intrigue has just celebrated its fifteenth anniversary and we're proud to continue to bring to you thrilling romantic suspense that leaves you breathless!—plus your favorite ongoing miniseries—into the new millennium.

To start the New Year off right, Kelsey Roberts launches into the second installment of her new series, THE LANDRY BROTHERS, with *Landry's Law* (#545). Over the next year you can expect more exciting Landry stories. Don't miss any!

We're also continuing our amnesia promotion A MEMORY AWAY... This month a woman wakes up with no memory and morning sickness, but she can't remember who's the father in *The Baby Secret* (#546) by Joyce Sullivan. And if you love a good twins story you must not miss *Twice Tempted* (#547) by Harper Allen. Finally, Harlequin Intrigue newcomer C.J. Carmichael explores the life of a devoted man of the law and the woman for whom he'll break all the rules in *Same Place, Same Time* (#548).

It's romance. It's suspense. It's Harlequin Intrigue.

Enjoy, and Happy New Year!

Sincerely,

Denise O'Sullivan
Associate Senior Editor
Harlequin Intrigue

P.S. Starting next month, Harlequin Intrigue has a new look! Watch for us at your favorite retail outlet.

Twice Tempted
Harper Allen

HARLEQUIN®

TORONTO • NEW YORK • LONDON
AMSTERDAM • PARIS • SYDNEY • HAMBURG
STOCKHOLM • ATHENS • TOKYO • MILAN • MADRID
PRAGUE • WARSAW • BUDAPEST • AUCKLAND

For Wayne…
Moi non plus, babe.

Author's Note

The bridge in *Twice Tempted* is loosely based on the
John Weeks Footbridge in Cambridge, but poetic license
has been taken with its location and many of its details.

ISBN 0-373-22547-4

TWICE TEMPTED

Copyright © 1999 by Sandra Hill

This edition published by arrangement with Harlequin Books S.A.

Visit us at www.romance.net

Printed in U.S.A.

East Boston

Boston Inner Harbor

South Boston

North End

BOSTON

Beacon Hill

Boston Common

South Bay

Longfellow Bridge

Back Bay

Cambridge

Charles River Basin

Harvard Bridge

CAST OF CHARACTERS

Annie Ryan — She always gets her man — but what happens when there are two of them?

Matthew Logan — His twin's antics often get him in trouble — but this time they lead him to a lovely woman....

Lucky Logan — A handsome charmer, and thief at large.

Dave Cartwright — Matt's partner is used to unusual things happening when Matt is mistaken for his brother.

Dmitri Kortachoff — He suspects Annie's working for the wrong side.

Bridie — Annie's beautiful older sister likes to offer advice, wanted or not.

Mary Margaret — Annie's niece is an innocent pawn in a dangerous game.

Pat Ryan — Annie's father is proud of her record — but wouldn't mind her taking a safer profession.

Chapter One

Annie didn't think she could stand it if she let him get away. She'd never wanted any man as badly as she wanted Lucky Logan tonight.

His stride was deceptively loose-jointed and lazy, but those long legs, in worn and faded blue jeans that molded themselves to every muscle, set a pace that she was beginning to find exhausting. She'd been following him at a discreet distance for a couple of hours now, and although she worked out every day, at five foot three she had to take two steps for every one of his. Since she couldn't let him catch sight of her until the right moment, she'd been forced to keep dodging behind other passers-by or stopping hastily in front of store windows, pretending to study displays of clothing she had no interest in buying, then hurrying to get him in view again. Once or twice she'd thought, with a heart-stopping fear, that she'd lost him.

She wasn't the only woman watching him with more than a passing interest, she noted with a possessive flash of irritation. Even as the thought crossed her mind, a jogger in thigh-hugging bicycle shorts and a T-shirt with the word Harvard stretched tightly across her chest tossed her auburn ponytail and veered slightly in Lucky's direction to give him a better look.

He's mine, college girl, Annie thought aggressively. *So just wheel that aerobicized little tush around and back off.* The redhead glanced flirtatiously at Lucky and then passed him, heading towards Annie. Even before he turned to watch her jog lightly away, Annie had dropped to one knee and was pretending to tie a shoelace, the bill of her Red Sox ball cap hiding her flushed face.

That had been close—too close. Whether he'd consciously noted her appearance or not, he might have caught a glimpse of her out of the corner of his eye, she thought in chagrin. Of course, he'd been focusing his attention on a pair of tanned legs in spandex, not on the shrimpy blonde in the ball cap and scuffed sneakers hovering in the background of his view, but even so, she was letting her personal feelings jeopardize the task she'd set herself for tonight. Sure, she wanted to introduce herself to Lucky Logan—but at the right psychological moment, and on her terms. For the love of Mike, Annie told herself disgustedly, she didn't want to scare the man off before she'd had a chance to talk to him!

She chanced a quick look upwards through her lashes and saw that he'd set off along the jogging path once more, his hands stuck in his pockets and his head turned to watch the last of the scullers on the river, their oars dipping in and out with military precision as the setting sun turned the placid surface of the water to fire. Straightening up, she dusted off the knees of her jeans and hurried after him, this time taking the precaution of keeping a little farther back. Lucky was moving more slowly now anyway, like a man with no worries on his mind and no particular place to go.

Of course, he couldn't know he had an unbreakable date with *her* this evening.

He really was a devastatingly attractive man, she thought in appreciation. She'd seen him mostly from a rear view ever since she'd started following him, but even that hadn't been a hardship. As her sister Bridie would have said, the man had buns to die for. His shoulders, straining the seams of a faded navy sweatshirt, looked like they belonged on a linebacker, and below the raggedly cut-off arms of the sweatshirt he had the biceps of a jock. He fit right in with the joggers and the in-line skaters who were speeding along the path, but there was still something that set him apart. The redhead hadn't been the only woman to spare him a prolonged glance.

Earlier, Annie had been pretending to study a rack of postcards outside a souvenir store and she'd watched him approach. Half-hidden behind the display and jostled by tourists trying to decide whether to choose a view depicting the Boston skyline or a card showing a statue of Paul Revere, she'd had the chance to study Lucky's features as he'd walked by. Lost in thought, he'd had his brilliant green eyes narrowed against the sunlight, half-veiled by his lashes. Lashes a model would kill for, she'd thought, fascinated. On Logan, they only served to emphasize the hard masculine planes of his face, the almost sensually chiseled cut of his mouth. He'd been yanked from his reverie by a toddler running into his knees, and while the child's mother apologized, Annie had watched in fascination as that mouth relaxed into a grin, perfect teeth flashing white against the tan of his face. He'd raked a thick strand of midnight-black hair out of his eyes and had bent down to lift the startled toddler back into her mother's arms, seemingly oblivious to the fact that the little girl's fingers had been sticky with chocolate and had left starfish-shaped imprints on the front of his sweatshirt.

Gorgeous. Good with children. The man was almost perfect. She gave a deep unconscious sigh. She didn't meet too many like him in her line of work. Well, she'd be getting to know Lucky a whole lot better before the night was over, she told herself with a surge of satisfaction. From the first moment she properly introduced herself to the man, Annie guessed, she was going to be the most important female in Lucky Logan's life.

It looked as though that moment had almost arrived.

In the last half hour, the joggers and strollers had thinned out, but though she'd lost the cover of the crowd she felt less exposed now than she'd been earlier. Dusk was falling quickly, and already a faint mist was rising from the river beside her. Lucky became a broad-shouldered shadow up ahead, and even when the ornate park lamps came on, piercing the growing dusk with hazy disks of yellow, she still had to concentrate to keep him in sight. But that was good, she thought, speeding up a little. That meant that he wouldn't be alerted to her presence ahead of time.

A chill rippled through her that had nothing to do with the dampness rising from the Charles River or the growing coolness of the late-spring evening. *How would he react?* Her glance darted from the deserted park on one side of her to the water, flowing dark and silent, on the other. If anything went wrong, she was on her own. She chewed nervously at the underside of her lip. She couldn't count on anyone or anything getting her out of a bad situation if Lucky decided he didn't want to go along with her plans. All she could count on was herself.

That was enough, she thought with grim determination. She wanted Lucky Logan. She was going to get Lucky Logan. Once she put her proposition to the man, he'd have no choice but to go along with her, no matter what his private feelings on the matter might be. She could be very convincing when she had to be, Annie reflected, a wicked half-smile lifting the corners of her mouth. No man yet had walked away from her when she'd poured on that irresistible persuasion.

And although he didn't realize it yet, Lucky was already cooperating with her.

In the daytime, the massive stone bridge across this narrower stretch of the river was a charming anachronism, a graceful half-moon curve from one bank to the other, rising at its highest about fifty feet above the Charles River. But its fairy-tale appearance couldn't hide the fact that the river below picked up strength as it flowed under the stone arch. Even experienced scullers found this part of the river a challenge. Annie'd brought her niece, Mary Margaret, here in the past and together they'd watched the rowing teams straining their muscles to negotiate the treacherous current.

And although the bridge was small compared to some of the others that criss-crossed the river, such as the Longfellow or the Charleston, it still seemed dizzyingly high when you were standing in the middle of it looking down. She couldn't have asked for a better place to confront Lucky and limit his chances of running out on her if she'd chosen the location herself.

Fortunately for her he'd walked into the trap of his own free will.

Keeping to the shadows wasn't hard. It was almost fully dark now. Still, she moved with the caution of a thief, careful not to make the slightest noise that would attract the attention of the man ahead of her. Following him onto the bridge, she halted in mid-step as he slowed near the crest of the span and looked casually around.

Barely daring to breathe, Annie held the uncomfortable position for what seemed like an eternity. Her weight balanced on one leg while the other froze in the stride she hadn't completed as she wondered frantically whether he'd heard her.

Apparently not, she told herself in relief as he turned to lean on the stone balustrade and look out over the water. She allowed herself to start walking again, but her heart was still racing and she felt an almost uncontrollable impulse to bend down and massage her thigh muscle. She resisted the impulse and tried to ignore the cramping twinge in her leg as she crept silently closer to him.

It was nearly time. One wrong move now could wreck everything she'd been working for. Her plan was to get a little nearer to where he was standing, lost in thought, under the dim gleam of one of the lights on the bridge. At the critical moment she would step out of the dark and—

Lucky lifted his gaze from the river, his whole attitude changing from studied casualness to a tense alertness, like a wolf scenting danger long before it appeared. Annie's breath caught in the back of her throat. But this time the man she was watching so intently turned his attention to the far side of the bridge, as if he'd heard something or seen a movement coming from that direction. Slowly he pivoted until his body was facing away from Annie. His arms hung loosely at his sides. It was an oddly open stance, as if he was trying to appear as non-threatening as possible.

And it was enough to convince Annie. The man was vulnerable. The situation was perfect. The time was…*now*. Stepping quickly from the shadows, she brought both arms up in front of her, elbows locked and the heels of her hands pressed together in a steadying grip.

"Freeze, scumbag!"

It was a pickup line that never failed to work…especially when she was aiming her Glock 19 semi-automatic at her quarry. Even as Lucky Logan spun around in shock at the sound, Annie lined up her sights on his torso.

"I said *freeze!*" The damp air had gotten into her lungs and her voice broke on the shouted command, she heard with a spurt of annoyance. Damn! She needed all the authority she could muster at a time like this. Psychology was everything at the moment of confrontation, and since she didn't have the bulk and the height to impress the skips, she tried to rely on her voice. She cleared her throat impatiently and advanced.

"Keep your hands away from your body, Lucky. Turn and assume the position against the bridge."

"What the—" He darted a quick look over his shoulder as if to gauge his chances of escape, but then focused his attention on Annie. "Who the hell *are* you, lady? What's this all about?"

"It's a retrieval." Never taking her eyes off him, she slid one hand around the back of her belt and felt for the pair of cuffs hidden under her windbreaker. "I'm Bail Enforcement Agent Annie Ryan, and I'm here to take you in."

She was close enough to him now to see the interplay of emotions on his features—surprise, disbelief, and then a dawning realization that what she was saying was true. But what she really needed to see in a skip's eyes was acceptance of the situation. That meant they were ready to start cooperating.

Lucky wasn't exhibiting that at all. It wasn't a good sign.

"A bounty hunter?" he exploded incredulously. "A damned *bounty* hunter?" He glanced once more over his shoulder and then took a step towards her. "Look, you've got no idea what you're screwing up here—"

"Stop right there, Logan!" Annie stopped fumbling for the cuffs and her hand flew back to the butt of her gun, steadying her aim. "No stupid moves or someone gets hurt—and it's not going to be me. You're probably thinking you've got a real good chance to take someone my size.

That could be the biggest mistake you make in your whole life.''

Under the careless strand of blue-black hair that fell across his forehead, his eyes narrowed. The lights reflecting on the river threw back a shimmering glitter into his pupils, and for a long, tense moment she thought that she was going to have to use her weapon. She didn't want to, but sometimes you just didn't have a choice, she thought warily. She wasn't about to let her scruples get in the way of surviving another working day and going home tonight to the family she loved.

Even as her finger got ready to tighten on the trigger, she saw the look she'd been hoping for enter Lucky's eyes, and some of the tenseness drained out of her.

"You're telling me I missed a damned court date?" One corner of that well-cut mouth lifted wryly, and with a shrug he turned wearily towards the stone railing of the bridge. "Don't you ever cut a guy some slack?"

"Cutting slack isn't in my job description. You were due to appear before Judge Deakin today, and when you didn't show, the rest was inevitable." Keeping a few cautious yards between them, Annie once more reached for her cuffs. "It's nothing personal, Lucky."

That wasn't strictly true, but by this time Logan had his back to her, bracing himself against the railings. He couldn't see the quick color that came to her cheeks as she let the lie slip out. *Face it, Ryan, you were interested in the man before you even laid eyes on him,* Annie chided herself as she unclipped the pair of handcuffs from her belt. The steel bracelets were cold and slightly damp from the chill of the fog that rose around them. *One of the last romantic criminals—a world away from the perps you usually hunt down. No wonder you asked Lew to assign Logan to you.*

An international jewel thief, wanted in half the capitals of Europe and more than a few states right here in the good old U.S. of A., Lucky Logan was a legend, and a colorful one. It didn't hurt that the man was heart-stoppingly good-looking, either. But at that, she reined in her thoughts decisively. Intriguing and attractive as he undoubtedly was, Logan was still a skip and her paycheck was riding on bringing him in. She couldn't afford to let herself think of him any other way.

"Keep your left hand on the railing and put the other one behind your back, Lucky," she instructed him. That had been one of the details she'd absorbed earlier today while she'd been tailing him—the man was right-handed, so that was the first wrist to be cuffed according to procedure, even though the inch-thick file on Liam "Lucky" Logan had contained no mention of violence. No, he wasn't going to be a problem at all. Except for that one moment when she'd first confronted him, he hadn't given her any reason to think he might not comply with all her instructions and go along with her peaceably.

His reaction was almost a let-down. It wasn't that she'd hoped for a fight, but she'd expected *something* more from the fabled Lucky Logan. Some last-ditch maneuver, a totally unexpected and daring dash for freedom. After all, the man had his reputation to live up to, didn't he?

A reputation that was probably as unearned as the rest of his possessions, she told herself pragmatically. She of all people should know better than to invest a perp with some kind of romantic aura. It was better this way for both of them. Logan wasn't a fool. He'd have the best lawyer money could buy in court for him tomorrow, and by evening the odds were he'd be out again on bail—although not with the bonding company she worked for. Lew Jacobs was a great believer in "once burned, twice shy."

Of course, even Jacob's Bail Bonds had been taken in by the man standing in front of her.

"A river, a bridge, the moon..." Lucky's words were pensive, but there was a smile underlying them. "And a blonde beside me."

He'd turned his head to look at her, and the smoky green of his eyes picked up the reflections from the water again. "It's crazy, isn't it? A romantic setting like this, and you're holding a gun on me."

His voice was hypnotically low, so low that Annie found herself straining to hear him. She almost leaned forward to catch his words, until she realized that was exactly what he wanted her to do. She drew back abruptly.

She'd underestimated him.

Logan wasn't resigned to being brought in—he was about as resigned to capture as the wolf he'd reminded her of a few minutes ago, facing a dog-catcher. He'd just been lulling her suspicions while he considered his options.

But his options were nil, and she intended to see they stayed that way.

"You're not my first, Logan," she said tensely. "I've seen all the tricks and heard all the lines. Don't even *think* of it."

For the first time the man in front of her looked at her as if he were really seeing her.

What he saw wasn't too prepossessing, she knew. She'd borrowed a T-shirt from Mary Margaret that morning, since she'd found out at the last minute that all of hers were in the wash, and under the dark blue, partially unzipped windbreaker was a faded picture of a leprechaun wearing a green hat and holding a shamrock, with the words Kiss me, I'm Irish on it. The rest of her wasn't exactly a sight to inspire fear either. From beneath the Red Sox cap, wind-tangled blond strands curved against her temples and the nape of her neck in what her sister, Bridie, resignedly called her Tom Sawyer haircut. Instead of a steely and threatening gaze, her gamine look was emphasized by wide-set, violet eyes.

Her appearance was definitely a professional liability at a time like this, but on the other hand, when she was tracking down a skip, no one ever suspected her of being an agent. She'd brought in perps that none of Lew's other employees had even been able to get close to.

She couldn't get a date, Annie thought wryly—all the eligible men in the neighborhood where she'd grown up and still lived looked at her and saw only the pint-sized tomboy with scraped knees and a killer pitch that they'd played sandlot ball with. But she was hell on rounding up any male with a rap sheet.

Like Lucky Logan. The slight smile on his face had been replaced by irritation. "Look, any other time I'd trot along with you to the authorities and give myself up, but not tonight. Prior engagement," he said through gritted teeth.

The man was everything they said he was, she thought with reluctant admiration. "Right. Dinner with the Kennedys? Tickets for the Boston Pops? Or maybe a reunion with your good buddies down at the 5th Precinct? Guess which one I'm betting on, Lucky? Come on, you know you'll be able to resume your social obligations by tomorrow night—but right now you're under arrest."

"You're like a miniature bulldog." He shook his head slowly, those smoky green eyes locked on hers as if he was trying to read her mind. "There's no way I'm going to talk you out of this, is there?"

"No way at all," Annie agreed smoothly, forcing herself to ignore the "miniature bulldog" comparison. She held out the cuffs while still covering him with the Glock, and jerked her head at the bridge parapet. "Let's get this over with."

"Yeah, I guess I don't have a choice," he said, so glumly that she actually found herself feeling a little sorry for the man. He turned once more towards the railing and stared disconsolately down at the black water glinting far below, and sighed heavily. "Hell of a way to end an evening, though."

He knew how to push all the right buttons, she thought in annoyance. All she was doing was her job, for heaven's sake, but somehow she was beginning to feel like the bad guy here. If he hated being behind bars so much, why didn't he go out and find an honest career, instead of trying to blame her for taking him in? She took a step towards him. *Cuff him, hand him over to the boys in blue and collect the receipt for him, Ryan,* she told herself briskly. *Then go home and put those green eyes and that roguish half smile right out of your mind, girl.* The man was dangerous, no matter what the file on him said.

It happened in an instant.

So swiftly that he seemed to become a blur of movement, Lucky Logan vaulted lightly to the top of the stone balustrade. For a split second his silhouette was poised there against the moon as she instinctively leapt forward to stop him. And then, just as her frantically reaching fingers brushed against the denim of his jeans—

He stepped off the bridge into the void.

"*Logan, no!*" The scream tore at her vocal cords, but the gathering fog muffled her words as effectively as if she'd shouted them into cotton batting. As she rushed to the parapet and looked over in numbed shock, she was just in time to see a dark shape plunge cleanly through the swift-moving current below.

The man was certifiable!

Why? Why had he done it, why had he taken such a desperate, crazy chance? Straining her vision against the mist and the night, waiting fearfully to see if he'd made it, the unanswerable questions raced through her mind.

Whether he was an expert swimmer or not, he'd had no idea what lay directly below the bridge, or how far out the pilings extended underwater. Even now he could be dead or unconscious. With fingers that felt suddenly numb and clumsy, Annie jammed her gun back into her shoulder holster and shoved the handcuffs into the pocket of her windbreaker, never taking her rigidly fixed gaze from the unbroken blackness of the water far below.

He'd had no reason to jump—no reason to take his life into his hands in such a last-ditch bid for freedom. He'd known as well as she had that re-booking him was just a formality, that with the legal hired guns he could afford he'd be out again within twenty-four hours. He wasn't a murderer or a rapist—and even they were in and out of the system with alarming rapidity.

But Lucky was a thief, and not just an ordinary break-and-enter hack. His modus operandi was well known, his targets never anything less than the cream of the world's most precious jewels. There would have been no problem with granting him bail once more, on the unspoken understanding that he'd be pulled in immediately if there were a major jewel theft committed in the city. On top of that, he'd already stolen the only gem in Boston that would interest him.

That was why he'd been in jail in the first place—because of the Rubicon sapphire.

He wasn't going to make it, she thought desperately. Her eyes were blurred with tears from the chill wind that was coming off the river, and she impatiently scrubbed the back of her hand against them. Lucky had been underwater for over a minute now, and even if he'd let himself be carried along by the current, she would have seen him break the surface of the water farther on.

He'd thrown his life away for a damned *jewel*—a jewel that by all accounts he'd only had in his possession for a few hours. She felt a spark of helpless anger at the futility and waste of it all.

According to the police report, lifting the fabulous Rubicon sapphire had involved delicate manipulation of an infra-red alarm system, a nerve-wracking encounter with the small army of burly guards responsible for the security of the priceless Imperial Russian treasures on exhibit at the Danninger Museum, and finally a death-defying scramble across treacherous tiled roofs in the dark.

But with his usual nerve and skill, Lucky Logan had pulled off the caper of a lifetime—almost.

An hour after the heist, he'd left his luxurious tenth-floor hotel suite with every intention of catching the next flight out of the country. He'd flashed his charming smile at the only other occupant in the elevator, a *very* pregnant woman, and pushed the button for the lobby.

At which point his fabled luck, at long last, had run out. The elevator had jammed between floors and the woman had gone into hysterics and then labor. While workmen tried to get the elevator operational again and a television news crew set up cameras in the lobby, Lucky had helped bring a seven-pound two-ounce baby girl safely into the world.

He was a hero for about two minutes after the elevator doors finally opened, but even as a reporter from News at Eleven was asking him how it felt to witness the miracle of birth first-hand, a sharp-eyed cop was checking the description of the Rubicon thief with Lucky's features and running his name through police computers. The news clip had ended with him being Mirandized and led away in cuffs, even though the police apparently hadn't found the Rubicon on his person.

Bail had been high, but an anonymous friend had put up ten percent and Annie's boss had covered the rest. No one had thought the man would run.

They'd read him all wrong, Annie thought with a sinking heart as she stared at the black glitter of the river. His file had been filled with enough examples of the man's daring escapades to demonstrate that with Lucky Logan, you had to expect the unexpected.

All she knew of him had been gleaned from a handful of newspaper clippings and police reports, and from their brief confrontation a few minutes ago. However quixotic and romantic, he'd been a thief and a criminal and the two of them would always have been on opposite sides of the law. He wasn't anything like her—he took dangerous risks and lived for the moment, while she did everything in her power to minimize the risks that were unavoidable and plan carefully for the future.

But when she'd looked into his eyes, she'd felt as if he was the first man who'd really seen the true Annie Ryan. It had been a disconcerting, oddly exhilarating feeling, as if she had escaped for a few moments from a cage she'd been in for a long, long time. None of that mattered now, though. She'd forced him into taking one last gamble, and he'd lost.

Even as the thought crossed her mind, she saw his head break the surface of the water. The wet tracks on her cheeks dried immediately in the night air and her eyes narrowed in disbelief.

Keeping his face turned to the shadows, Lucky swam just enough to stay afloat, the moonlight delineating the muscles in his upper arms as he allowed the current to carry him downstream away from her. If she hadn't been watching so intently she never would have seen him.

"*Damn* you, Logan." Her grip on the railings went slack with relief, but over-riding that emotion was a growing feeling of angry humiliation. While she'd been standing here going crazy with worry, he'd been trying to get away without alerting her. And she'd actually been stupid enough to convince herself there could have been some kind of *bond* between them.

He'd done it again—slipped free from a seemingly impossible trap with all the style and insouciance he was noted for. He'd pulled it off a hundred times in the past: escaped from a millionaire's zealously guarded mansion without arousing even a whimper from a pack of Dobermans; walked away from the palace of a dictator disguised as one of his bodyguards; shuffled wearily past an army of security, dressed in the worn robes of a simple country priest, in one of Europe's most tightly-guarded museums.

But this time he'd slipped by Annie Ryan. And despite her reluctant admiration for his daring, there was no way she'd let him get away with it. The only bond between them that she would allow herself to recognize from now on was the bail bond he'd violated and she was determined to enforce.

The stone railing had been about waist-high on Logan. For Annie it was an effort to swing one leg over it, and when she did she felt her heart swoop nauseatingly as she nearly overbalanced. She closed her eyes instinctively, her legs feeling like rubber.

"You were right, Lucky," she murmured shakily. "Hell of a way to end an evening."

She didn't want to do this. As she opened one eye and peered nervously down, all she could focus on was the ghostly white gleam of her sneaker-clad foot on the edge of the bridge. If she looked past it there was nothing but empty space, and she didn't want to look at empty space. If she let herself actually look at the drop below, Annie knew, she'd probably solidify here, straddling the bridge, until someone found her in the morning and peeled her off her perch. Looking wasn't a good idea.

"So don't look, Ryan. Just swing the other leg over and push off," she told herself bracingly. "If he did it, so can you."

The only thing wrong with that line of reasoning, Annie thought as she gingerly pivoted the weight of her body onto the leg on the outside of the bridge and then started to inch her other one over the stone rail, was that cat burglars were used to high, dangerous places. Remembering that earlier might have saved her from what she was going through now, she reflected in disgust as the thigh muscle in her awkwardly extended leg began to cramp up.

"You forgot he was a skip. It's your job to bring skips in, Ryan," she grunted under her breath as she maneuvered her suddenly unwieldy leg over the rail. Her fingers felt slightly slick, as if they'd been rubbed raw by her death-grip on the rough stone. "Annie Ryan always gets her man, and Lucky Logan *isn't* going to be the first exception."

With that, her foot slipped and she felt herself falling off the bridge.

Chapter Two

His lungs bursting, Logan made himself stay underwater for as long as possible before coming to the surface and gulping in some sweet, badly needed air. A bounty hunter! Of all the dirty tricks fate had played on him in the last few days, this had to take the prize. She looked like a kid still in junior high—except for the solid piece of iron she'd been training on him. The way Annie Ryan handled that gun told him he wasn't dealing with a rank amateur, but a professional as dedicated and single-minded as himself, even if the two of them didn't exactly have the same goals in mind.

When he'd come to that realization, he'd known he had no choice but to pull an unexpected stunt like jumping off the bridge. Anything less and she'd have had the cuffs on him before he'd known what was happening. She was good.

But he was better, Logan thought.

Despite the fact that it was all in a day's work for him, he'd had to force himself to make that leap. It was one of the best-kept secrets in his very secretive life that he had no head for heights—and neither did the bounty hunter, from the way she was peering over the parapet at him when he shot a look back over his shoulder.

She swung one leg over the railing as he watched.

He coughed furiously as he swallowed a mouthful of river water in consternation. *What was her problem?* She'd given him a good scare up there on the bridge. She'd thrown a monkey wrench into his arrangements—he was going to have to do some fast talking later on tonight to salvage the situation—and she'd forced him into taking a chilly moonlit swim just to stay out of the hands of the law. So why couldn't she call it a night, like any sensible person would, and admit she was beaten?

The fog swirling up from the river thickened for a moment, obscuring his view. He found himself treading water nervously, wondering whether she'd actually have the nerve to make the jump.

What had he called her? A miniature bulldog? He'd seen on her face when he'd made the comparison that it had stung, and at the time he'd wished he could take back the words. But she'd stood there covering him with her weapon and barking out orders at him, and he'd *known* she had no intention of letting him go. All that fierceness coming from someone who looked more like a teenage babysitter than a coldly dedicated hunter had seemed somehow incongruous. Like Gidget with a gun, he thought ironically.

But appearances were deceiving, as he knew only too well himself. And for a moment there on the bridge, he'd been positive that the real woman behind those big violet-blue eyes was absolutely nothing like the Annie Ryan she presented to the world.

So what had driven her into a profession where every day she pitted herself against criminals on the run? Did she have some kind of death wish? Logan didn't think so. The woman who'd confronted him on the bridge was too vibrant, too invested in life to take it casually. Which left his original question unanswered: what compulsion drove Annie Ryan, bounty hunter?

There was a story there he'd never hear, he thought. He was just as driven as she was, and in a few minutes he was going to have to get the hell out of here.

Just then the mists parted like a piece of shattered silk, and he saw that she'd continued to maneuver herself over the stone parapet. She wasn't backing off, he thought in reluctant admiration. God knew what was going through her mind as she clung like a limpet to the cold stone of the bridge while forcing herself to get into position to jump. But he figured quitting wasn't part of it. She had a job to do, dammit, and if it meant jumping into the Charles River in the dead of night, then Annie was about to jump.

It was too bad her job entailed taking him in, or he just might have stuck around. It was always instructional to watch a professional doing a job with meticulous dedication.

With a small shock of self-discovery, Logan realized that he was actually putting off his escape.

He pulled himself up short and deliberately shut his mind to further musings. He had to stop wasting valuable time daydreaming about a woman he didn't intend to meet again. He started swimming for the nearby bank, but found it impossible to drag his gaze away from the small figure on the bridge.

He saw it happening as if someone was running a movie in slow motion. The foot that was wedged into the stone on the outside of the bridge slipped. By then Annie's center of gravity had shifted enough so that when she started to overbalance, her body began to fall inexorably away from the bridge. Oblivious to the bone-chilling cold numbing his limbs, Logan watched helplessly as both of Annie's legs swung into space.

All that prevented her from falling was her grip on the stone railing. And it was apparent that, with all her guts and courage, even Annie Ryan couldn't fight the forces of gravity that slowly weakened her precarious hand-hold.

"Dammit, Annie—push off!"

He barely knew that he'd shouted the words at her. She didn't have a chance if she slid straight down, he thought urgently. She was bound to hit one of the carved medallions that protruded from the structure, and even a glancing blow could knock her unconscious long enough so that she wouldn't survive in the water. The only recourse she had now was to shove herself clear of the bridge while she still could.

And time was running out for her. Maybe it was his imagination, but he swore he could see her hands slipping slowly on the damp stone. If she didn't act now…

Two white blurs—those dumb little-kid running shoes that she was wearing, he thought disjointedly—swung, in what must have been an incredible effort, back up to the stone facing of the bridge, but even as they did he saw her grip fail and the top half of her body fell backward into thin air.

She'd left it too damned late. She'd left it too late, and now she was going to smash into the bridge while he watched, and there was nothing—*nothing*—he could do about it. Logan bit down hard on his bottom lip, not noticing when the warm taste of blood mingled with the cold river water he'd swallowed. He began swimming back upstream. All that was left for him to do was to track her fall with his gaze and pray that he'd be able to recover her body before the river swept it away. He forced himself to keep his eyes fixed on her as her arms flew out in a useless attempt at saving herself.

Then the icy hand that was painfully squeezing his heart relaxed as he saw Annie's feet give a mighty shove even as she started her free fall.

It was enough to propel her safely out from the protruding and potentially lethal facade, and he found himself grinning stupidly as she hit the river with a splash. The woman was nothing less than amazing. She'd managed to twist herself around like a cat while she'd fallen, handling the situation as coolly as a paratrooper making his hundredth jump.

"That's my girl, Annie. Now just come up for air so I can get the hell out of here with a clear conscience," he said under his breath. It was a damned shame they'd had to meet like this, he thought with sharp regret. Annie Ryan intrigued him—there was no use pretending she didn't. The contrast between that urchin-like exterior and the forged-steel personality would have been worth investigating. But there was no chance they'd ever meet again. He'd see to that.

Still…if only he'd had this one night with her. If they'd met under different circumstances, he could have asked her out for—aw, hell—a cup of coffee or something. Yeah, he would have liked that, Logan thought with sudden surprise. He would have liked that a lot. But somehow he had the feeling that a single night wouldn't be nearly long enough to get to know a woman like Annie Ryan.

Smooth move, Logan, he muttered to himself. *You find a woman worth taking all the time in the world over, and it turns out she's the bounty hunter assigned to bring you in.* He had to get a normal life, he thought in disgust. However, right now he had to concentrate on dumping the blonde that intrigued him so much, not picking her up.

The mist cleared. The moon, full and yellow, hung in the sky like a stage prop in a low-budget little-theater production and, like an actress making a belated entrance, the woman who had occupied his mind for the last half hour popped to the surface of the river. Her hair was plastered over her features as she glanced wildly around and caught sight of him, but even so he could see that her mouth was wide open. She looked furious.

"I said freeze, Mister!"

Thrashing around in the water, she fumbled with the zipper of the windbreaker she was wearing. The next minute, to Logan's stupefaction, she was levelling the damn Glock at him again.

Didn't she *ever* give up? He couldn't believe the tenacity of the woman. There she was, sinking underwater again, still holding that cannon in both hands and bawling out instructions at him. With some reluctance, he realized that although he'd forgotten their respective roles long enough to indulge in a few foolish daydreams, she obviously hadn't veered one inch from her plan to take him in. But she'd never get off a decent shot while she was struggling to stay afloat and she was professional enough not to risk it. While she was bobbing around in the middle of the Charles and threatening him with a gun she wasn't going to use, he might as well strike out for dry land.

And put Bail Enforcement Agent Ryan completely out of his mind while he was at it, Logan thought wryly.

He swam a couple of yards closer to shore and looked back. He couldn't hear her yelling at him anymore, and for some reason he felt uneasy. He was just in time to see a blond head sinking for the third time beneath the water.

For crying out loud—she couldn't swim!

"Of all the damned stupid—" Logan bit back the rest of his sentence and abruptly changed course, heading with powerful strokes towards the spot where Annie had disappeared. He'd been right the first time, he thought grimly. She was a bulldog. A crazy bulldog, who didn't know when to quit. Coming after him off that bridge had been one thing. That had taken *cojones,* and he didn't care if the term was sexist or not. It fitted Annie Ryan. But coming after him when she knew damn well she couldn't survive in the water was just plain insane. What had she been hoping—that she'd land close enough to him that she could hitch a tow to shore before snapping the cuffs on him?

A pale glimmer just beneath the surface of the river caught his eye and he dove. Her hair floated eerily around her head, soft strands moving lazily back and forth like some aquatic flower. A few feet away in either direction and he'd never have seen her, despite the moonlight, he thought with a flash of fear. All that fiery determination and courage would have been quenched in a matter of minutes.

It didn't bear thinking about. Reaching for the collar of her windbreaker, he resolutely shut his mind to what might have been and focused on the task at hand. As he surfaced with her he shifted the position of his arm into a classic life-saving clasp, keeping Annie's head above water but making sure she wouldn't impede his progress if she regained consciousness while he was still trying to get her to shore. The cold made him clumsy, and he could feel his own strength rapidly ebbing away.

She was heavier than he'd have guessed from her size and slight build, Logan thought. Then he remembered the ironmongery she'd been carting around. A gun, handcuffs—he wouldn't be surprised if she had an Uzi and a machete strapped somewhere out of sight. He felt his foot stub against something and it took a moment to realize that they'd reached the near bank. With the last of his strength he dragged her unconscious body onto the mud and clambered up beside her.

She lay there, her face white and her arms flung out awkwardly at her sides. At the edge of the water her sneaker-clad feet pointed defenselessly at the moon, and Logan's heart turned over.

There was no way he was going to let Annie Ryan slip away from him. If he had to trade his own soul for hers he was going to make sure she came out of this.

"You've got a damn *job* to do, Ryan! You've got a skip to bring in—you can't give up now!"

His voice was hoarse and his hands were shaking, from cold and from desperation. Hastily checking that her airway was clear, he was about to press his mouth to hers when her eyes, just inches away from his, flew open.

"I'm not drowned, Logan." She sounded defensive, her flat South Boston accent suddenly noticeable. "My leg cramped up and then the cold got to me, but I'd have gotten out of the damn river myself."

She stared defiantly up at him like a street-corner tough, her hair matted with mud, a piece of river-weed draped across her cheek, her stupid Kiss Me, I'm Irish T-shirt sticking to her body, and he felt a fuse deep within him start to burn. Five minutes ago she'd been planted under-water like a water-lily and now she was telling him that she'd have gotten out of the damn "rivah" herself? That was taking Southie moxie way past the limit, he thought, ready to explode.

Then he saw the shadow that flitted briefly behind that stony gaze.

She'd been afraid. And she wasn't going to let *anyone*—least of all the skip she'd been tracking—know it. The fuse of frustration inside him sputtered and died.

"Yeah, I figured that," he lied. He couldn't resist pick-ing the piece of weed off her cheek, but he kept his touch impersonal. Her skin felt like satin. Her eyes narrowed like daggers.

"No, you didn't." It sounded as if she was spoiling for

a fight. "You thought I needed saving. You were about to give me the kiss of life, Logan—admit it."

What did she want from him? Was her pride so touchy that she couldn't accept the olive branch he was offering? *Not when it's so obvious, Logan,* he told himself with rare insight. That was it, he realized. For Annie, being patted on the head and placated like a child would be the supreme insult, and that's what it must have seemed to her that he was doing. He already knew that behind that blond urchin haircut and those blue-violet eyes lurked a tiger, rather than a cute kitten. How was he supposed to show her he recognized the fact?

"Either that, or you were about to make an extremely tasteless move on a woman you thought was unconscious," she continued with cold sarcasm. "Which was it, Logan?"

He couldn't help himself. He'd given up hoping for any sign that she was grateful he'd saved her from drowning, but now she was accusing him of being some kind of weird pervert. Maybe another man would someday get past her defenses, but it obviously wasn't going to be him. Not tonight. Not ever.

"The tasteless pass, of course," he said shortly, before he could stop himself. "The erotic T-shirt got me all hot and bothered."

"The erotic—" Annie squinted down at her chest suspiciously. Her eyes widened and a corner of her mouth quirked upwards in surprise, but when she spoke her voice held the tough, no-nonsense tone that he'd come to expect from her. "Oh, right. I can see how it might arouse a man."

"Well, it was wet, sweetheart. And don't forget that I thought you were in no state to protest," Logan drawled.

An urgent voice in his head told him it was time to cut and run, that as soon as she got back her strength she'd be whipping out those handcuffs again. He ignored it.

''Yeah, I was planning a pretty exciting night for myself before you came to,'' he went on uncontrollably. His words were sharper than he'd intended but dammit, her accusation still rankled. He knew to her he was just a skip, like all the others she hunted down, but was her opinion of him *that* low?

''Logan. Shut up for a second.''

She was still giving out orders, he noted, but for the first time since they'd met she sounded tentative. That drill-sergeant voice had softened to a smoky contralto. When she continued her tone sank even lower, until he could barely hear her.

''I guess you just saved my life.'' It wasn't easy for her to say, he could tell. Although he was still poised over her, somehow she managed to avoid his eyes. ''What I'm trying to say is—'' she came close to stumbling over the word, but finally she forced it out ''—is…*thanks*.''

A few minutes ago he'd been chilled to the bone. Now he felt like he was being stroked with midnight-blue velvet, as that husky whisper wrapped around him. Then she looked up at him.

This time he was the one who wanted to look away. It was like having a searchlight turned onto the most hidden recesses of his soul, revealing every secret he'd ever hoped would stay hidden, Logan thought apprehensively. Her gaze was that uncompromising, that direct.

Now he knew how she'd felt out there in the river, going down for the third time. At a certain point you didn't want to fight it anymore. You just let it wash over you and welcomed the sensation.

His eyes held hers and it seemed like time crystallized into this one fragile moment. The moon shone full on her face, turning her features to alabaster. The lushness of her bottom lip seemed incredibly ripe, the thick sweep of her lashes was thrown into mysterious relief by the light flooding down on them, and even the tangled honey strands curving towards the delicate bones of her temples didn't look cute or tomboyish anymore. They made her look like she belonged in a rumpled bed, waiting for him, he thought with a sudden surge of raw desire.

Her pupils widened slowly, and in that moment Logan could tell that he wasn't alone in feeling the mood between them inexplicably and irrevocably shift down to a more elemental level. He was so close to her that he could hear the tempo of her breathing deepen and slow as it feathered against his skin, and suddenly he knew that his last shred of control was about to give way altogether if he didn't put the brakes on now.

"You'd better bring the gun out, sweetheart." He tried to defuse the situation with a light tone. It didn't work. He went on hoarsely. "It's about the only thing that'll stop me from kissing you right now."

"I think I'm lying on it," Annie said in a husky whisper, not breaking their gaze.

She didn't look a damn bit like a little kid right now, he thought with the part of his mind that was still functioning. She looked like some kind of river nymph with her wide, moonlit eyes staring challengingly up at his. Drops of water beaded her skin like small, perfect diamonds floating on cream.

And that was part of his persona, wasn't it? The famous Lucky Logan never could resist a perfect gem, he thought hazily. He ran his thumb gently along her top lip and brought it away wet, as if it were sparkling with liquid jewels, and then he lowered his mouth slowly to hers to steal the rest of them.

HE TASTED wet and cool, Annie thought as Lucky's mouth came down on hers. Like a lover in a dream, unreal and magical…in fact, the whole situation was dreamlike, so perhaps she really had drowned and this wasn't actually happening. Certainly the real Annie Ryan would never let a near-stranger go ahead and kiss her, the way she was doing with Logan, but there was no air of reality to this scene at all. She'd drowned, she thought languorously. She'd drowned and she was being kissed by a man who didn't exist.

Except that his lips were no longer brushing hers. Without warning his kiss deepened, and just as immediately she found herself opening her mouth to receive him, to draw him in. Suddenly nothing was dreamlike. Everything was sharply real, every sensation almost painfully acute.

How had she ever thought he felt cool? His mouth was hot and she could feel an answering heat in herself, building up from some secret part of her that she hadn't even known about, a part of Annie Ryan that was totally unlike the rest of her personality. A bright sliver of fear shafted through her. She was *always* in control, but right now, right here with this man, she had the crazy impulse to abandon every ounce of control she had and act on her most basic desires.

Short strands of his hair fell forward in blunt wet blades against her skin. Acting almost of their own volition, her hands moved up to his face, the unshaven line of his jaw scraping like carbon grit against her palms, and her fingers weaved into that cool midnight-black silk, sliding through it and pulling him deeper into her. He tasted like Bushmill's whiskey splashed into strong black coffee—sweet and intoxicating and burning. She could get drunk on this. She was half-way there already. Through the thin nylon of her windbreaker she could feel the heat of Logan's outspread hand lifting her from her prone position to meet his mouth more fully and the tightening of his biceps against the side of her breast where his arm encircled her.

It was like falling from the bridge all over again. It was a weightless, reckless feeling.

But she wasn't reckless or impulsive, and before tonight, she'd *always* kept her feet firmly planted on the ground. Life was random enough as it was—the only way a person could protect herself and the ones she loved was to play by the rules and try to make sure the rest of the world did too.

Right now the two of them were breaking every rule in the book.

It had to stop. The thought drifted through her mind and she clung to it like a drowning woman clutching a life line. No matter how good this felt, it couldn't be right. Pulling slightly away, she looked up into his face...and felt her determination waver.

The devil-may-care Lucky Logan that she'd seen throughout the day, the casually tough man who made his living stealing from other people and slipping away into the night before they'd even realized they'd been robbed, *couldn't* be the man who was even now looking at her as if she was the most valuable thing he'd ever seen. The hand that had been around the back of her head slowly moved to the pulse-point at the side of her neck and then continued a stroking path to the corner of her mouth before she could put her weakening intentions into words.

"I finally figured out what makes you look so sexy," he whispered. His voice was hardly louder than the faint breeze sifting through the leaves of the trees in the park beyond. "Everything else about you looks like it belongs to Doris Day, but you've got a bad-girl mouth, sweetheart." His smile flashed wickedly in the shadows as he lightly traced her top lip with the tip of his middle finger.

"Wide and full and erotic, especially teamed up with those couple of freckles on your nose. Pure hell on defenseless males like me."

The surge of desire that Annie thought she'd conquered ran through her with greater force than ever. His finger was brushing her parted lips and what she wanted to do more than anything was to take it gently between her teeth and draw it into her mouth. She wanted to have some part of him inside her, she thought urgently. They were lying on the soaked grass of a riverbank, her hair was flecked with mud and her clothes were wet and cold. None of that mattered. She was never going to see the man after tonight. She didn't have to care about him, worry about him, make him a part of her life—but she wanted to take this further. She wanted to live on the edge with Lucky Logan for one night.

It was the stupidest impulse she'd ever had, she thought abruptly. And if she didn't break this off right now she might just carry through on it.

"But I'm not a bad girl, Logan," she said, shifting position slightly and slipping one hand into her windbreaker pocket. "I'm one of the good guys."

He realized what she was doing a split second after the cold steel snapped around his wrist and those dark green eyes narrowed in instantaneous reaction as the cuff ratcheted into place. Then he was on his feet and half-way up the bank, the loose cuff gleaming in the moonlight. Lucky Logan was about to make another lightning-fast escape.

Not if she could help it, Annie thought grimly. Lunging towards him on her hands and knees, she wrapped both arms around one of his legs.

"Don't even try it, Lucky! You're under arrest and I'm taking you—" The rest of her sentence was lost as she tugged at his leg and he lost his precarious balance on the slippery grass. Both of them fell backwards into the shallow water at the edge of the river.

Normally she'd care, she thought. But since she couldn't possibly get any wetter or muddier tonight, what did it matter where she took him down?

"Come on, Annie!" Logan gasped. "I thought we had something going here! You're not seriously thinking of selling me out now, are you?"

He dodged as she made an abortive grab for the free-swinging cuff, and the move took them into deeper water. It was only up to his knees, but she was wading through it up to her thighs. That old height thing again, she thought in frustration. Why did it always seem to work out that her skips were all over six feet tall?

"I'm not selling you out, Lucky," she panted, facing him. "I'm just doing my job. You steal jewels and I put you back in jail. Hey, you're right—we *do* have a relationship going for us."

"I like smart-mouthed women." He waded back a few feet from her, almost stumbling on the muddy river bottom, but never taking his eyes from her. "And I like the way you kiss. But let's forget about this bondage stuff, Annie, and keep things nice and normal."

He was *trying* to get into deeper water. He knew as well as she did that the odds were rapidly shifting to his favor the farther in he went. With another step or two he'd be completely out of her reach and able to dive into the Charles again. He'd saved her life—without Logan she'd never have made it out of the river tonight. She was grateful to him for that. She owed him for that. But it wasn't enough to erase the principles of a lifetime.

And neither was her ill-advised attraction to him enough to make her forget how things really stood between them. She liked the way he kissed, too, Annie thought. Her lips still felt soft and swollen, and if she touched them with the corner of her tongue she could still taste him on her. She'd lied to him just now—the relationship between them was something a lot less complicated than that of a skip and a bail agent. If circumstances shifted half a degree into an alternate reality, she and Logan wouldn't be here facing each other like antagonists. They'd be making exquisitely slow love together with the whole night ahead of them.

Her legs felt weak. She knew it had nothing to do with the cramp she'd suffered earlier, and with an effort she brought herself back to the real world.

It was time to take off the kid gloves and treat Lucky Logan like she would any other skip. Reluctantly she reached inside her jacket and pulled the Glock out of her shoulder holster.

"The position, Lucky. This time let's try it against the riverbank."

Chapter Three

"I could have taken it away from you when you were unconscious. I should have."

Lucky's words were the first either of them had spoken for over half an hour. Squelching through deserted city streets on their way to where Annie had left her car hours earlier, both of them had maintained a chilly silence. He hadn't taken too well to finally being captured, she thought wearily. She didn't feel that great about the situation either. She'd told him to shorten the rangy stride that she'd had so much trouble keeping up with before, and with his hands behind his back and his pace accommodating hers, he gave the impression of wearing leg-irons and chains.

He wasn't trying to make any part of this easy for her. But knowing he was manipulating her didn't make her feel less guilty.

"Then why didn't you?" she snapped. "You've lifted gems from right under the noses of armed guards, Lucky. What stopped you from taking a gun away from a semi-drowned woman?"

"God knows," Logan replied shortly. "Chalk it up to a bad mistake in judgment. You looked so damned helpless."

"I'm from South Boston—helpless gets weeded out pretty quick in my neighborhood. You picked the wrong woman to play the strong, chivalrous male with.'' Her tone was distant. ''That's my car over there.''

She jerked her head at the dirty brown Buick sitting all by itself under a streetlight in front of a run-down group of stores and a laundromat. This section of the city wasn't a dangerous one, but signs of impending decay were ominously noticeable. Several of the storefronts were boarded up and graffiti had been spray-painted on the sides of some of the buildings. The interior of the laundromat with its rows of washers and dryers was brightly lit, obviously as an attempt at security, although it was closed for the night.

At least the area was deserted, Annie thought thankfully. She hated doing her job in front of a hostile audience. She could hear a siren wailing far away and a motorcycle cutting the silence a few streets over, but apart from that the night was surprisingly quiet.

There was a ticket on the Buick's windshield and she let her breath out in a sharp sound of annoyance. She was tired, muddy and shivering. In the next fifteen minutes she'd be turning her skip in at the nearest police station and she actually felt guilty about it. Did she need any more aggravation right now? *I don't think so, Ryan,* she thought tiredly. *But you can bet it's not over yet.*

She had to stay alert for this last part of her job. Her prisoner was cuffed and she was armed, but that didn't mean that she could relax. The next step was going to rile him even more than being escorted from the river at gunpoint, Annie thought with grim certainty. Skips always hated it when they were told to get into the back seat and lock themselves to the length of chain bolted to the frame of the Buick.

In the end, even Logan would have to comply. So why did she find the image of him shackled to solid steel like a chained wolf so repugnant?

Maybe because you never got up close and personal with a skip before, Ryan. Maybe because you let the lines between you blur a little—make that a lot—and Logan stopped being just a job to you.

She brought the unwelcome train of thought to an abrupt halt. Some other time she'd try to figure out why she'd behaved so uncharacteristically with a man she hardly knew, but right now she couldn't afford to let herself think about what had happened between them on the riverbank.

"This is where you picked up my trail?" Logan asked. He'd moved closer to her and for one irresponsible second she wanted to touch him. She stepped away, maintaining the distance between them. "How'd you know where to find me?"

"Pure, dumb luck," she answered, raising her voice a little as the motorcycle she'd heard earlier downshifted with a throaty rumble a couple of streets away. She kept him in the corner of her vision as she reached over and ripped the ticket out from under the wipers. "I was looking for another runner—Benny Lopez. His girlfriend works at the laundromat and I've found him there before."

"But this time instead of finding Benny you saw me walking down the street." He looked peeved. "Hell, I was just killing time this afternoon. I could have turned down the next block instead and you'd never have laid eyes on me."

"Maybe you should think about changing your nickname," she told him dryly. "But I would have found you eventually—you just made it a little easier for me." She unzipped the side pocket of her windbreaker and pulled out a heavy set of keys.

"No wonder it was so hard to haul you to shore." Lucky raised an eyebrow and nodded at the key-chain, a small gold-tone statue of a dog with most of the gold worn off.

"I should have guessed you were carrying bullion along with everything else."

Flustered, she looked at the cheap figurine and then closed her fingers around it, hiding it from his gaze. "Oh, that. It's supposed to be a collie, though it doesn't look much like any dog I've ever seen. My niece bought it for me one Christmas because it reminded her of the dog we had at the time."

"A guard dog to watch over you on the job?" Lucky's voice had lost its edge, and the green eyes were curious.

"Something like that." Annie didn't like the direction the conversation was taking and she deliberately didn't volunteer any further information. He was entirely too observant, she thought with a twinge of dismay. She had that key-chain in and out of her hand several times a day, and he'd been the first person to ever comment on it.

This way, at least Buddy'll be with you when you're working, Aunt Annie. He can protect you from the bad guys.

It had been several Christmases ago, Annie remembered, and Mary Margaret must have been what—four years old? No, she'd been five. The year after that, the real Buddy had been run over by a car and the little girl had sobbed as if her heart would break. It had been too soon after the other accident that had torn her whole world apart, and although only a few months earlier she had sat dry-eyed and seemingly uncomprehending through her father's funeral service, the loss of Buddy had affected her so much that both her mother and Annie had been desperately worried about her. At one point Bridie had even considered sending the child to a counsellor.

Annie unlocked and opened the driver's-side door and then used a second key to open the rear passenger door. The locks worked independently, and there was an iron grille separating her from the skips she transported. Most of the time the elaborate precautions weren't necessary, but her father had an ex-cop's healthy respect for safety procedures, and when she'd started as a bail enforcement agent she'd promised him never to let herself get careless. It hadn't completely reassured Patrick Ryan about his daughter's choice of career, but it had eased his worries a little.

"See that second pair of cuffs attached to the chain on the floor, Logan?" Annie cleared her throat as he threw a careless glance towards the back seat. "Get in and snap the open one around the connector shackle of the ones you're wearing. I'll be watching, so don't think you can fake it."

He'd ducked his head a little to look inside the car, but now he straightened to his full height and pivoted slowly to face her. The interest he'd shown a moment ago when he'd asked about the key-chain had vanished. The man who'd kissed her as if he was giving away his very soul had gone. There wasn't even a trace of the easy-going good humor that he'd shown earlier in the day. Annie forced herself to stand her ground, but for the first time she was uncomfortably aware of the tightly leashed power he'd kept under control until now.

"No." The one-word answer was flat and uncompromising, forced out between barely parted lips. A muscle in his jaw moved as he stared back at Annie.

"Don't give me that, Logan." She met his stare with one of her own and kept her voice even. "I've got a one-woman arsenal here. You know if I have to use the Taser I will, so don't force me."

She would, too, Annie thought grimly. Sending a jolt of electricity through a man didn't make her feel good, but it was better than having to take him down with a bullet after he'd gotten the jump on her. Logan knew the rules. If he chose to disregard them, he was going to have to live with the consequences.

And so would she.

"Don't push me, Annie." The tense set around his mouth tightened, but to her relief his voice had lost its dangerous edge. "I'll get in the damn car like a model prisoner, but I won't secure myself to the chain. It's an old phobia, okay?"

The sound of the motorcycle grew louder, but she noted it with only part of her mind. *She owed him.* He didn't have a rep for violence, and all he'd tried to do so far was escape, not disarm her or catch her off-guard. And for God's sake, she'd given him a much easier opportunity back at the riverbank. Maybe the man had been in a car accident once, maybe he just couldn't stand the thought of being totally helpless if something happened. She wasn't about to pry, and she wouldn't insist on the extra precaution. In her heart of hearts, Annie thought, she didn't really believe he'd hurt her. That's what it all came down to.

"Logan, if—"

He moved with frightening speed for such a big man. Before she knew what was happening, he'd grabbed the open rear door of the Buick and slammed it powerfully against her, knocking her backwards into the open driver's space.

Her head hit the steering wheel hard. A bright flash of pain shot across her field of vision and for a second she couldn't move as she nearly lost consciousness. Then instinct took over. Even as she slid sideways onto the driver's seat the Glock was in her hands, the trigger in firing position.

"Down on the ground, Lucky! *Now,* dammit!"

She'd *trusted* him! How could she have been so stupid as to trust a skip? It was her first coherent thought.

"*Drive,* Annie! Start the car and *drive!*" Logan was in the back seat, his face close to the wire grille. His voice was harsh and cracked. "He's coming back!"

"You *bastard!*" Her breath was shallow and she could hardly get enough air to talk. "If I even see your eyes blink you're a dead man, Lucky. Don't move!"

Take a deep breath, Ryan. Then go shut the rear door, get back in the car, and dump his sorry butt in the nearest lock-up. And hope you never see his lying face again.

He reached his cuffed hands over and slammed his door shut. Before he'd even finished she had the gun aimed through the grille at him. Her nerves were as tightly strung as piano wire and her head felt like someone had taken a sledgehammer to it.

"I'm telling you for the last time, Lucky—stay where you are and don't—"

"Drive or duck, Annie. That biker's coming back and he's gunning for us." He jerked his head at the windshield. "And whatever he's packing's got a hell of a lot more firepower than that Glock of yours. Look at the laundromat."

"What biker—"

She didn't trust him anymore, but as the ringing in her ears subsided she realized that she could hear the throaty rumble of a motorcycle getting closer. It had the distinctive coughing sound of a Ducati. She'd heard it earlier, just before Logan had attacked her.

"The Italians sure know how to build a bike, Annie. It sounds like the devil's percolator and it drives like a bat out of hell. One of these days Bridie's gonna buy me a Duke for Christmas, right darlin'?" Sean had been tinkering with the old Suzuki he'd bought and his mild blue eyes had glinted mischievously as he'd teased his wife and Annie. Motorcycles had been his passion.

She thrust the memory aside. Out of the corner of her vision she cautiously took a quick look at the laundromat—and gasped. Its bleak fluorescent lights shone down on a scene of destruction. The front window hung in shards and inside, rows of broken dryer windows hung on their hinges like smashed glass eyes.

If the line of fire had been a foot lower it would have stitched its deadly seam right across her—except that Logan had knocked her down out of harm's way.

"Assault rifle. The only reason he missed us is that he almost lost control of the bike, but he'll compensate for the kick-back this time. For the love of God, Annie, will you get us the hell out of here?" His face was white under his tan. "This is going to turn into a shooting gallery again in a few seconds, and we're sitting ducks."

"But why? Who *is* he?"

"I don't know! Let's *go,* sweetheart!"

He was lying, she thought in sudden certainty. Or at least not telling her the whole truth.

The sound of the motorcycle filled the empty street with an ever-increasing scream. Tearing her gaze away from the laundromat, she saw that it was only a block away and coming up on them—*like a bat out of hell, Sean. You were right.* Annie slammed her door and snapped the Glock's trigger back to safety, tossing it on the seat beside her before jamming her key into the car's ignition. The sweetly reassuring growl of the souped-up V-8 engine sprang into life.

"Grab something back there and hold on, Lucky," she said between gritted teeth. "It's going to be a bumpy ride."

It was their only chance, she thought, as the Buick shot onto the street, its tires squealing. She let the engine revs build and then shifted smoothly to second gear, mentally thanking Sean again. Her brother-in-law had taught her all she knew about driving fast in an emergency, and she couldn't have had a better teacher, Annie thought. The most important thing he'd taught her was to close her mind to everything else and concentrate on the road. She quickly considered her options.

There were no handy cross streets to escape onto between them and the motorcycle. Making a U-turn and heading in the opposite direction would take time they didn't have—the biker would close the gap between them long before she'd outrun him.

"What the *hell* are you doing?" Logan's voice was right by her ear, his face as close to hers as the grille allowed. "We're heading right for him, Annie—he'll get us as we pass him!"

"Trust me," she said tersely. "I know this area."

There were only about fifty feet between the Buick and the motorcycle now—she could see the rifle strapped to the side of the machine and the full-face helmet the biker wore. It obscured his features completely. *Could be a woman, for that matter,* she thought briefly. *But I'm not planning to find out.*

Just as the biker reached down for his weapon, she hit the brakes and spun the steering wheel violently. The back end of the Buick slewed around sickeningly until they were facing the side of the street. Without even letting the car rock to a stop, she pressed down on the gas pedal and they shot forward.

"Are you insane?" Logan was staring straight ahead and their eyes met briefly in the rearview mirror. "What's your plan, Annie? Because if my choice is between taking a chance on that maniac's shooting skills and driving straight into a brick wall, let's turn back now."

"Breathe in, Logan—it's a tight squeeze." She shut everything else out of her mind as she aimed the Buick into the darkness between a boarded-up shoe store and the grimy facade of a restaurant. She'd lost Benny Lopez down here once, after sitting for three and a half hours in this greasy spoon and drinking at least six cups of vile coffee while waiting for him to show. Afterwards, angry with herself, she'd scouted the area to ensure that Benny wouldn't get the drop on her the same way again. She'd discovered that she could have followed him in her car down the narrow alleyway beside the restaurant with at least a couple of inches left over on either side of the Buick.

Of course, she'd been taking it slow when she'd tried it that time, not barreling along at full speed in the dark. Annie hit the high beams just as they slipped in between the two buildings and the alleyway jumped into sharp relief. Through the windshield the hood of the Buick seemed enormously wide and unmaneuverable and the crumbling brick walls pressed in on the car like two pieces of bread on a ham sandwich. Annie jumped as a discarded bottle exploded beneath the tires. It was all she could do not to jerk the steering in reaction when she saw a cardboard box in their path.

Okay, Ryan, keep the darn wheels straight and don't freak out here. Sure, the walls are right up to the car windows, but you can do it.

Somewhere behind her on the street, she knew the biker would have overshot the alley opening. But he'd realize soon enough where she'd gone, and he wouldn't have any trouble at all guiding a motorcycle through the narrow passage. With any luck, though, she and Lucky would be a couple of blocks away by then.

The side-view mirror scraped against the wall and snapped off.

"You're doing good, sweetheart. You're doing great."

His voice was a soothing murmur by her ear. Her hands

took a firmer grip on the wheel. Overcorrecting could be fatal, but for a moment the impulse had been almost irresistible. Logan seemed to know instinctively how she felt.

The next moment the end of the alleyway shot up in front of them and they were safely through, jolting over the curb.

"Ever thought of driving a taxi?" Logan's dry comment was casual enough, but his voice sounded rusty and strained. "If this bounty hunter gig doesn't pay enough, you could moonlight on the side."

"It pays just fine." She felt light-headed with relief and delayed reaction and her next words were spoken without thinking. "Bringing you in is going to cover the check for my sister's operation."

"Operation? What's the matter with her?"

She'd forgotten his cat-like curiosity, she thought in chagrin. For a while there they'd been on the same side, but she wasn't going to open up enough to him to tell him about Bridie. She didn't want him learning anything about her family, even though he'd sounded as if he really wanted to know…and even though for a moment she'd really wanted to tell him.

It was an unwelcome revelation. Instinctively she shrugged it away. She wasn't about to let him get *that* close to her. What had happened to Bridie was still too fresh, too painful to discuss with a near-stranger.

Jeffrey Haskins had been out on bail, awaiting his trial on a drunk-driving charge—his fifth. Although he was in his early twenties, he'd been released into his father's custody, and Haskins Senior had had the responsibility of seeing that his son didn't have access to liquor or a vehicle. The night that Jeffrey had run a red light and ploughed into Sean's motorcycle, he'd had an open bottle of Southern Comfort on the seat of the Porsche he'd been driving.

Sean Connor had been killed outright. Bridie hadn't

walked since. It had been the second time the Ryan family's world had been ripped apart, and Annie had vowed it would never happen again.

Her father. Bridie. Mary Margaret. They were all she had left of the people she loved, and if eternal vigilance was the price she had to pay to keep them safe then Annie knew she'd do it gladly. That was what love was all about.

"Your sister—what's the operation for?" Logan's quiet question pulled her back to the present and Annie knew that he was watching her in the mirror. She turned down a one-way street, trying to get her emotions under control.

"She was in an accident." Her reply was clipped and businesslike. "But I'd rather ask the questions right now, Lucky—especially since we both almost got killed back there. I get the feeling that you weren't particularly surprised when that maniac came out of nowhere and started shooting up the street, so level with me. Who was he? Why was he gunning for us?"

"Your verb tense is wrong," Logan said shortly. "He still is."

Even before he'd spoken her subconscious had picked up the throaty rumble of the bike, and by the time she'd verified the single headlight in her rear-view mirror Annie realized that escaping this time from the unknown biker was going to be almost impossible. They were in an industrial area and except for the motorcycle, the Buick was the only vehicle around at this time of night.

"You seem to know your way around this part of town," Logan said. "Can we lose him by slipping down a side street?"

She thought rapidly. The surrounding neighborhoods were blue-collar residential with shoddily built row houses jammed shoulder to shoulder. Children would be sleeping in bedrooms. Their parents would be watching the eleven o'clock news in their living rooms or getting ready for bed themselves. People would be walking their dogs, leaving for work on a graveyard shift, getting a late-night snack out of the refrigerator. A stray bullet tearing through a peaceful home could turn this quiet neighborhood into a scene of tragedy in an instant.

"I can't do that," she said slowly. "We'd be putting innocent people in jeopardy, Lucky, and that's out of the question. We're going to have to ditch the car and take our chances on foot. The Buick's fast but he's faster—and a lot more maneuverable."

In the mirror she saw him scan the passing buildings, most of them surrounded by chain-link fencing. His features looked harsh in the dim light. "I didn't scoop you out of the Charles just to watch you get shot."

The biker was gaining on them fast, even though the Buick's accelerator was pressed to the floor. In a minute the killer would be within range. She felt an icy trickle of sweat between her shoulder blades at the thought.

"You're not responsible for me, Lucky. I'm responsible for you—or had you forgotten that fact?" she snapped. "And if you'd told me from the start that someone was gunning for you, I could have taken precautions, called for help. He *is* gunning for you, isn't he?"

"Yeah, it's me he wants. At least, that's the only theory that makes sense," Logan said. His breath was warm against the back of her neck. "This isn't your fight, Annie. And no matter who's responsible for who, I don't intend to let you get killed over something that's got nothing to do with you."

"It's the first time all night we've agreed, Lucky, because I don't intend to die—" Her reply was cut short as a burst of gunfire came from behind them, and the steering wheel jerked out of her hands. She struggled to regain control of the car and was forced to slow down.

''He's blown out a tire. I've got to pull over and then we'll make a run for it.'' The slapping thump of the destroyed tire sounded almost louder than the screaming of the motorcycle's engine and she shouted to make herself heard. ''Lucky? Are you ready?''

There was no answer from the back seat, and all of a sudden Annie realized why. It was the reason why the gap between her and the motorcycle was getting larger, even with her reduced speed. The biker had stopped following her. The back door of the Buick was swinging open.

Lucky Logan had escaped—but this time he'd run into danger to lead it away from her.

Chapter Four

"Don't tell Pa any of this, Bridie." It was the next morning and Annie's face was white with fatigue. She'd changed into sweat pants and another of Mary Margaret's T-shirts, this one with a Tyrannosaurus Rex roaring across her chest. Bridie wheeled expertly across the kitchen floor to the washing machine and added softener to the rinse cycle.

"I would if I thought it would do any good," she answered tartly. "But he hasn't been able to talk you into changing careers yet, so I'm not going to worry him with it. The police didn't find the biker or this Logan fella?"

She had the same flat accent as Annie, only in her it was more pronounced. To look at her, you'd expect the bell-like vowels of the Queen's English to come out of that perfectly formed mouth. She looked like an angel that had stepped from an old stained-glass window. Everything about her glowed, from the cloud of strawberry-blond hair that fell gently to her shoulders to the porcelain complexion Annie had always envied.

An angel who'd not only lost her wings, but whose ability to walk had been stolen from her. Annie started to get up from her chair to help, but sat back down again as Bridie waved her away impatiently.

"You're bushed and I don't appreciate being treated like

an incompetent, sis.'' The angel facade shattered with her blunt words. ''So drink your tea and tell me the rest of the story before Pa gets up.''

''There's nothing much more to tell.'' She automatically stirred another teaspoon of sugar into her mug. ''I had to file a report at the police station and they told me that there'd been no trace of Logan when they reached the area. The biker obviously took off when he heard the cruisers coming.''

''So you lost a skip. This Logan—why didn't he scram when he pulled you out of the river?'' Bridie was pouring a capful of fabric softener as if the task took all of her concentration, but her forget-me-not blue eyes darted a limpid look at her sister. Annie blew on her tea noisily.

''I had the cuffs on him.'' She didn't meet Bridie's innocent blue gaze.

''But you said you had to pull your gun on him to cuff him. He could have gotten you to shore and then left before you knew what was happening—or did he have to give you the kiss of life?''

''I told you, I wasn't anywhere close to drowning, and no, he did not have to give me mouth-to-mouth. He was going to, but then I opened my eyes.'' Annie took a hasty swallow of tea and immediately regretted it. She gulped it down and felt it scald her esophagus all the way to her stomach. Bridie wheeled back to the table and took a delicate sip from her own mug.

''Was he as much of a babe magnet as his photo in the paper? The *Globe* ran a blurry little black-and-white picture when he was arrested for stealing the Rubicon, but even so, he looked like a darlin' to me. Totally edible, sis—even if he is a bad boy.''

The trouble with her sister's angelic looks, Annie thought, was that they masked a basically devilish personality. And Logan's curiosity was nothing compared to Bridie's. One way or another Bridie was going to get the full story out of her, so she might as well cave in and spill the details now.

"Okay." She thumped her mug of tea onto the oilcloth-covered table. "The man kissed me. Satisfied? He was a babe magnet, as you so maturely put it, he kissed me and I kissed him back. He kisses great, if you want a rating on the experience too." She knew that the heat in her face had nothing to do with the tea she was drinking, and she gave her older sister a peeved glance. Bridie's creamy complexion never changed. Heck, Bridie could find herself naked in the middle of Boston Common and Annie would bet that that pale skin wouldn't hold the faintest touch of pink.

Her own face felt like it was on fire.

"There was a full moon, he'd just saved my life and he said my T-shirt turned him on," she added weakly.

"Sweet Mary and all the saints." Bridie was staring at her intently, all mischievousness gone. "You fell for him, didn't you? You fell for a skip."

"I did not fall for a skip. I felt a momentary surge of lust for a skip, and if I make it to Mass this Sunday—which I doubt—I'll confess to Father Murphy, say ten Hail Marys and forget all about it. I did not fall for a skip. Falling for a skip would be an incredibly stupid thing to do, not to mention that I'll never see the man again." She lifted her steaming mug of tea, remembered just before she burned her mouth again, and put it down. "He's gorgeous. Very sexy. It was a shallow reaction on my part."

Bridie was rolling her wheelchair back and forth, an inch at a time. It was a habit she knew drove her sister crazy, because the wheels gave a tiny squeak every time she did it. It was something she did when she wanted Annie off-balance in an argument, Annie knew, but this time she wasn't going to crack.

Bridie's chair moved back an inch, and then forward again. Her attention stayed on her tea. The wheels squeaked again.

"All right! There was a brief moment when I felt something more between us—but then I came to my senses and pulled the Glock on him. Is that what you wanted to hear?"

"You're nuts." The wheelchair came to an abrupt halt. "You'd die rather than admit that you might feel something for him. Don't forget who you're talking to, sis—you'd never have let the guy touch you if you hadn't liked him just a little bit. Why is it so hard to admit it? What are you so afraid of?"

"Afraid? I'm not—"

"You're petrified of attaching any importance to a relationship," Bridie interrupted. "Okay, so this probably won't go anywhere, what with him a jewel thief on the run and you hunting him down. But darn it all, Annie, the man saved your life—what? Three times in an evening? You must have wished just for a second that you'd met under different circumstances."

"What I felt for Logan was purely carnal," Annie insisted. "Don't try to make it into Romeo and Juliet, even if there was a faint similarity to the balcony scene."

"What's purely carnal, Aunt Annie? Is there any toast, Mom?"

Both sisters spun around as seven-year-old Mary Margaret, in grubby blue jeans and a pajama top, came into the kitchen. Bridie's eyes met Annie's over the mugs they both hastily raised to their mouths.

"Sometimes your Aunt Annie uses words she doesn't really understand, sweetie," Bridie said, swallowing with difficulty. "Why aren't you properly dressed?"

"I wanted to wear my leprechaun shirt, but I couldn't find it." Mary Margaret padded lightly over to the counter in her bare feet and looked over at her mother. "Can I put the bread in myself?"

"Just don't try to get it to pop up before it's done. And bring it over to the table to put the jam on." Bridie watched out of the corner of her eye as the little girl carefully dropped the slices into the toaster. "You'll have to wear something else today—your aunt was fooling around in your T-shirt last night and got it dirty."

"You always borrow my stuff, Aunt Annie." Mary Margaret sounded fed up. She put her hands on her non-existent hips and faced them. "Sometimes I think you buy me clothes too big just so they'll fit you. Isn't that my T-Rex shirt?"

"Sorry." Annie looked down guiltily at the dinosaur lurching from one breast to the other. "How about we go to the Science Park this afternoon and after we make our hair stand straight up at the electricity exhibit I'll buy you a new tee? Kid-size only, I promise."

"Could we go to the Aquarium instead and look at the eel garden?" Mary Margaret was busy slathering grape jelly on her toast. She looked up just in time to see her mother making gagging gestures at her aunt, and frowned defensively. "They're not gross, Mom. They're cool. Maybe I could get a T-shirt with eels on it." She took a huge bite of toast and looked up expectantly, her mouth ringed with purple.

"Puh-leese!" Bridie rolled her eyes dramatically. "What if they come to life in the water the first time I have to put it in the washer?"

"Like that would happen," Mary Margaret said scornfully, but with a gleam of interest in her eyes. "Anyway,

Aunt Annie's not afraid of eels. She'd zap them with her Taser, right Aunt Annie?''

"The electric ones might zap me right back. Besides, your Mom would just switch the washer over to spin and dry them right back onto your shirt where they belong, champ,'' Annie said lightly. "Okay, it's a date—the Aquarium after lunch, but not unless you get that revolting purple off your face. It looks like you're wearing some kind of punk lipstick.''

"Cool!'' Mary Margaret yelped, cramming the last crust into her mouth and sliding off the kitchen chair. "It goes with my tattoos.''

She ran out of the kitchen and Bridie looked over at her sister in resignation. "Great. Stick-on tattoos, punk lipstick. Next she'll be wanting a nose-stud. I wasn't like that at her age. She takes after you, not me.''

"I put one green rinse on my hair when I was young and wild, and I have to hear about it for the rest of my life,'' Annie said. "Sorry sis, but the kid's all you, through and through. Don't forget that little rosebud on an unmentionable part of your body.''

She regretted the words as soon as she'd said them. Bridie, about to move away from the table, stopped, and the light in her eyes dimmed. Then she saw Annie's stricken expression and gave a wavering smile.

"That was for Sean. We can talk about him, sis. It hurts more not to.'' She looked down at the chair she sat in, at her feet, in fluffy pink slippers, resting uselessly on the metal footplate. "That drunk took a lot away from me, Annie. But he couldn't rip the memories out of my mind, and he couldn't take my darling man away from me completely. The only way that could happen is if we try to pretend he never existed.''

Annie started to say something comforting, but her sister's head jerked up. Her eyes were shiny but her voice was fierce and low. "Sean *did* exist. He was my husband and I loved him completely, from the very first day I saw him in high school. We made a child together. We laughed together. We argued, we worried, we made love together. I was his and he was mine, and he still is. So don't stop talking about him on my account, because sometimes I feel like I'm the only person in the world who remembers him at all!"

"I remember when he took that old motorcycle apart on the living room floor, and when you asked him what he was doing he said it was performance art." Patrick Ryan walked into the kitchen and casually poured himself a mug of tea, not glancing at either of his daughters. At fifty-nine, he still looked like what he'd been for thirty years—a Boston-Irish beat cop. Only a close observer could notice the stiffness in his left arm, and the fact that it never moved higher than the level of his waist. He pulled out a chair at the kitchen table and sat down. "He was a lad, that boyo. He could charm the birds right out of the trees."

Bridie stared at her father for a long second, the anguish on her features slowly fading. She smiled, her eyes still bright with unshed tears. "He was that, Pa, wasn't he? He was quite a lad, my Sean." She turned from the table, her leanly muscled arms propelling the wheelchair with ease. "I can't be sitting around here in my robe all morning gabbing with you two. I've got to finish those bridesmaids' dresses for the Connelly wedding today, and if you can spare the time, Pa, maybe we could nip out this morning and pick up some groceries."

"My day's free," her father said easily. "We'll leave whenever you're ready, Bridget Catherine."

She made a face at him and wheeled out of the room. Annie could hear the soft swish of the rubber tires on the polished wood of the floors as she left. She met her father's eyes.

"Thanks, Pa. You're quite a lad yourself. I don't know why I find it so hard to talk about Sean in front of her."

"You do it from the best of motives." He gave her a wry smile. "Always trying to wrap this family up in cotton wool, aren't you? And then you go out and take on a career that's guaranteed to turn my hair white with worry."

"I don't wrap everyone in cotton wool," she protested, ignoring the last half of his sentence. "How do I do that? By being glad you didn't get involved in that corporate security company with your old pals?"

"It might have been exciting. O'Neil and Russell aren't shooting it out with industrial spies every day, but their agency is picking up a lot of important contracts around Boston." He looked over at her and shrugged with his right shoulder only. "But until they get a larger staff, I guess there would be a little leg-work involved. I'm probably not capable of taking the punks down by force anymore. Good thing I'm needed around here, isn't it?"

"We wouldn't have made it without you to hold us all together when everything seemed so hopeless. After Sean died, Bridie couldn't go on living in Cambridge alone with Mary Margaret, and I didn't mind giving up my tiny apartment to move back home." Annie darted a look to the doorway and kept her voice down. "But some things, like lifting her in and out of her chair and converting the house for her disability, would have been physically beyond me, Pa. She needs you. We all need you here."

"Bridie *needed* me," Patrick Ryan corrected his daughter. "Have you taken a good look at your sister lately, darlin'? There's not much she needs physical help with these days, and after her operation she should be almost as mobile as you and I, God willing."

"If it goes well," Annie said in an undertone. "But what if it doesn't?"

"It will. We have to think that, for her sake," he said with an edge in his voice. "We have to respect her decision to go through with it and support her."

"But it's so risky!" She raked a distracted hand through the short strands on top of her head, making them stick up in disarray. "Sometimes I just wish she could accept—"

"What? That she'll never walk again because her sister's determined not to let her take a chance? No." Her father's eyes, the same blue as Bridie's, bored into her. "We all have to live our own lives, Annie. Maybe bad things will happen to one or another of us—they have in the past and I'm sure they will again. But loving someone doesn't have to be a burden. Let Bridie go and accept the fact that you can't keep everyone safe all the time. Don't put your sister in a cage, however protected and comfortable it is. She won't thank you for it in the long run."

"I'm ready, Pa. Where's the list?"

Bridie's entrance prevented Annie from defending herself, but after her father and sister left the house, she felt a spurt of resentment. Even when Mary Margaret, a ball-cap turned backwards on her head and her pockets bulging with marbles, announced that she was going next door to play, Annie's response was subdued, her mind still on the unfairness of her father's accusations.

He'd practically come out and said that she didn't *want* Bridie to get better! It just wasn't true! And if he thought that she saw loving her family as a burden, then he was way off the mark. She cupped the teapot with her hand, scowling. She was still exhausted from the night before, and somehow this morning had turned into "Pick on Annie Day," she thought childishly. First Bridie, then Pa. She wouldn't be surprised if Mary Margaret gave her a stern lecture on some aspect of her personality at the Aquarium later today.

She smiled reluctantly. Not Mary Margaret. She thought the sun and the moon rose and set on her fabulous bounty hunter Aunt Annie. The remark about zapping the eels had been typical of her hero-worship, although it wasn't something Annie wanted to encourage. She didn't like to present what she did as glamorous. Mary Margaret had to learn that real criminals weren't like the bad boys on television and the movies.

Most of the skips Lew's agency went bail for and had to bring in were just plain dumb. They were thugs, nothing more and nothing less. Okay, Lucky Logan was the exception, she thought grudgingly. But even he was basically a thief when you looked past the daring escapes and the extravagant life-style.

She shoved the vision of a pair of dark green eyes and a sexy smile out of her mind with difficulty.

There was another reason why she didn't want Mary Margaret placing too much importance on her job. Occasionally, she wondered if Bridie felt her daughter was starting to compare the two of them. Having a mother in a wheelchair was sometimes hard for an energetic little girl to take. Annie had taken over some of Bridie's role—last summer she'd coached the pee-wee girls' softball team—and she was aware of how easy it would be for Bridie to feel that her disability was creating a wall between herself and her daughter.

Bridie was a great mom, Annie thought fiercely. She didn't want Bridie thinking otherwise.

Which didn't mean that sometimes Bridie's insight wasn't way off base—like this morning. Annie snorted. She'd been dead wrong about Annie's feelings for the gorgeous Mr. Logan. Clearing the table with more vehemence than she usually gave to household chores, Annie groped for the word she was looking for. *Lust.* That was it, pure and simple. Couldn't a woman admit to being strictly interested in a man for his body in this day and age? Did that mean she was afraid of anything deeper?

"I think not, Ryan," Annie mumbled to herself, pouring hot water and detergent into the sink and snapping on a pair of bright yellow rubber dishwashing gloves. She flexed her fingers like a surgeon. "If you ever see Lucky Logan again you'll be back in your respective roles of skip and bail agent, and there won't be any hearts and flowers getting in the way of you taking him in. A one-night stand would have been interesting, but I'm not about to start picking out silverware patterns."

Just as she plunged her hands into the suds, the doorbell rang, and she cut off her monologue with a pithy expression she'd picked up from one of her skips and only used when she was completely alone. Saturday morning. It had to be someone selling something, and of course Murphy's Law dictated that he couldn't have come two minutes earlier, before she'd girded herself for battle with the breakfast dishes. She started to tug the rubber gloves off, but then decided that wearing them might emphasize the fact that she'd been interrupted in her work.

"We don't need any more magazine subscriptions, no matter how sorry you feel for them, Ryan," she told herself sternly as she walked to the front door. "Whatever he's selling, you don't need, want, or have to have. Be *firm.*"

She opened the door, suds dripping down her arm, and looked straight into the brilliant green gaze of Lucky Logan, skip at large.

"Ms. Ryan?" Glancing down at a notepad he was holding in his hand, he frowned dubiously. "Ms. Annie Ryan, Bail Enforcement Agent?"

"You owe me a pair of handcuffs, Lucky. But don't worry, I've got a spare. Step in while I get them." She kept her voice cool to hide her stupefaction. The man had the nerve of the devil, showing up like this when he knew she would take him in on sight! What was he trying to pull here?

Instead of the sweatshirt and jeans she'd seen him in before, he was wearing a well-cut charcoal-gray suit. The snowy cuffs of a dress shirt protruded an exact quarter-inch from the sleeves of his jacket, the white contrasting markedly with the tan of his hands. His shoes were black brogues, polished to a high shine. In them she could see the garish yellow reflection of her dishwashing gloves.

She hastily peeled them off, her puzzlement growing. Lucky didn't have a hair out of place. The wayward strand that had kept falling into his eyes last night was neatly groomed.

"I'm not Lucky, Ms. Ryan."

His voice was the same as she remembered, she noted with a small sense of relief. Same dark-honey tones, deep and smooth. If he hadn't been a thief he could have made a pile of money doing voice-overs for commercials, she thought appreciatively. He could sell anything to any woman with that voice.... She pulled herself up short and narrowed her eyes at him. It was time to get down to business. She didn't know what his little con game was, but as she'd told herself earlier, she wasn't buying.

"Not lucky enough to get away from me a third time, no," she agreed. "Or are you turning yourself in?"

He snapped his leather notebook shut decisively, carefully replacing it and the silver ballpoint pen he'd been using into an inside pocket of his jacket. From another pocket he pulled out a flat wallet-like case and flipped it open.

"Matt Logan, Federal Bureau of Investigation, Ms. Ryan. Lucky is—'' his eyes flickered closed for a split second as if he had a headache "—Liam, alias Lucky, is my brother."

He was good, she thought, impressed. The ID looked pretty real, but of course he'd have access to the best forgers. For whatever reason, the man had come to her to turn himself in, but he just couldn't resist putting on a show to add to the fund of stories about the mysterious Lucky Logan. He had style.

And even in a suit and tie, looking like the perfect stuffy FBI agent, he was pure male. A tom-cat swaggering along the top of a fence couldn't exude more appeal to the female of his species than Lucky Logan did to the average woman.

The average non-bounty-hunting woman, of course. To her he was attractive, sure, but basically just a skip. Just a skip, she repeated mentally, dragging her gaze from those smoky green eyes.

"Yeah, that would be your evil twin brother, right?'' she retorted. Retreating into the hallway a pace, she felt around the back of the door. Hanging on a coathook was a heavy jacket that she'd worn a couple of days ago, and in the pocket was a pair of—

"Just like old times by the riverside, huh?'' Moving swiftly, she locked a handcuff around one strong tanned wrist. The other cuff she attached instantly to a sturdy drainpipe running down the outside of the house.

Lucky sighed, not struggling. "Actually he *is*,'' he said wearily.

"Just let me get my car keys and leave a note for the family and I'll be right with you, Logan,'' Annie said. "Oh, and I have to run next door and ask Mrs. Singh to look after my niece while I'm downtown handing you over. Is what?'' she asked belatedly.

"He *is* my twin brother. I personally don't think we look that much alike, but as you can imagine, it hasn't helped my career any."

This was getting stale, she thought in disappointment. "I got the joke. I just don't think it's funny enough for a whole act, Lucky. Now how about dropping it and let's get on with business. Wait here while I—"

"Jack?" Lucky called over his shoulder. "Can you explain things to Ms. Ryan?"

There was a dark blue Taurus parked on the street, and as she watched, a man got out of the driver's seat and started up the walk towards them. He was dressed as conservatively as Lucky, but he was a couple of inches shorter, about ten years older, and his sandy hair was thinning on top.

Joe Fed, definitely. He *had* to be the real thing, Annie thought in confusion. What the heck was this all about?

"Hold it right there, mister," she barked. "Toss your badge over and don't get any closer."

"She still thinks I'm my brother," Lucky said expressionlessly. "Give her your ID, Jack. The sooner she checks us out the faster I get off this drainpipe."

Moving slowly and carefully, the other man drew an identical wallet from his pocket and threw it gingerly over to her. Annie let it drop at her feet and then, without letting her gaze waver from the two men in front of her, she nudged it towards her with the toe of her sneaker.

"There's a phone right here on the hall stand. I'm going to call the feds right now and tell them to come and pick you two jokers up," she said tensely. "Until they arrive, I want you both to play a new game—statues. The first to move loses, because right beside the phone is my gun. Understand?" She was lying. In a home with a child, even a child as sensible and mature as Mary Margaret, it would be criminally irresponsible to leave a weapon out, but all she could hope for was that they wouldn't call her bluff.

There wasn't a chance they were telling the truth, but the FBI took impersonation of their agents very seriously. Within minutes they'd have someone here.

With a cold feeling in her stomach she prayed that Mary Margaret wouldn't show up before the feds did.

"Just make the call, Ms. Ryan," the second man said. He shot a disgruntled glance at Lucky. "Ever since they made him my partner this kind of thing's been happening all the time. They're probably sitting by the phone waiting for it to ring."

Lucky's features looked like they were carved from stone, but he didn't say anything. While she dialled the operator and asked to be put through to the local field office of the FBI, he stared straight ahead, as if he'd somehow removed himself mentally from the scene.

"Logan and Cartwright, yes." The female voice at the other end of the line sounded bored, as if she'd gone through this before. "Read me their badge numbers just to make it legal, but they're supposed to be contacting you today."

"Wait a minute." Annie felt like she was in some weird kind of reverse universe. This was too bizarre. "Are you seriously telling me that you have an agent called Matthew Logan, and he's a dead ringer for Lucky Logan, the jewel thief who stole the Rubicon a while back?"

"His brother. His twin brother," the switchboard operator said. She read off two series of numbers. "Those the badge numbers they gave you?"

"Uh—yeah. Yes, that's right." He was only a couple of feet away, and she darted an incredulous look at him. His brow was knitted and he was staring at his shoes.

"Cartwright's around forty, going a little bald up top,

about five-ten. And Agent Logan—'' the voice on the phone suddenly sounded human and dropped suggestively to a purr ''—Matt Logan's tall, dark and handsome, with green eyes to die for, right?''

Annie let her glance slide unobtrusively over at him. ''More like emerald, I'd say,'' she mumbled, one hand shielding the receiver. ''With flecks of gold or amber in them.''

''I've never gotten close enough to see the flecks.'' The female agent sounded slightly wistful. ''But one other thing—if you really have got Logan handcuffed to your house I'd advise you to release him now. The man's only drawback is that, where his brother's concerned, he's got *no* sense of humor at all.''

Chapter Five

It was an exact description, Annie thought as she slowly hung up the phone. But how could she have guessed that the man chained to her drainpipe wasn't the skip she'd spent most of last night with? Surely she should have been able to spot *some* small difference in the two brothers! After all, she'd kissed Lucky. How much closer could she have gotten to him?

Don't forget, for part of that time you had your eyes closed, Ryan. Now, his kiss—that you'd be able to tell from any other man's.

"I take it everything checked out?"

Matthew Logan's dry voice held a faint edge of impatience, and she jerked her attention back to him. The white cuff of his shirtsleeve had a small spot of rust on it from the old drainpipe, but otherwise he looked as immaculate as if he were waiting outside the office of the Director of the FBI himself.

"What? Oh, right." In consternation, she fumbled in her coat pocket for the key to the cuffs. "I'm sorry about all this, Agent Logan. Agent Cartwright, you can move now," she called out to the other agent. "Hold on a minute, Agent Logan. I can't seem to find—here it is."

She unlocked the cuffs clumsily, almost dropping the key

in her haste. She was acting like a ditz, she told herself. It wasn't her fault she'd taken him for his black sheep of a brother. Apparently it happened all the time. You'd think he'd be used to it, but the way he was pulling down the sleeve of his jacket and dusting off his cuff made her nervous. He didn't even crack a smile.

Lucky's, she'd heard, could charm the diamonds off a duchess's neck. She believed it.

"You filed a report with the police last night on my brother," Logan said. "Do you mind if we come in and talk to you about it?"

"Of course not. Come in." She sounded more like herself, she thought thankfully. Professional and competent. Then she saw a blur race through the legs of Agent Cartwright, heading for the open door.

"Watch the dog!" She slammed the door behind the two men, almost knocking Cartwright over and just in time to see a pair of pleading brown eyes looking up at her from the step. "He's a stray, and he keeps trying to adopt us," she explained lamely.

"I see." Matt Logan sounded supremely bored as they followed her into the kitchen. "You should call to have him picked up."

The idea had crossed her mind, but having him express it so dispassionately seemed somehow callous. "I haven't been able to bring myself to do it yet," she said. "My niece would never forgive me if I did, anyway."

Because Mary Margaret still thought that she'd weaken and let her keep the mutt, Annie thought. But Agent Logan hadn't come here to talk about dogs.

"Why is the FBI involved in this? I thought Logan— Lucky, that is—was the responsibility of the local law." She watched in fascination as Matthew Logan flipped open his notepad and withdrew his pen from his pocket. He uncapped it and wrote the date across the top of a new page.

All of his movements were economical and precise. While his partner Cartwright sagged into his chair like a tired bloodhound and nodded enthusiastically at her suggestion of coffee, he sat bolt upright and severely declined. Annie felt as if she'd tried to bribe a Doberman on guard duty with a doggie treat.

"The FBI is involved because my brother's behavior could very well cause an international embarrassment for our government," he said, still busy writing. He shot a brief look at his watch—a plain, stainless-steel chronometer that she thought was exactly what he would wear—and wrote the time beside the date and her name. "The Rubicon belongs to the Russians, as you know. If it hadn't been for a bureaucratic foul-up, we'd have had custody of him right from the start, and we would *not* have entertained the notion of bail for him."

It was his brother he was talking about, but the man sounded as if Lucky Logan was someone he'd never met—someone he would never care to meet in any capacity other than a strictly professional one. She knew she should be on the side of law and order, and she was—but even at his worst Lucky hadn't been half as aggravating as the man sitting beside her right now.

"The Russians. Of course, the Treasures of Imperial Russia Exhibit," she said. "It was quite a daring heist, wasn't it?"

"Foolhardy and criminal acts are my twin's speciality." Logan's green gaze, exactly like Lucky's, narrowed at her as she poured a cup of coffee for his partner and came back to the table with it. "You sound as if you find him glamorous, Ms. Ryan."

He was definitely disapproving, she thought with a touch

of annoyance. "Call me Annie, Matt," she said evenly. "Since we're both professionals in the same field, more or less. And how about you come right out and tell me why it was necessary to interview me in person. Was there something you thought I might have left out of my police report?"

"Great java," Cartwright intervened diplomatically as he hastily set his mug down. "Don't get us wrong here, Annie—nobody's accusing you of anything. It's just that this is a potentially explosive situation and we need to go over everything that happened last night. Maybe Lucky said something that you didn't think was important enough to write down, or maybe you can remember some minor detail that could give us an idea of where he might have been planning to go."

"He was planning to go to jail. I was planning to put him there. And the only reason my plan fell through was that somebody started shooting at us and Lucky escaped from my car while I was trying not to get us killed, gentlemen." Her voice was low and vehement. "I didn't give him a lift to the bus station and lend him fifty bucks to make his getaway, if that's what you're implying."

"Please don't take this so personally, Ms.—Annie." It sounded as if using her first name was abhorrently informal to Logan, but he went on. "However, there are some inconsistencies in your report that we'd like to clear up for our own peace of mind. You said that he wasn't secured inside the car, but as I walked up your driveway I couldn't help but notice you've got a steel eye-bolt on the floor of the rear section. Why wasn't he cuffed to it?"

"If you saw that you must have seen the grill between me and the skips I transport," she hedged. "It's not strictly necessary to secure them to the eye-bolt. The back doors can't be unlocked from the inside."

"If they're locked in the first place," Logan said. "Which they weren't."

"It was an emergency situation, as you'll note from my report. We were being shot at." Was the man deliberately trying to rile her? If so, he was making a big mistake.

"Perhaps I misunderstood. Jack, do you have a copy of that report on you?"

For the first time, Logan smiled at her, but it was nothing like Lucky's grin. Matt Logan's smile was politely perfunctory. It held no warmth, and his eyes stayed as coolly watchful as ever. Annie had the sudden fanciful notion that if she could somehow see behind that smile, she would find an intricate and finely tuned machine, tiny gears whirring as precisely as a Swiss watch, instead of a real flesh-and-blood man.

Lucky was a criminal. He'd lied, conned and tried to escape from her during their brief time together. But he'd also unhesitatingly risked his own life for hers. He hadn't taken the time to weigh all his options or consider the consequences of his actions—he'd acted.

Just like when he'd kissed her.

Bridie had been right—he *could* have dragged her to shore and then run. Those few crazy moments in the moonlight had cost him dearly and in the same situation, his by-the-book brother would never throw away his freedom on an impulse.

"Yes, here it is. The way I read this, you and Lucky were standing by the car having a brief discussion for a couple of minutes before either one of you realized you were in any danger. Would you care to tell me what that discussion was all about?" Logan's eyes bored into hers. "I would have thought that instead of chatting with the skip you were supposed to be escorting to the authorities, you would have been more concerned with following normal procedure and getting him safely secured for transport.''

''Matt, she's on our side,'' Cartwright interjected uncomfortably.

''Let me handle this, Jack.'' Logan didn't look at his partner. ''Well, Annie?''

There was no inflection in his voice at all. He sounded like an accountant trying to track down a possible discrepancy in a column of figures. He wasn't going to understand, she knew.

''He asked me not to secure him,'' she said wearily. ''He's your brother—you must know he has a phobia about it.''

''If one of your skips had a phobia about being cuffed, would you indulge him? I'm sure many of them have *phobias* about being put behind bars again. Does your concern for their psychiatric well-being extend to letting them go if they ask you nicely?''

''Of course not.'' She held onto her temper with an effort. ''But he doesn't have a rep for violence and I felt I was justified—''

''No, he doesn't have a rep for violence. It's one of his few redeeming features.'' Logan was rolling the silver pen between his fingers unconsciously, with short, abrupt movements. ''But he does have a rep for pulling off seemingly impossible escapes. And he's also got a quite a reputation with the opposite sex—not that there's any reason for me to believe that was a factor, from your notes here. They are complete, aren't they?''

No, Annie thought with a surge of white-hot anger. She hadn't mentioned anything about their encounter on the riverbank, and she wasn't about to now. It had nothing to do with Lucky's escape. It had nothing to do with his hard-eyed brother.

"Look—this was a unique situation," she said in a low, vehement tone. "As I stated in my report, he'd pulled me from the river that same evening. I felt I owed him for that, at least. The eye-bolt is an extra precaution that really isn't—"

"But you'll agree that if he'd been secured to it we wouldn't be here interviewing you and trying to find him," he over-rode her.

"Probably not. You'd likely be down at the morgue making a positive ID on your twin brother," she snapped, rising from her chair so quickly that it nearly fell over. She put both palms on the tabletop, bracing herself, and leaned forward, bringing her face to within a foot of his. Her eyes blazed pure violet. "But I don't think that would bother you at all, would it, Logan? Do you hate him that much?"

For a moment the echo of her accusation hung in the silent room. Logan's expression was rigidly set, his mouth a grim line. Only his fingers, so tightly clenched around the silver pen that the tan had faded to white around his knuckles, betrayed the strength of his emotions. Then Cartwright cleared his throat nervously in an obvious attempt to break the tension and the pen dropped from Logan's hand to the table. It rolled off onto the floor but he didn't seem to notice.

"I don't hate him. He's my brother—my twin," he said in a monotone. "I'm just doing my job."

He had something in common with his brother besides their looks, Annie thought—they were both liars. This wasn't just a job to Matt Logan, even if he'd managed to convince himself that it was. She'd exposed a nerve.

"He's still got the Rubicon," Cartwright said bluntly. "The Russians want it back—like yesterday," he added with a sour smile.

Shaken, she slowly lowered herself back down to her

chair. She stared at the two agents in bewilderment. "I don't understand. He didn't have it on him when he was arrested, and the word was that he'd probably already passed it on to his buyer."

"He couldn't have. There wasn't time." Logan was perfectly in control of himself again and he bent down to pick up his pen as if Annie's outburst and his reaction to it had never occurred. "He had to have hidden it somewhere safe and picked it up again when he was let out on bail. There wasn't even enough hard evidence to charge him with the Rubicon theft or else he never would have been released without handing it over. He was officially charged with the theft of a ruby necklace a year ago—a job he probably didn't do, but it was something to hang on him while the Rubicon job was being investigated."

"And you think he had it on him last night when I found him?" A suspicion was beginning to dawn in her mind.

"He's a man on the run. We've blocked his bank accounts, posted look-outs at his usual haunts. Any old girl-friends that we know about are being watched, and he'd realize that." He studied her intently. "We don't just think he had the Rubicon on him last night—we *know* it. He's got nowhere to hide the thing and he needs to unload it."

"Oh, my God…" She remembered the way Lucky had stood on the bridge before he'd known she was there. He'd held his arms away from his body and had seemed to be waiting for something or someone on the other side to approach him.

"I think I may have interrupted the hand-over," she said slowly. "He said I had no idea what I was screwing up for him. He said he had an appointment he had to keep."

Logan was writing as she spoke. He looked up. "Anything else?"

"I don't think so. I didn't take him seriously anyway—not until he jumped."

"Off the bridge," he said unnecessarily. He bent his head to his notebook again, but not before Annie saw the tiny twitch at the corner of his eyelid.

It was a giveaway. Whatever he said, however he acted, there was still some shred of feeling inside the man for his twin, she realized. In his eyes she'd seen a brief glimpse of fear for his brother's safety. What must it be like for him? He'd know the death-defying details of every one of those risky exploits. He'd know that it was just a matter of time before Lucky's nickname failed him. She felt a rush of compassion for the straight-arrow Matt Logan, always aware of but unable to prevent his brother's rashness.

Her compassion was snuffed out with his next words.

"If he gave it to you for safe-keeping, we'll find out sooner or later, Annie." He closed his notebook and laid the pen beside it neatly. "I know you're holding something back."

It took a moment for his words to sink in. When they did, she felt as if she'd been slapped across the face. It was the supreme insult. This man—this pompous, humorless, unpleasant FBI agent who probably had a picture of J. Edgar hanging in his office, she thought disparagingly—this Matt Logan was accusing *her* of being a criminal, no better than the scum she hunted down every day. How dare he!

"You got that right," she smiled thinly. "Guilty as charged, Agent Logan—I *have* been holding back on you. But I guess I'll have to come clean now." Out of the corner of her eye she saw Cartwright looking at the two of them like a man watching an accident about to happen. "I've been holding back my real opinion of you, Logan. I've been holding back what I'd really like to tell you to your face. I've been holding back, with great difficulty, my suggestion about where you might like to put that nifty little notebook and pen set of yours—"

"Annie, come on now. Matt's under a great deal of stress here but I'm sure—" Cartwright's bloodhound demeanor was more pronounced than ever, his mouth sagging in dismay.

"I'm under stress too!" she retorted. "I lost a skip last night and nearly got killed on top of everything else! Probably the only reason it wasn't a member of *my* family going down to the morgue today to make an identification was because Lucky Logan bailed me out of the situation, using his own life as collateral. *Lucky.* The good-for-nothing black sheep of a brother you feel so superior to, Agent Logan."

"I'll note your comments," he said stiffly. "Right now we need to—"

"You need to take a look at your attitude," she interrupted. "I'm damn good at my job and I won't have anyone implying that I'm not. I'll cooperate with you fully, and if I run across your brother again I'll do my duty—but after meeting you, he has my sympathy."

"If I see him first I'll convey the message, Ryan." He stood up, looking suddenly intimidatingly tough. All at once the suit and tie seemed like a civilized disguise, the correct manner nothing more than a mask. "And I appreciate your offer of cooperation, because we're going to search your vehicle. I take it we don't need a warrant?"

"It's possible Lucky might have stashed the stone there, Annie," Cartwright said into the silence. "*Without* your knowledge, of course." He shot an angry look at his partner.

"You really think I've got it, don't you?" She drew herself up to her full height and stared up at Logan. "Go ahead and look. Maybe you'd like to try for a strip-search while you're at it. Maybe you get off on flashing your tin badge at women and having them cower in front of you.'' She gave a thin smile. ''Don't mess with me, Logan.''

''A strip-search isn't necessary.'' Cartwright was already out of the kitchen, and Logan started to follow his partner. Then he stopped. ''But if it was, I wouldn't be using my damn badge to persuade you, Ryan. Count on it.'' He turned on his heel and walked out.

HE DIDN'T LOOK anything like the man who'd shown up on her doorstep earlier. The suit jacket was flung carelessly on the front lawn and the black brogues were scuffed and dusty. As Matt maneuvered himself out from under the Buick, Annie surveyed him with satisfaction. There was a smear of grease high on one cheekbone, and although he'd rolled his shirtsleeves up, the once-immaculate white fabric was creased and dirty. He'd lost a button. She could see it at the edge of the grass, but she didn't point it out to him.

''You know, I'm not absolutely sure now that Lucky did have an opportunity to reach down under the car,'' she mused. ''Oh, well. Better safe than sorry.''

Logan stood up and turned away from her, his shoulders set. He had a large oil stain on his back. ''Find anything, Cartwright?''

''A little over a dollar in change, two empty potato-chip bags and a couple of paperbacks,'' Cartwright said. He glanced at the covers and held them out to Annie. ''This must be how you fill in those long hours on stakeout, right? Interesting mix—*Maximizing Your Firing Capacity* and a Harlequin romance.''

She took them from him. ''I'm a woman of many facets, Jack. Just like the Rubicon, which I take it you *didn't* find.'' She stepped back to place the books on the porch and felt something under her foot. She looked down.

"I'll get that if you don't mind," Logan said through his teeth. He bent down and tugged his notebook out from under her sneaker. His hair was falling into his eyes and as he shrugged into his jacket he raked it back in frustration.

"It looks like we're finished here, unless you want to take a look under the hood, Matt," Cartwright said mildly. His partner turned a cold stare on him and said nothing. "Well, that's it, then. We appreciate you letting us take up your time like this, Annie, especially since it looks like we were barking up the wrong tree anyway."

Logan was already on his way to the Taurus at the curb. He stopped at the driver's side. "On behalf of the Bureau, I echo that." It seemed an effort for him to choke the words out. "Here's my card in case you remember anything else you feel inclined to share with us."

He wasn't even bothering to use her name anymore, Annie thought. All he wanted to do was to get the hell out of here and forget he'd ever met her. She smiled pleasantly. She could afford to be magnanimous now. Matt Logan was a beaten man.

"You bet. *If* I remember anything."

As Logan handed her his business card, Cartwright climbed into the passenger seat of the Taurus. Logan shifted position so that he was blocking the other agent's view of them and as she reached out to take it from him he moved swiftly, imprisoning her wrist in a strong grip.

"Why?" His voice was barely above a whisper, harsh and urgent. "You're not the type to risk everything for a kiss in the moonlight, so what is it about him? Is it just the thrill of the forbidden, flirting with the wrong side of the law? Is it his romantic reputation?"

"Let me go, Agent Logan. You're way out of line here." She tried to pull her hand from his as she ground out her command, but he only held it more firmly. His face was inches from hers. Someone watching them from the other side of the street might think they were lovers, prolonging a reluctant farewell. His head was bent towards her and his mouth was close enough so that if she rose up slightly on her tiptoes, she'd be able to kiss it.

He'd respond if she did, she knew suddenly. He wouldn't be able to stop himself. What was between them was too bright and sharp for mere dislike. It ran deeper than that; so deep that on some barely conscious level she knew that if she and Matt Logan were ever forced together in the future they'd either be at each other's throat or in each other's bed.

She knew which option she'd choose. She could handle him as an enemy.

"I've seen it a hundred times in the past. He's charming, Annie. He lives on the edge and I guess that's attractive to a woman. It worked on you, didn't it?"

Abruptly he released her hand and stepped back. She felt as if the world around her had suddenly lost a hairbreadth of focus—just enough that her senses no longer felt so painfully acute. The real man who'd revealed himself to her for the last few seconds had vanished behind the unreadable mask of the perfect agent again.

"You've got the stone. You know where to reach me."

He turned on his heel, got into the Taurus and drove off. She watched him come to a full stop at the intersection half a block away, put on his turn signal and pull smoothly and unhurriedly into traffic.

He drove like he did everything else—with absolute precision and not an ounce of passion. But it was all a lie. Maybe he thought he and Lucky were nothing alike, but the wild streak was there in both of them. Lucky's was visible. Matt's was buried so deep that he probably didn't even know he had one.

But she'd caught a glimpse of the fire that raged in him. He was right to keep it locked away under that icy exterior, Annie thought with a slight shiver. If he ever unleashed it completely the flames could end up engulfing not only himself, but anyone who was foolish enough to get close to him.

"Aunt Annie! Can Ranjeet come with us to the Aquarium this afternoon?"

Mary Margaret's plea broke into her troubling thoughts, and she looked up to see that her niece was in the middle of a game of marbles on the Singh's driveway, two doors down. She strolled over to watch, glad to return to normalcy.

"Hi, guys. Who's winning?" she addressed the semicircle of rumps hunched over in concentration.

"Me," Mary Margaret said with callous honesty. She'd tucked her red-gold hair up under her cap and was preparing to shoot again. With her baggy jeans and unlaced high-tops, she looked as tough and feisty as the rest of her companions, all boys. But appearances could be deceptive, Annie thought with amusement. Mary Margaret was tougher.

"*Yes!*" The little girl pumped a grubby fist into the air and turned to her aunt. "Big Blue wins again. Can Ranjeet come with us?"

"Sure, if his mom says it's okay," Annie answered distractedly. "What do you mean, 'Big Blue?'"

"My new marble. Go ask her, Ranjeet." Mary Margaret looked up as another player prepared to shoot. "It's awesome. I left my catcher's mitt in your car Monday after practice and when I got it this morning, I found Big Blue in the thumb. Do I have to ask the other kids on the team if they lost it, Aunt Annie?"

She held it out for Annie to see and, bending down

slowly, her aunt took it from her. It was blue, all right. And big—almost obscenely so. Mary Margaret was right. Even begrimed with grease and dust, it was awesome.

It was a long way from the Imperial Court of St. Petersburg to a cutthroat game of marbles in a Southie driveway, but judging from the pile of recently won aggies and cat's-eyes beside her niece, the Rubicon sapphire was still performing like an aristocrat.

Chapter Six

"Back away from the chocolate chip cookies and nobody gets hurt, lady."

Annie spun around guiltily as Bridie wheeled herself noiselessly into the kitchen. Her sister was wearing a quilted dressing gown and her hair hung over her shoulder in one thick braid. She frowned at Annie in mock disapproval.

"Those are for that do at your darling niece's school on Monday. Although if her behavior at the dinner table tonight was any indication, maybe chocolate's not a good idea."

"She was all wound up from our trip to the Aquarium. Who knows, you might have a future marine biologist on your hands," Annie said, snaffling another cookie. "Last one, I promise."

"She was a brat." Bridie sighed and took a cookie for herself from the plate. "I really shouldn't. I can't burn the calories off like you can. So are you going to tell me why that visit from the FBI upset you so much today?"

"Gosh darn, let's see," Annie stared up at the ceiling in intense concentration. "Agent Logan practically dismantled my car in the driveway looking for the Rubicon sapphire, accused me of lying to him and finally told me that I was holding it for his brother, whom I'd apparently fallen for at first sight so hard that I was willing to break every law in the land for him. Apart from that, he was charming.''

''Nothing like Lucky?''

''He looks like him, but when the personality gene was handed out he must have been somewhere else spit-shining his shoes,'' Annie said sarcastically.

''Of course, when the honesty gene was handed out, Lucky wasn't in line either, was he?'' Bridie said. She nibbled delicately at her cookie and looked up at her sister quizzically. ''Too bad you couldn't put the two of them together in one man. You'd have Mr. Perfect.''

''Or maybe the experiment would go wrong and you'd end up with an arrogant, overbearing jerk who lied his head off,'' Annie mused.

They stared at each other. Bridie was the first to crack, but in a moment both of them were laughing so hard that she was holding onto the arms of her chair for dear life, and Annie was doubled over.

''Darn!'' she swore weakly. ''Obviously it's been done before.''

''Many times,'' Bridie agreed, gasping for breath. ''Remember Duke Krasinski?''

''Oh, my God—the date from hell. What was I thinking, to go out with him?''

''I don't think it officially counts as a date when it only lasts forty-five minutes and he has to get his nose taped at the emergency ward, does it?'' Bridie asked.

''That was an accident. I was nodding off in the middle of him droning on about his promotion and the next thing I knew there was a hand half-way up my skirt. I was so startled my head just jerked up involuntarily.'' Her laughter subsided into a sigh. ''I sure know how to pick 'em, don't I?''

Absent-mindedly she reached for another cookie but Bridie's hand shot out and slapped her wrist. "It works out exactly the way you want. You'd run a mile if you ever met someone you could get serious about. That's why you were so attracted to Lucky—because you know there's no future with a thief on the run." She looked up at Annie soberly. "And if you don't expect a future with someone, then you're not worried about them being ripped away from you, right?"

"That's getting old, sis. Drop it, okay?" Annie turned away in irritation and poured herself a glass of milk. She suddenly wished it was something stronger, but she hadn't felt much like eating today and milk was probably a safer bet than a shot of Pa's Irish whiskey—especially since she was going to need all her wits about her later on tonight, she thought nervously.

Still, there were times when Bridie's big-sister concern came close to driving her to drink. Even with her back turned she could feel those periwinkle-blue eyes on her as she drank her milk.

"Mom's death wasn't your fault, Annie," Bridie said. "She never would have wanted you to close yourself off like this."

The quietly spoken words were tender and her tone was gentle, but to Annie it was as if her sister had tossed a grenade into her lap. She felt her whole body go rigid, and she spun around to face Bridie in shock.

"Is that your theory? That I feel responsible for what happened to Mom?" she snapped. Her lips felt numb and the words seemed to tumble out by themselves. "Because if it is, you'd better turn in your mail-order psychiatric degree. Unless the truth is that *you've* always blamed me a little bit for that night!"

"That's crazy and you know it!" Bridie's expression

was stunned, her face white. "No one ever blamed you except yourself. For heaven's sakes, Annie, you weren't much older than Mary Margaret at the time she was killed—what were you supposed to do?"

"Exactly." Annie slammed her milk glass down on the counter sharply. She swore briefly. "So why would you think that what happened all those years ago is still affecting me? I grew up without a mom. I missed her—I still miss her, just like you and Pa miss her. Just like you miss Sean. Does that make you responsible for *his* death?"

She regretted the words as soon as they were out of her mouth, but it was too late to retract them. It was too late to erase the stricken look in Bridie's eyes, to take back the pain she'd caused her. But she had to try.

"Bridie, I'm sorry. I didn't mean to—"

"It *was* my fault that Sean was killed," her sister said in a whisper. "That drunk was behind the wheel—but Sean wouldn't have gone out at all that night if I hadn't persuaded him to. I wanted some time alone with him, just the two of us, and his parents had offered to look after Mary Margaret for a few hours so I thought…" Her voice broke.

Annie knelt swiftly by her sister's wheelchair. "Of course it wasn't your fault. How can you even think that?"

"He'd had a long day at work. He was tired, maybe his reactions were slower than usual, maybe he might have been able to do something—"

"He was in the middle of an intersection when a drunk driver sped through a red light, for God's sake!" Annie said urgently. "Bridie, Sean never had a chance! There was *nothing* he could have done to prevent that accident! Nothing *you* could have done."

"It doesn't have to be logical." Bridie met her sister's gaze. Her hands gripped the arms of her chair tightly. "I know in my mind that I really wasn't responsible, but some nights I lie in bed alone and my heart just keeps crying out for him. That's when I think, what if I hadn't asked him to take me out for a ride? What if we'd just…just stayed home?''

Annie wrapped her arms around her sister's strong shoulders, feeling them shake. She'd had no idea that Bridie'd been carrying such a burden of guilt for all this time. Even so, Annie should never have lashed out at Bridie the way she had. What had prompted her to react so defensively? Bridie had been off base in her assumptions about the way their mother's death had affected Annie, but she'd only brought up the subject out of concern. *And I came back at her with the sharpest weapon I could find,* Annie thought in shame, *as if I was under attack. As if I felt threatened.*

''I went down to the jail that night,'' she said, prying up the fingers of Bridie's hand with difficulty and holding them in her own. ''I went down looking for Jeffrey Haskins. I think I wanted to kill him.''

Bridie raised her head slowly and looked at her. ''You never told me this. What were you thinking of, Annie? You would have been charged with murder!''

''The doctors didn't think you'd make it through the night. Sean was dead. Haskins had destroyed my family.'' Her eyes were dark with memory. ''I hadn't been able to prevent that from happening, but I thought I could make sure he never had the chance to do it again. Then I ran into Dave Bunt.''

''Pa's old sergeant.'' Bridie was returning her grip, her eyes fixed on her sister's set face.

''Yeah. He knew me well enough to see that something was wrong, and when he asked me what I was doing, I told him.'' Annie made a sound that might have been a laugh. ''I guess I was a little crazy at that point. He drove me home and stayed the night, and never reported the incident.''

Bridie closed her eyes briefly. "Thank God."

"I do," Annie said. She felt the steel of the wheelchair cold against her thigh as she knelt there and she took a deep breath. "Most of the time."

"Does Pa know about this?"

"No one knows except Dave Bunt, and now you." She swallowed past the lump in her throat that suddenly made it hard to speak. "I guess I want you to know that I don't always do the right thing, sis. But I love you even when I'm being horrible. I'm sorry for what I said."

"I've always known that." Bridie looked up, her smile faint but visible. "Just like you know I love you even when I'm being an irritating big sister, right?"

"Right," Annie laughed weakly, relief flooding through her.

"Pa should be back from his block safety meeting soon." Bridie tucked a stray strand of red-gold hair back into her braid and propelled herself over to the kitchen counter. "What the heck—I can whip up another batch of these tomorrow. Let's put on the kettle and have tea and cookies waiting for him."

"For an irritating big sister, sometimes you come up with pretty good ideas," Annie said huskily.

"Once in a while." Bridie looked up at her, her eyes bright. "But the best one I ever had was when I was five years old. Know what it was?"

"What?" Annie paused, the kettle in her hand.

"I told Mom and Pa I wanted a little sister for Christmas instead of a doll. They said they'd see what they could do." She cleared her throat, turning to the counter and peeling back the plastic wrap from the plate of cookies. From outside came the sound of the van turning into the driveway.

"No returns or exchanges after all this time, sis." Annie's voice was soft and her hand touched the bright rose-gold of her sister's hair so lightly that Bridie didn't notice. "You've left it too late to take me back now."

SHE'D LEFT IT too late to take the Rubicon to Matt Logan, Annie thought nervously a few hours later. But she'd never intended to. From the moment she'd first laid eyes on the thing, glittering through its coating of grime in Mary Margaret's hand, she'd known exactly what she was going to do.

She sat on the edge of her bed in the dark, looking down through the open window at her car parked directly below. She was a bounty hunter, dammit! If fate handed her a second chance to bring her skip in, she'd take it.

There's the little matter of possessing stolen goods, Ryan. What makes you so sure Logan won't have you charged with that when he finds out you had the Rubicon and didn't tell him? He wouldn't, she answered herself. Not if she delivered his brother at the same time she handed over the stone.

It was a trap, with the Rubicon as bait. Matt Logan might have had his suspicions that Lucky had stashed the sapphire during that wild ride last night, planning to come back and retrieve it. But, despite the fact that he'd thought she was lying to him this morning, he had no hard proof that his theory was correct. The only person who knew for sure that Lucky would be back to collect his ill-gotten gains was...

Me, Annie thought in satisfaction. And I'll be waiting for him. She heard a faint noise from down below and froze, straining her eyes to see through the darkness. It came again, a curious whining sound. Then she saw the small figure trotting disconsolately down the drive to the sidewalk and she relaxed. The mutt was persistent, she thought with reluctant admiration. He'd been hanging around for weeks now, and he hadn't given up yet. If Mary Margaret hadn't gone through so much in the last few years she might even have caved in and allowed him to become part of the family. But it was too soon—the child was still too emotionally vulnerable. She'd never forgive herself if she let Mary Margaret have a pet right now and something happened to it.

The house was quiet, and when she glanced at the faintly luminous dial of her watch she saw that it was after two o'clock. If he was going to show up at all it would be soon, she thought, moving closer to the window and feeling the cool night air on her face. He'd go directly to the Buick and the baseball glove that she'd replaced on the seat, and when he did, she'd creep down the back stairs and have him covered before he even realized that the sapphire wasn't there.

She darted a swift look at her dresser where the Rubicon gleamed coldly in the moonlight.

He'd *used* her. She shifted position slightly, still keeping to one side of the open window. She'd thought that he'd risked his life last night to draw the shooter away from her, but his priority had always been that damned stone. He'd been protecting it, not her.

"I don't owe you a thing, Lucky," she murmured under her breath. "You played me for a fool right from the start, but it won't happen again."

The worst of it was, there *had* been some truth in what Bridie had said this morning. Annie's face warmed as she remembered how vehemently she'd denied her attraction to Lucky, and how easily her sister had guessed that she was lying to herself. She might as well admit it—she hadn't been able to forget that kiss all day, hadn't been able to control the slow heat that ran through her every time she thought of it. His hands on her, the taste of him, the way his wet clothes had clung to that leanly muscled body like a second skin.... And the look in his eyes when he'd held her as if he didn't want to let her go. While she was at it, she thought uncomfortably, she might as well admit that what she'd felt for the man hadn't been exclusively physical.

She *had* fallen for him a little, despite everything she knew about him. How stupid could she get?

He was undeniably good-looking. Those eyes, that midnight-black hair, those broad shoulders that even his immaculately cut jacket couldn't completely conceal, Annie mused. He was devastatingly—

She pulled herself up short. She'd never seen Lucky in a suit—for some reason, it was *Matt* Logan she was visualizing. And that really was ridiculous, because if there was one man who was definitely *not* on her fantasy list, it was Agent Logan.

There was a soft *click* as the door to her Buick was opened.

He was there! Adrenaline surged through her as she saw the shadowy figure in the driveway leaning into the unlocked car, but she controlled her racing pulse and stood up, keeping to the edge of the window frame where she could see but not be seen. It was Lucky, all right. Her plan had worked and he'd walked straight into the trap she'd laid for him.

Hastily slipping out of her room and down the back stairs, she pulled her Glock from her shoulder holster. One of the few things she and Matt Logan agreed on was that his brother wasn't a violent offender, but the gun would persuade Lucky that running wasn't an option. All she had to do was hand him over to the police tonight like a special delivery parcel, and then tomorrow she'd have the satisfaction of watching Agent Logan's chiseled jaw drop as she told him she'd got both Lucky *and* the Rubicon back.

She edged round the corner of the house, thankful that her father and Bridie were sound sleepers and that for the past few months the nightmares that Mary Margaret had suffered from after the accident seemed to have stopped. She didn't want her family involved in this at all, no matter how charming a criminal Lucky was.

She rounded the last corner of the house and stepped into the driveway, the Glock preceding her as she trained it on where Lucky was—where Lucky *should* have been. Although the door to the Buick was still open, there was no one there.

A slight movement caught the corner of her eye, and she looked up just in time to see the dark silhouette slipping in through her open bedroom window.

He was in the house! Suddenly it didn't matter what Logan's rap sheet said—her heart felt like it was going to explode as she spun around and headed for the back stairs at a run. Her father and Bridie had their rooms on the first floor, but Mary Margaret's room was just down the hall from hers. Dear God, what if she came wandering into the bedroom while Lucky was there? Who knew how he'd react if he was startled?

If anything happened to Mary Margaret, Annie knew she would never forgive herself. As she crept down the hall she noted with relief that the little girl's bedroom door was closed. She felt almost weak with reaction, and then anger kicked in. Nobody got this close to the people she cared about!

She pushed her door open and raised the Glock. "Freeze, Lucky. And this time don't try any swan dives."

She flicked the switch by the door on with one hand, and the shaded lamp by her bed spilled a warm golden glow into the room. He was dressed in a black sweater and jeans, and he had his back to her. One leg was already thrown over the windowsill. He did as she said, and froze.

"Maybe it's time for me to look into another career," he said conversationally, still not moving. "I think I'm losing my touch."

"You'll lose more than your touch if you don't stop talking and get back in the room," Annie said repressively. "I'm in no mood for lighthearted charm, Lucky. Or sudden moves. Keep your hands in plain view and take it real slow."

"Did I forget our anniversary or something, sweetheart?" Logan gripped the sides of the window frame and straightened up to his full height. "I mean, last night you were going to hand me over to the cops, but you still laughed at my jokes."

The man was impossible. "I was being polite. I forgot my manners when I found out you'd used my car as a hiding place for your loot, Lucky. Turn around."

"It was a spur of the moment decision." He pivoted slowly and faced her, and although she'd been prepared for it, the full force of his magnetism struck her like a blow.

He didn't have to steal, she thought helplessly. All he had to do was ask nicely, and most women would hand their jewelry over. That little half smile hovering at the corner of his mouth was the clincher, but the silky wool sweater, its sleeves pushed halfway up strong forearms, and the button-front jeans riding those lean hips didn't hurt either.

In her softly feminine room his overwhelming maleness was an almost physical force. Contrasted with the white-painted window trim his skin looked dark gold, and the lace of the curtains seemed more fragile as he leaned against them and met her suddenly uncertain gaze.

"I never planned on involving you further," he said slowly, his green eyes regretful.

Okay, now *that* was a lie, she thought briskly, forcing herself to ignore the husky note in his voice and concentrate on the words. She felt as if she'd just been doused with ice-water. It was a welcome jolt back to reality.

"Give me a break," she said bluntly. "You had every intention of involving me. That's why you broke the dome-light in the car—because you knew you'd be sneaking back here tonight if you could, and you didn't want it coming on when you opened the door."

The half smile slipped and then he rallied. "A stray bullet. I'd say we both had a narrow escape last night."

"It was crushed, not shattered. You had to have done it while I was busy trying to dodge that maniac on the bike, which takes this out of the realm of a spur-of-the-moment decision." She gave him a half smile of her own. "Any other lame excuses I can shoot down? I'm on a roll here, Lucky."

"It's not just that I put the damn jewel in the car, is it? It's because I brought this whole mess too close to your family." He wasn't smiling this time, and suddenly his expression was more like his brother's than his own. "I'm sorry for that, Annie. I realized you'd discovered it when I found that the baseball glove was empty, and then I saw the open window. Like I said, I must be losing my touch— I'd thought I'd be in and out in a second. But I'd never have hurt anyone in this house—including you."

He had a patent on phony sincerity, she told herself dubiously. But somehow she found herself believing that this time, at least, he was telling the truth. If she wanted to blame anyone for this, she should be blaming herself. Using the Rubicon as bait had been her plan after all, and what was bait for if not to attract a catch? She'd been too self-confident, too sure that she could confine the take-down to the driveway, but she shouldn't have taken even that much of a risk. Now she was stuck in her bedroom with a jewel thief who could make Houdini look like a butterfingers. What the heck was she going to do with him?

They couldn't leave the way he'd come. Maybe Lucky Logan could scale walls with ease, but there was no way she could cover him and make it down herself without breaking her neck. And she wasn't about to lead him through a sleeping house in the dark, she thought, her unease growing. It would be too easy for him to escape, especially since there was no way he'd believe she would use her gun. He'd proven last night that handcuffs weren't a deterrent when he felt like making a fast departure.

There was only one solution, but she refused even to consider it.

"You're trying to figure out what to do with me now, aren't you?" He was studying her with interest. "You've decided that we can't leave by the window and you won't risk playing blind-man's-bluff with me in your house. Which means that you're probably going to keep me here in your bedroom until morning, right?"

"In your dreams, Logan." Her response was nervously automatic, but he was right. What else could she do? She'd painted herself into a corner. And if she was forced to keep him here all night, what in heaven's name was she going to cuff him to?

"You'll have to cuff me to the bedstead," he said thoughtfully. "It's about the only thing that's sturdy enough. You're right, this *is* like in my dreams—my dream last night, anyway."

"I don't want to hear about it, Logan." She could feel the color rising in her cheeks. "Maybe you're under the mistaken impression that I invited you here for a sleepover, but to me this is a simple problem in logistics. One—I need to keep you locked up until I can get you out of here safely. Two—To do that I'm going to have to cuff you. Three— I'm *not* cuffing you to my bed. So all I have to do is find something strong enough to secure you to for a few hours and my problem's solved.''

Nothing could be farther from the truth, she thought. If she was actually considering spending the night with Lucky Logan, her problems were just beginning. She darted a quick look at him from under her lashes and felt the now-familiar weakness in her knees, the molten warmth spreading through her veins. Maybe if she'd never kissed him in the first place she wouldn't be feeling so vulnerable now, but she had. She remembered exactly how it had felt, and ever since last night she'd been aching to experience it again.

Staying away from him would take all the will power she had and then some, but there really wasn't any other option. She'd just have to cuff him to something strong enough so that she could concentrate on standing guard over her own impulses for the next few hours.

She looked expectantly around the room she'd slept in since she was a little girl, as if it might have possibilities she'd never seen before. Out of the corner of her eye she saw that slow, heart-stopping grin spread across his features.

''I like sleeping on the left side, sweetheart,'' Lucky said.

''THIS IS COSY.'' He was propped up with four feather pillows behind his head, his long legs almost touching the ornate iron footboard. ''You don't have to cover me with that cannon all night. I can't go anywhere.''

He shouldn't be able to, she thought, eyeing him from across the room. His right wrist was encircled by heavy stainless steel, and the other cuff was snapped around solid Victorian iron. She'd seen the bed in the window of a Charles Street antique dealer last summer, and although it had been more than she really should have spent, she hadn't been able to resist it.

The man attached to it right now was another story, she told herself. Nothing he said was about to make her relax her vigilance.

"I take it this wasn't the way it was in your dream." As soon as she uttered the words, she knew they were a mistake.

"Well, there were handcuffs." He slanted a lazy look at her through half-closed eyes. "But you were wearing them. And not much else, as I recall."

The sensually teasing note in his voice did nothing to dispel the erotic image that flashed through her mind. He'd fantasized about her. He'd *dreamt* about her. She'd affected him the same way he'd affected her, and he'd known the same dry-mouthed frustration she'd been feeling since they'd broken off that kiss last night. But he'd continued the encounter between them in his imagination…

With an effort she turned the conversation back to a safer subject.

"Your brother told me you had a reputation, Lucky. I'm immune to you now that I've been warned."

"Matt?" His eyes flew open and he seemed suddenly tense. "He talked to you about me? What did he say?"

"He came here looking for information and the Rubicon." She sat back in the overstuffed easy chair a few feet away from the bed, hoping he hadn't noticed her momentary susceptibility. "There's no love lost between you two, is there?"

"We were separated when we were just kids. Our parents died in a plane crash and we were brought up by different branches of the family.'' He shrugged. ''We don't have much in common.''

''You don't seem to have anything in common. Tell me, was he always so stuffy and strait-laced?''

''Is that the way he seemed to you?'' He frowned. ''I guess he does give that impression at times. My mother's side of the family took him in when we were orphaned, and they were old money—wealthy and conservative. He spent most of his childhood at boarding schools.''

''That would have been hard on him,'' Annie said slowly. ''First losing his parents and his twin, and then being shipped off to school like an unwanted package.'' It explained the spit-and-polish demeanor that had irritated her so much, she thought.

''My mother's parents were a lot older than the grandparents who adopted me. Matt always cared for them, and they did their best by him.'' Lucky grinned. ''But I got the fun side of the family.''

''Your father's parents? What were they like?''

''Sam was a trapeze artist when he was younger—he's my grandfather. Yvonne, my grandmother, was the daughter of minor royalty, without a penny to her name but with a face so beautiful that people would stop in the street and stare at her.'' He smiled. ''That's what Sam says, anyway. It's not hard to believe—she's still lovely.''

''So you were brought up in a circus?'' she asked curiously.

''Hell, no. Yvonne made Sam quit the trapeze act when they got married, and they became the most famous husband-and-wife team of jewel thieves of their day.'' He lay back on her satin pillows, obviously enjoying her stupefaction. ''I'm carrying on the family business, sweetheart.''

She was startled into laughter. ''No wonder you two are

like night and day!'' she said. ''Doesn't he sometimes wish your positions had been reversed?''

''He'd never admit to it, but the life he leads has got to drive him crazy once in a while.'' Lucky raked his free hand through his hair. ''I mean, look at him—always having to be so careful, so conservative, just to live down the blot on his family tree. He nearly didn't get into the Bureau because of his background, and he's had to fight for every promotion. Having him on my case is probably a test of his loyalties—they insisted on calling him in on this.''

''Why wouldn't they? One of their agents is the brother of the criminal they're trying to find—of course he'd be assigned to you.'' She was surprised to hear an edge in her tone, and she lowered her voice. ''The one man who knows you better than anyone else and you didn't think he'd get involved?''

''And the one man who might not be completely objective about putting me behind bars.'' He looked up, black hair falling into his eyes and his mouth thinned to a humorless line. ''If he hadn't been given the case he would have asked for it.''

''He wanted the chance to hunt you down? But why?'' If it was anyone other than Agent Logan, Annie thought, she wouldn't believe it. But after their conversation today she'd known he was being driven by an overwhelming emotion where his brother was concerned.

''Who knows?'' A shadow crossed his face. ''Maybe he's got some crazy notion that he can save me from myself. Maybe he's doing it because he cares.'' He shrugged, but she had the impression that he wasn't as unaffected as he was pretending to be.

''And maybe he's doing it because his whole life he's been confined to a stifling mold, and you've always been a free spirit. Maybe he can't stand that," she suggested, her eyes narrowing as she recalled their encounter.

"He really got to you, didn't he?" Lucky looked taken aback at the vehemence of her reaction. "What was it about him that riled you so much?"

"That damned notebook!" she retorted heatedly. "The man must sleep with it. It's probably the most meaningful relationship he has."

"That's it? That's your main objection to him?" He was sitting bolt upright on her bed now, leaning towards her and only restrained from coming closer by his shackled wrist. He looked incredulous and she felt compelled to explain.

"Oh, it just seemed typical of his whole persona—uptight, by-the-book, meticulous." She frowned. "I got the feeling he forces himself to act that way—that he's afraid if he relaxed that iron control even a little, he might never be able to get it back again."

"That's crazy. That's like saying he's as wild as I am, only he won't admit it," he said flatly. "I know him, and believe me, Matt's exactly what he appears. He's nothing like me." He nodded at the dresser, his features relaxing into his usual casually amused expression. "And that damned blue rock isn't exactly going to bring us closer."

He'd obviously said all he was going to about the relationship between him and his brother, Annie thought, stifling her curiosity with difficulty. Even the Rubicon was a preferable subject.

"Strange that you didn't have it on you when you were picked up by the police," she probed delicately. "What a busy few hours you must have had—stealing the world's most valuable sapphire, preparing to skip the country, delivering a baby in an elevator. When exactly did you hide it, and where?"

"If I tell you all my secrets you won't find me mysteriously attractive anymore," he said with an infuriating smile. "And I still have high hopes for this bed, sweetheart. It's warmer than that riverbank last night."

"What happened on the riverbank was a one-time-only deal, Lucky," she countered, willing her gaze away from his with an effort. "Chalk it up to the moonlight and the fact that you'd just saved my life."

He looked thoughtful. "That's all it takes? Because if we switch off this lamp I figure there's still plenty of moon out tonight. I saved you more than once, so you still owe me."

"From the biker, you mean? I'm glad you brought that up." She stood, suddenly needing to put some distance between them. Sitting there, letting that rough purr of a voice wrap itself around her was altogether too dangerous. He was evading all her questions with ease, and it was time she re-established the lines between them before they blurred completely.

"You can keep all the other secrets you want. But when someone comes that close to killing me, I have this insatiable curiosity to find out more about him. Who was the shooter, Lucky—the person you were meeting on the bridge when I showed up? Was he after the jewel?"

She was beginning to think he wasn't going to reply when he finally spoke.

"He wasn't my buyer," he said heavily. "I'm guessing he was a third party who somehow found out about the deal I'd arranged and was there to hijack the stone."

"Who *was* your buyer? How do you know this biker wasn't working for him, trying to double-cross you?" she demanded, not satisfied with his cryptic explanation.

"I can't tell you that." He looked up at her, his expression closed and unreadable. "You'll just have to trust me on this one, Annie."

He'd manipulated and maneuvered her for long enough, she thought with growing heat. And she'd cooperated all the way down the line, letting herself be swept away by her hormones every time she looked at him. Even now she wanted to give him the benefit of the doubt, wanted to forget that the two of them were on opposite sides, but if she didn't take a stand now, she never would.

"Trust you?" She forced a low, incredulous laugh, and had the satisfaction of seeing that she'd disconcerted him. His eyes darkened. "After you left the hottest piece of stolen goods in Boston on the back seat of my car? After you got me on the FBI's list of suspected accomplices? I don't think so."

"I risked my life for you when I took off on foot last night," Lucky said. He swung his legs off the side of the bed and started to stand, but then he was jerked back by the handcuff. He swore under his breath.

"You risked your life for the Rubicon. You led that biker away from the stone, not me. All I was to you was a convenient patsy—and I fell for it, dammit!" She leaned over the bed, her face close to his. "Was that what the kiss was all about? An insurance policy to keep me on your side if you needed to?"

"For a smart woman you can be awfully dumb sometimes," he ground out. There was no trace of his normal lazy attitude now, Annie noted. She was seeing the real Lucky at last, and he was mad enough to discard his evasive tactics and tell her the truth for once.

"I didn't plan on hauling a bounty hunter out of the river last night. I didn't plan on taking one look at her when I did and feeling like I'd just had the breath knocked out of me. And I certainly didn't plan on kissing you—in fact, that was just plain stupid on my part.''

''It was stupid on my part too!'' she hissed back. ''I've been thinking about you all day, replaying every minute of what happened between us and wishing we hadn't stopped when we did. Don't you think I *know* how crazy that is?''

Their faces were only inches apart, both of them glaring at each other. She was so close to him that she could feel the heat he gave off and see the specks of hazel in those furious green eyes. He smelled like plain soap and water, she thought foolishly. Then she saw the faint ridge of color ride high on his cheekbones under his tan and the hazel in his eyes deepened to a tawny gold.

''Maybe we're both not too smart.'' His voice was a husky whisper. ''But I bet we'd be hell in bed together. Get rid of the damn gun and kiss me, Annie.''

Chapter Seven

Last night she'd had an excuse, however flimsy, for her uncharacteristic behavior with this man, Annie thought. Tonight the only excuse she had was that she just couldn't say no to him—not when he was sprawled there on the edge of her bed, holding her with that steady green-gold gaze.

"Stop looking at me like that, Logan," she said. She heard the unsteadiness in her own voice. "It's not fair."

"I don't give a damn about fair. I'll use everything I've got to have you, even if it's just for one night." Without breaking eye contact with her, he moved a fraction of an inch closer. Before she knew what he intended, the tip of his tongue licked against the curve of her lower lip. "No holds barred, Annie," he said as she caught her breath. He tasted her again. "I'm not the Logan who follows the rules."

Slowly he reached out and pulled her to him with his free arm. She felt the hard solidity of his chest against her breasts and only stopped herself from falling into his lap by bracing one knee on the bed. Her leg was trapped between the lean muscles of his thigh and the pillows, and her arms were around him.

Behind his back she was still holding the Glock.

"Okay, I do have one rule," he whispered into her hair. "Tell me this isn't what you want too, and I'll quit right now."

"I don't know if I want this. All I know is that I've been thinking about it since we first met." She felt boneless and light-headed, as if her body was about to disobey her mind and melt against him. She pulled back with an effort. "But that doesn't change anything."

"It changes everything." His cheek was lightly sand-papered with stubble and as he moved from her hair to her lips it felt as if she was being stroked with tiny rough wires. He didn't kiss her, although his mouth was touching hers and she could feel the warmth of his breath and the slight movement of his lips as he spoke. "I'm a liar. I come from a long line of thieves and con-artists. So I don't expect you to believe me when I tell you that everything changed for me last night when I first saw you."

He closed his eyes briefly and she felt his lashes, like thick silk brushes, fan against her. He was so close it was as if he was speaking directly into her soul.

"You'll think I'm lying when I say that for the last twenty-four hours I've been telling myself to stay the hell away from you, and it hasn't worked. But you'd never have caught me tonight if I hadn't wanted you to, Annie. I knew what I was doing. I knew I was trading my freedom for a few hours with you, and whatever you decide I know I made the right choice." He kissed her finally, but so lightly it was more like a sigh at the sensitive corner of her mouth. He stared straight into her eyes; his own gaze wide and sincere.

"So…am I telling the truth, or not?"

"You're probably lying. It's what you do." She whispered the words against his skin, her eyes locked directly onto his. Just as she had on the bridge last night, she had the impossible conviction that she was looking past all the outward layers to the real man behind them—flawed and imperfect, but with a core of strength and his own personal inviolate integrity. With sudden certainty she knew that this was a watershed moment that would only come to her once.

She could turn away. Maybe she *should* turn away, let the moment pass, choose the safe course of action. It would be the right thing to do. Letting this go any further would be foolhardy. It wasn't anything she'd done before—setting aside all her values, everything she'd always believed in, for a few hours with a man she'd probably never see again.

But if she could see into his soul, he could see past *her* defenses and shields the way no one else had ever done. She didn't know how she knew it, but she did. It was as if on some elemental level the two of them had no secrets from each other and no need for secrets, like lovers meeting again after being too long apart.

Behind his smoke screen of lazy teasing was the fact that he'd been willing to trade his freedom for one night with her. He'd felt that inexplicable recognition too. It was all worth it to him, no matter what. And if she let herself look past her own hesitation and apprehensive qualms, she knew that in her heart of hearts it was worth it to her too.

Just this once. Just this once, and just with this man.

She stood up and took a step back, placing the gun on the dresser and still not taking her eyes off him. He looked like a thief, dressed all in black so that he could disappear into the night. But he wasn't stealing anything from her. Whatever he received from her she was giving him of her own free will, and she had every intention of taking what he had to give in return.

There was going to be no holding back tonight. It would only be worth it if they both took it to the limit.

She moved back to the bed and a corner of his mouth

lifted. "Absolutely no chance this damn cuff's coming off, is there?" He didn't sound hopeful.

"No chance in this lifetime," Annie replied steadily. "We'll just have to figure it out as we go along."

He gave that killer smile, his eyes dancing wickedly. "You're going to have to do most of the work, sweetheart, since I'm at a disadvantage here."

"Your police file says you're a resourceful man, Logan," she said solemnly. "Prove it."

She was watching him so closely that she saw the rhythm of his breathing deepen, saw the faint pulse beating at the side of that tanned neck. He put one hand out and hooked his fingers into the waist of her jeans.

"Make me, Annie."

This time she let herself fall against him, and as they tumbled back onto the pillows he swung his legs up onto the bed and reached around to hitch her more securely against him. His hand, cupping her inner thigh and wrapping tightly around her jean-clad derriere, sent a shock of pure desire spilling through her.

And then his mouth opened against hers and she felt a white-hot heat race like lightning along her nerve-endings, electrifying all her senses. When they'd kissed last night she'd been afraid of losing control, but now she felt a dark and urgent need to cast off the last of her inhibitions. She felt his tongue deep inside her and she met it with her own, her fingers tangled in his hair, pulling him closer.

"Take this thing off." He pulled away from her, his breathing shallow. "I have to feel you."

The heat inside her started to turn to ice. "I can't do that. And if you thought—"

"The sweater, Annie." He cut across her words abruptly. "I'm beginning to like the bondage, sweetheart, but rip the damned sweater. It's the only way I can get it off."

With one swift movement he pulled it over his head and stared defiantly up at her. She saw what he meant. Without uncuffing the wrist that was still secured to the bedstead he couldn't draw his right arm out of the sleeve. His eyes glittered in the lamplight, humor replacing the spark of frustration.

Mad, bad, and dangerous to know. The quote fit Logan perfectly, Annie thought. He was sin personified. He was everything the nuns at St. Margaret's had warned them about when she'd been a schoolgirl, and everything that a grown-up woman had schoolgirl fantasies about. And now it was time to make those fantasies come true—*all* of them.

With both hands she held the seam of his sweater and pulled. The fine material resisted and then gave way completely, ripping jaggedly along the seam until it separated, slipping away from his body. She pushed it to the floor and let her gaze linger on him.

His skin was dark gold, smooth and taut over tightly defined muscle, like some primitive sculpture meant to capture the essence of virility. The same black hair that sprinkled his forearms made a light tracery on his chest and triangled down the flat surface of his stomach, disappearing at the buttoned fly of his jeans. It was…irresistible. *No holding back,* she told herself, putting aside the last flicker of apprehension that constrained her. *To the limit—everything you've ever wanted or dreamed of wanting.*

Slowly she bent her head, keeping her eyes on him and watching his reaction. Like a cat at a saucer of warm milk, she licked the silky pelt. He tasted like salt and skin.

A shudder ran through him and she heard him gasp. His left hand sank into her hair and she felt his fingers tighten. She flicked her tongue again, teasingly, and then she gave a tiny nip just under his ribcage. Logan's eyes were closed but his lips were parted, and he grasped her shoulder and pulled her up to him.

"You're a biter, sweetheart," he breathed. His lashes lay against his skin like shadows. "That's good."

As he spoke he was fumbling one-handedly with the buttons on her shirt, and then he jerked at it impatiently, opening it through sheer force. Annie saw him open his eyes, and she felt suddenly as exposed as if there were a spotlight on her.

She was wearing a chocolate-colored bra, and the dark-brown lace was a sharp contrast against the pale cream of her breasts. He held his breath for a second, looking at her, and then he let it out in a sigh. He touched her with a feather-light stroke, nudging past the lace.

"You're beautiful," he said simply. He moved her bra strap off her shoulder and took the weight of her in his hand, his thumb circling her nipple. He watched in fascination as it tautened under his touch, and then spoke softly. "Let's make love, Annie. I want to do everything with you. I want it to last all night long."

He raised his head and took her breast gently into his mouth, continuing with his tongue what his hand had been doing. She bit her lip and arched her back, tiny bursts of sensation exploding through every part of her body. Her hair felt damp on her forehead.

"Let's make love." There were other ways he could have put it, but his words had been old-fashioned. *Romantic.* Making love meant more than just the physical act—it involved a certain tenderness. It was two people committing to each other, Annie thought, even if it was only until the moon outside her window faded into dawn.

She reached down and undid the first button on his jeans, the denim tight with his need already. "Let's make love, Logan. All night long."

"Wait, Annie." His voice was barely under control. He looked at her hungrily, half leaning on one elbow, his expression haunted. "I didn't come here planning this. What I mean to say is—I'm not the kind of guy who carries one in his wallet in case he needs it." He managed a rueful smile that somehow looked forced. "Not since I was an optimistic teenager, anyway. Do you have anything?"

"I've got a sister with an offbeat sense of humor," Reaching over to her night-table drawer, she pulled out a package. "Valentine's Day last year—her way of telling me to get a social life. I hope they don't glow in the dark." She peered closer at the fine print on the side of the box and her eyes widened. Logan saw what she was looking at.

"Just my size, sweetheart." He laughed at her expression and then pulled her down onto his chest as if he was handling spun glass, the teasing note in his voice softening to tenderness. "This is going to be right, Annie. For both of us."

He was a big man. She felt ridiculously small on top of him, and then it was as if the pieces of a puzzle had fallen precisely into place. Her hair swung forward as they kissed, blond against the darkness of his, and when at last there was nothing between them except the touch of skin against skin her hands slid over his body as if they'd known him before, finding the secret places, the sensitive spots, that seemed to set him on fire. Straddling Logan, and feeling his hand against the softness of her inner thighs, Annie closed her eyes and caught her breath in a small gasp. Nothing could get better than this, she thought as his fingers pressed hot against her, moving back and forth with her. She felt a melting pressure building inside her, and when suddenly he stopped, she felt as if she'd been poised on the edge of a highboard ready to jump and had abruptly been pulled back.

"I want to taste you," he urged her huskily. Without waiting for her to move closer, he half lifted her with one hand, his arm slick with sweat and corded with muscle. And then all she knew was that she'd never felt anything like this before, she'd never known that she could want anything this badly, and she wasn't sure if she could stand it.

She was there, back on the high-dive, and suddenly she was plunging through space, gasping and shuddering and feeling as if the very air against her skin was too much to bear.

"Wild honey." Logan was kissing her stomach. It felt like he was rubbing her with velvet the wrong way, rough and silky at the same time. "You taste like wild honey, Annie. Get your Valentine's present and let's celebrate the holiday now."

He was funny and sweet and sexy and inventive in bed, she told herself with an inner rush of pure desire. And he was all hers for tonight. With hands that seemed all of a sudden clumsy and nervous, she tore open the package and paused. She looked up at him pleadingly.

"Not one-handed, I can't. I can see there've been some serious gaps in your education, sweetheart."

"I'm an Irish Catholic girl from Southie, Logan—what the nuns didn't teach us we learned all by ourselves." She slipped the thin latex over him triumphantly. "That's where you bad boys come in."

"Yeah, this is where the bad boy comes in," he breathed. "Take me, Annie."

She felt him start to enter her, hard and full, and for a second she panicked. She couldn't do this. She was just too small, or he was the wrong size for her, but it wasn't going to—

He was in, gently moving and watching her through

green-glazed eyes, and she realized that the flicker of pain had gone as soon as she'd relaxed. Now there was just a feeling of completeness, of absolute satiation. She moved her hips against his tentatively, her knees gripping him. He swore faintly and his words were slurred and low.

"We can do this fast or slow, but if you want slow tell me now. Tell me before it's too late, Annie."

"I want it fast this time." She looked at him through her hair and bit hard on her bottom lip to keep from crying out. "I don't think I can wait any longer."

She saw the heat rise under the tanned skin of his face and then he was holding her and going deeper. She was bent over him, her mouth open against his, feeling him thrust and withdraw over and over again and matching his moves with her own. His breath was torn and shallow, and then those eyes opened briefly and locked onto hers.

"Come with me, sweetheart. I don't want to go crazy alone."

It wasn't Valentine's Day, she thought disjointedly, it was the Fourth of July, because fireworks were exploding inside her, incredible pinwheels of brightness bursting one after another through every fiber of her being. She was high in the night sky, almost touching the moon, and then she was flying down through the air only to climb skywards again.

And then she wasn't airborne any longer. She was lying in her own bed, lying on top of the man she'd just made love to—his mouth on her hair, one strong arm keeping her close, the other still locked to an extravagantly Victorian, deceptively fragile-looking iron headboard. And on the dresser across the shadowy room the cool blue of a sapphire glittered in the moonlight.

THE HEADBOARD had been difficult to get free from, Logan thought, grimacing and rubbing his wrist. Of course, most of the night he'd had no desire to slip out of his bond. Even now he wished circumstances were different and he could stay, but he couldn't afford to wait another minute. It was time to leave her.

He picked up the ruined remains of his sweater and balled it up in his hand absently, his whole attention focused on the woman curled up like a sleeping kitten in the tangled mass of sheets. Annie Ryan. Two days ago he hadn't even known she existed, and now she was the most important thing in his life.

And when she found out what he'd done, he wouldn't have a chance in hell with her.

She stirred and he held his breath, not moving. She murmured something and clutched at a blanket, her breathing slow and regular again. It had sounded like she'd said his name, Logan thought. He'd like to think so, at least. It would be something he could take away with him, one last treasure he could steal from her. Without lifting his gaze he knew that the Rubicon was an arm's length away, sitting on the dresser beside her gun.

It was worth a king's ransom. Once he had thought it was worth risking his neck for. Now it was just a piece of blue stone that was going to take the woman he loved away from him. His eyes darkened in memory as he remembered the way she'd been poised above him, her neck thrown back, those short blond tendrils curling in towards her cheekbones. She had a habit of biting her bottom lip in passion that had driven him mad with desire all night. The last time they'd made love, just as the absolute blackness of the night was starting to seep away, he'd held her so tightly he'd been afraid he'd hurt her.

He was going to rip her world in two, and there wasn't a thing he could do about it. He had a job to do. It was all he knew, all he was good for after so many years. Right now he hated it, almost as much as he hated himself.

All she'd remember were the lies he'd left her with. She'd never know that when it had counted, he'd told her the truth.

The next minute he was out the window, melting into the dying night...

SHE'D DREAMT that she'd called his name and he hadn't answered, but that's all it had been—a dream, Annie thought drowsily. She'd wakened twice in the still hours of the dark and he'd been there, rousing at her lightest touch, wanting her. And taking her. She stretched luxuriously, and slid her bare leg over to his side.

He wasn't there.

Her eyes flew open in shock and the first thing she saw was the window, still slightly open. A faint dawn breeze lifted the sheer gauze of the curtains and touched her skin.

She was icy cold, but it had nothing to do with the temperature in the room. *He'd gone!* She started to sit up. Somehow he'd escaped from—

There was a dull clanking sound and she fell back onto the bed. Around her wrist was the silvery bracelet of the handcuff that had secured him—still sized for him and slipping easily from her hand. She felt a spark of anger fan to life inside her, but immediately it was overshadowed by another emotion.

Dear God, the Rubicon! How was she going to explain her reckless irresponsibility to Agent Logan? She'd probably spend the next five years in prison, she thought in irrational panic. And somewhere out there Lucky would be living high, thanks to a daring theft and a stupidly gullible woman. How could she have been so trusting, when she'd known from the start the kind of man she was dealing with?

It wasn't there. She knew in her heart it wasn't there.

Slowly she turned her head and looked at the dresser in defeat.

The next moment she was flying across the room, hardly daring to believe what she saw. Not until she'd picked it up and its solid weight lay in her hand could she accept that it was real.

She wasn't wearing anything and the room was cold, she realized belatedly. Hurriedly lowering the window and scrambling back under the covers, she stared at the jewel in her palm, her thoughts chaotic. What was it supposed to be—a fair trade? Was that why he'd left it, but seized at his freedom? And had all the rest been his way of sweetening the deal for both of them?

She didn't want to believe that. The imprint where his head had lain was still on her pillows; she thought she could still smell the scent of him, faint but unmistakably male, lingering in her bedroom. Her lips were swollen from his kisses. How could it have meant nothing when she could still taste the man, Annie thought in desperation. He couldn't have been just using her after everything he'd told her last night.

I'm a liar. I come from a long line of thieves and conartists.

But he hadn't lied to her. She'd lied to herself. She'd used every flimsy scrap of argument she could muster to persuade herself that throwing all her scruples to the wind was justified. She'd even halfway convinced herself that she was a little in love with him, and that had been the biggest lie of all.

Or was it? He'd left her the Rubicon. Who could blame the man for escaping from custody when he had the chance? She wouldn't be feeling this betrayed if all she'd felt for him was desire, Annie told herself with brutal honesty. Would she?

She forced the unwanted thought aside quickly and stared at the huge sapphire still clutched in her hand. For whatever reason, he'd left her this, and now she had to deliver it to the other Logan—the Logan who'd never understand, who'd never lose his head or his heart and who was so dedicated that he wanted to see his own brother behind bars. She wasn't going to let him know what a fool she'd been, she decided, drawing her knees up and wrapping her arms around them for a warmth that she suddenly needed. If she'd learned one thing from his twin, it was how to lie.

As she laid her head on her knees the Rubicon, shimmering wetly, fell from her fingers and onto the empty bed.

"HE SHOULD be here soon, Ms. Ryan."

The receptionist at the FBI field office was too professional to show curiosity, but Annie knew she had to be wondering about her. She fidgeted nervously on the edge of an uncomfortable molded-plastic chair, wondering where the heck Agent Logan was. All she wanted to do was hand over the stupid hunk of rock that was jammed into the pocket of her jeans and get out of here, and the man had to pick this day to be late for work.

She was not looking forward to meeting him again. Annie stared at the floor glumly. She noticed her shoelace was dragging and bent over to tie it.

"You wanted to see me?"

A pair of gleaming brown oxfords was inches from her face, and she resisted the startled impulse to jump to her feet. He'd caught her off-balance, but she didn't want to let him know that. She'd need all the psychological advantages she could get in the coming confrontation. Tying her laces in a neat bow and evening out the loops with a fussy flourish, she looked up casually and felt her assumed confidence take an immediate nose-dive.

The one psychological weapon he had that she'd overlooked was the fact that he was Lucky's twin. It didn't seem possible that those strong, capable-looking hands now holding a briefcase and a sheaf of papers weren't the same ones that had stroked and teased her all night long. That unexpectedly erotic mouth, firmed to a polite line—hadn't that mouth covered hers, hadn't it spent hours doing indescribably delicious things to her body in the dark? Starting with her toes, and working up to—

She jerked herself back to the present and the man who was actually standing in front of her.

"Could I have a few moments with you in your office?" she asked. She glanced over at the receptionist who was signing for a courier delivery, and lowered her voice. "I, uh—I've got something I think you might be interested in."

She sounded as if she was trying to sell him dirty pictures, she thought in embarrassment. But if her furtiveness struck him as odd, he didn't show it.

"Of course. Follow me, Ms. Ryan." He smiled remotely. "Annie, I mean."

She didn't like hearing him use her first name, she thought, trudging along a seemingly endless hallway behind him. She wished she'd never insisted on it now. Except for the toneless inflection, Matt's voice was too similar to his brother's for comfort. Annie closed her eyes and immediately she could hear Lucky gasping out her name, over and over again as the two of them moved together on her bed.

But the Logan she had to concentrate on now was Matt. He didn't have the dash and charm of Lucky, and for that she was grateful. Even without being distracted by him it was going to be hard enough making her glossed-over account of how she'd come into possession of the Rubicon sound convincing. Those cool green eyes probably never missed a trick, she thought despondently. He'd take one look at her face and know she wasn't telling the whole truth.

He was wearing mismatched socks. As he stopped in front of a door with his name on it and took a key from his pocket she nearly barreled into him in astonishment. Mr. Perfect had one dark brown and one navy sock on, she realized as he ushered her into his office. They were pretty close in tone, but they definitely didn't match. It was as shocking as if any other man had forgotten to put his pants on, Annie thought, stupefied. And now that she took a closer look at him, she realized that his hair was still damp from his morning shower and his perfectly knotted tie was a tiny fraction askew. Maybe he was human after all.

"Sit down. Can I get you anything? Coffee?"

He raised one eyebrow inquiringly and she shook her head. "Nothing, thanks. I don't want to take up too much of your time."

That was an understatement—she didn't want to be here at all. But maybe it wasn't going to be as gruelling as she'd expected, she thought. The socks were a tip-off that Matt Logan wasn't infallible. For the first time since she'd woken up this morning she began to think there was a chance of getting out of this without having to spill all the details of her personal life to Lucky's brother.

She was about to speak when he forestalled her. With his first words she felt her eyes widen in shock.

"Before you say anything, Annie, I want to tell you I'm sorry for leaving you the way I did. The situation got out of hand and both of us let our emotions take over, but that was my fault. I shouldn't have let things go so far." He looked down at his hands and gave the desk blotter a nudge, lining it up with the letter-tray and appointment book that sat beside it. ''I couldn't blame you if you didn't want to see me again after everything that's happened between us.''

Chapter Eight

She felt as if she'd just had the wind knocked out of her
as she stared at him in stunned recognition. How had Lucky
managed to pull off this incredible masquerade right here
at his brother's office? He was taking an insane risk—Matt
could walk in at any moment. But that wasn't the worst
danger he was in, she thought with growing outrage. Things
got out of *hand?* He shouldn't have let it go so *far?* Is that
how he intended to dismiss last night—and her?

The man was in a lot deeper trouble than he knew.

"You were more than cooperative, allowing us to search
your car like that, especially without a warrant, and I'm
afraid that my frustration in coming up empty-handed had
affected my attitude by the time Cartwright and I took our
leave of you." He looked up and met her blank gaze.
"Again, my apologies. Now, what was it you needed to
see me about? Annie?"

She was sitting there with her mouth slightly open, she
realized belatedly, closing it with a snap. God, Matt Logan
must be wondering what was the matter with her! He'd
been apologizing for their confrontation *yesterday,* she
thought in relief. And she'd been about to demand an explanation of why he'd made love to her all night long and
left her this morning! Her blood ran cold when she realized

how close she'd come to making a total fool of herself in front of him.

Suddenly she didn't want to deal with the Logan men anymore. *Either* of them.

"Here's the Rubicon." She stood up briskly and pulled a plastic dinosaur out of her pocket. "Oh. Hold on a minute. Here—no, wait."

He watched silently as she tossed the dinosaur, a small penknife, and a piece of string covered with lint onto his immaculate desk. Digging deeper, Annie triumphantly pulled out a plastic sandwich bag secured with a twist-tie and placed it on the center of the blotter, which had been pushed sideways by the dinosaur.

"My niece found it in her baseball mitt. I didn't know until after you'd left, but at least you've got it now. I guess the Russians will be glad to see it back, won't they?" She jammed the rest of the junk back into her pocket and glanced at her watch. "Can you sign some kind of receipt saying that I've handed it over to you? I've got a full schedule ahead of me today and I'd like to get going as soon as—"

"What the hell is this stuff?" His unflappable facade showed a tiny crack as he unwrapped the sandwich bag and held the Rubicon gingerly in his hand. It was covered with a flaky substance.

"Bread crumbs. I couldn't find a clean bag," she said impatiently. "So like I said, if you can just give me a receipt—"

"I can't do that. The only person who can sign for the Rubicon is Dmitri Kortachoff, the exhibit director." He dropped the sapphire back into the sandwich bag and dusted the crumbs from his hands dismissively. "This isn't an umbrella you're dropping off at the lost and found, Annie. At the very least I'm going to have to take a statement from you and then we'll arrange to hand the jewel over to Kortachoff together.''

He picked up the phone. ''Mrs. Hendricks, can you put me through to Dmitri Kortachoff? Try him at his hotel first.''

He motioned to Annie to sit down again while he spoke and reluctantly she sank back into her chair. She might have known it wasn't going to be that simple, she thought. Any minute now he'd be dragging out that notebook and wanting to know everything she'd done from the minute he'd pulled out of her driveway yesterday to when she'd shown up at his office today. He'd certainly want to know why she hadn't notified him as soon as she'd realized that Mary Margaret's Big Blue was the Rubicon sapphire.

''He can meet us in fifteen minutes at the museum.'' Logan hung up the phone and drummed his fingers on the desk, frowning. ''He's understandably eager to see the Rubicon right away, so I'll have to get your statement later.''

She had an idea. ''Why don't you just deliver it yourself, and I can give my statement to Cartwright?''

He shook his head decisively. ''I'm the agent in charge. It's my case.'' His gaze sharpened as her face fell. ''Do you have a problem dealing with me because of yesterday? I've expressed my apologies, but all I'm asking for now is an hour of your time so we can wrap this up.''

He was already halfway to the door, not waiting to hear her objections, and Annie knew she wasn't being given a choice. In his own civilized way he was just as persuasive as Lucky, she thought as she followed him out the building and into the parking lot. She felt as if she'd spent the last forty-eight hours being manipulated by one Logan or another, and she was getting tired of it.

She just had to hold on for another hour or so and her involvement with him would come to an end, she told herself staunchly. Surely she could bear his abrasiveness for that long. And if she found his company hard to take, she could derive some comfort from the fact that he obviously didn't enjoy hers either. The short drive to the Danninger Arts Museum was marked by an uncomfortable silence. Not until they pulled up across from the charmingly historic building that was the temporary home for the visiting exhibition did he speak, but when he did there was an odd note in his voice that put her instantly on guard.

"I was way out of line saying what I did about you and my brother."

He got out of the car, and waited for her to do the same. They crossed the cobblestoned street to the sidewalk in front of the museum, Annie tense with an apprehension she didn't fully understand.

"We ran a background check on you—and before you explode, it wasn't my idea. It's standard procedure in a case of this magnitude." He shrugged broad shoulders. "You came up squeaky clean, Annie. Obviously not the type to be swayed by a little sweet-talk and a charming smile." He flashed one of his own at her, but it didn't reach his eyes. That green gaze studied her carefully, noting her reaction.

He reminded her of some big cat. A tiger, so assured of his own power that he could afford to toy with his prey before he moved in for the kill. He could even afford to let her think she was safe, that she'd out-maneuvered him— but it was all an act.

He knew. She had no proof, nothing but a gut feeling to go on, but somehow she was sure that Matt Logan knew exactly how she'd spent her night. It was in his voice, his eyes, his double-edged comments. He knew.

He watched her appraisingly for a second. Then he broke off the eye contact between them abruptly, glancing upwards with obvious reluctance. She followed his gaze and repressed a shudder—Lucky had scrambled over this treacherous-looking roof not long ago, in the dark, with a pack of security guards at his heels. Beside her Logan paused, the muscle at the side of his jaw suddenly tense, the corners of his mouth visibly white. His whole attitude was so changed that she wondered if she'd merely imagined the silent confrontation that they'd just had.

"I'll say this for him—he seems to have overcome the fear of heights he used to have when we were kids. One false move and he'd have fallen all the way down those slate tiles to the ground." He took a deep breath, switching his gaze to the Jaguar parked on the cobblestones in front of the elegant row of old homes, most of them now displaying discreet signs with the names of galleries and privately owned museums. "That's Kortachoff's car. He's here already."

She'd read about the Treasures of Imperial Russia exhibit when it had opened. The major museums had vied for the honor of hosting the visiting show, but the Russian exhibit director had chosen the exclusive location of the Danninger as a fitting setting for his exquisite collection. He'd been right in one way, Annie thought as she and Logan passed through the delicate wrought-iron gate and mounted the shallow steps. Polished brass fittings gleamed against the dark-green paint of the door, the walkway was ornamented with manicured box shrubs in antique urns, and the Italian Revival brick of the building gave off a mellow glow in the morning sunlight. It wasn't a czar's palace, but the quiet elegance seemed more suitable than a large public museum as a temporary home for the imperial gems.

But Kortachoff must have regretted his decision the minute he'd been notified of the Rubicon's disappearance. Though the security in this building was state-of-the-art, it still would have been easier to crack than that at Boston's famed Museum of Fine Arts, Annie mused. Heisting the Rubicon from this place must have been child's-play to a master thief like Lucky. The fact that all the buildings on the street were attached would have been an added bonus. He'd simply skipped from roof to roof until he could make his final getaway.

They were ushered inside by an armed guard and she felt immediately out of place in her jeans. Logan, with his Brooks Brothers' suit, tailored so perfectly that the shoulder holster he was wearing was barely noticeable, fit right in, projecting detached courtesy and tough ruthlessness in equal measure. When he flashed his badge at the guard the man immediately escorted them along a sumptuously appointed hallway and up two sweeping flights of marble stairs, finally ushering them into the exhibit room.

"The Director will be with you in a moment," he said in a thick accent. "You will wait for him here, please."

He closed the door behind him as he left, and Annie found herself gaping at her surroundings. Originally this must have been a small ballroom, she thought, turning slowly around and taking in the spacious sweep of white marble floor, the gracious Palladian windows opening onto a tiny balcony over an enclosed courtyard, the huge and glittering chandelier that cascaded like a frozen waterfall from the exact center of the high ceiling. The walls were hung with pale-blue silk and small gilt chairs were scattered about, upholstered in the same material.

But the setting, breathtaking as it was, paled in comparison to the blinding display of jewelry around her. Glass cases, each one individually lit, seemed to float at waist-height on clear columns. Inside, nestled on white velvet as if they were resting in snow, blazed the Treasures of Imperial Russia—a necklace of pigeon's-blood rubies, a bracelet set with square-cut emeralds, pearls and diamonds and smoky topazes encrusted on a tiara that must have been cruelly heavy on the tsarina who'd worn it so long ago. From every corner of the room jewels flashed and glowed—it was like Aladdin's cave.

In the middle of the room, directly under the brilliantly lit chandelier, sat a display case apart from the others.

It held a large gold egg, paved with diamonds and hinged in the middle. A Fabergé egg, she realized, extremely valuable in its own right. Some of them had been equipped with musical workings, some had held miniature scenes constructed entirely of precious jewels.

This one was exquisite—and empty.

"Typical Lucky," Logan drawled, but his eyes were chips of ice. "He leaves the egg there to make a good newspaper photo the next morning, and to show he's above stealing anything but the cream of the collection."

"Or maybe he left it there because he knows exactly how to push your buttons," she said absently. "Maybe it was personal."

She'd spoken without thinking, but she could have inadvertently hit on the truth, she realized. She looked up at the man beside her.

"He did this to somehow get back at me for something?" He smiled disbelievingly, but his eyes narrowed beneath the straight dark brows. "He didn't break my toy train set, for God's sake—he stole the Rubicon. He's not a boy anymore, and this wasn't a prank."

"I know that." His attitude was insultingly patronizing. Coupled with the fact that his very size made her feel at a disadvantage, she wasn't about to let him get away with insinuating that she wasn't thinking straight when it came to Lucky. "I also know that this wasn't a homicide. The man didn't injure anybody. He stole a big damn stone, but you're acting as if he should be shot on sight."

''Get one thing straight, Annie. I'm not the bad guy here.''

There was no heat in his words. He was leaning negligently over the display case, not even facing her, his hands casually in his pockets. And he was furious, she knew.

They were right back to where they'd been yesterday— on opposite sides of an unscalable fence, the damped-down antagonism that for a while they'd tried to cover with awkward courtesy flaring up again. What was it about her that infuriated him so much? Was it the fact that he knew she'd been attracted to the brother who was his exact opposite?

That was it, she told herself slowly. Every time Lucky's name came up in her presence his facade of stiff good manners fell away to reveal a rawer emotion, as if she was somehow part of what he felt for Lucky. She'd known yesterday that his reaction to her was stronger and more complex than simple dislike. It held another, more dangerous component that he wasn't admitting even to himself.

Maybe it was time she brought it out into the open, she thought with a flash of anger.

''I'm just saying you're probably not the most impartial investigator that could have been assigned to this case. Lucky might be using that against you,'' she said coolly. ''You're so blinded by family rivalry that you can't even see it.''

''Rivalry? There'd only be rivalry if we were competing against each other for something,'' he said, turning to confront her. His hands were still in his pockets, his jacket pushed back, and across the crisp white of his shirt she could see the worn brown leather of his shoulder holster. ''And he's got absolutely nothing I want.''

''You're lying, Agent Logan. I've had a hundred skips hand me stories and some of them were pretty plausible. It's taught me what to look for.'' There was a knife-edge of challenge in her tone. "Is it that he lives the life you secretly wish you had? Is it that the rules never seem to apply to him, and you have to go by the book? Or is there something more involved here?"

He was standing so close that she could smell the faint scent of gun oil from the weapon concealed under his suit jacket. Suddenly apprehensive, she started to turn away from him but he reached for her wrist before she could move. His grip was strong enough that she was forced to meet his gaze.

"You fight dirty, Annie," he breathed.

He had the same erotic mouth as his brother, she noted inconsequentially. A pulse was thudding at the side of his throat and all of a sudden it didn't seem like a confrontation anymore. She swallowed, her mouth dry.

"Keep that in mind, Logan," she warned, her voice not as steady as she would have liked. "You don't want me as an enemy."

"So why don't you tell me what I do want you as?" he said evenly. "You've got theories on everything else about me—what's your guess on that?"

His thumb was moving on the inside of her wrist in unconsciously slow strokes. His eyes were locked on hers, dark green on dark violet, and the two of them were no more than inches apart. She felt a heat rising inside her that she told herself was anger.

She'd guessed right. Behind that glitteringly hostile gaze was a smouldering fuse of pure desire, whether he acknowledged it or not. All it needed to fan it into racing, explosive life was one move on her part. Her smile was enigmatic, but her words were calculated as she deliberately made that one move.

"I don't have to guess on that one, Logan. I know what you want, even if you won't admit it to yourself." She raised herself up on her tiptoes and pulled him closer, her fingertips resting lightly on the material of his suit. Her voice was low and suggestive.

"You don't want to fight with me. You want a *much* more intimate relationship with me—but you couldn't ever allow that to happen. That would be against the *rules,* wouldn't it?" she murmured confidingly. "And there's no guarantee that I'd say yes, so you're just not going to take that chance. But it's burning you up, isn't it? It's making it very, very hard to deal with me with any kind of impartiality or professionalism, and that's totally unacceptable to you." She looked at him and stepped back, releasing him. There was a flush of color on her cheeks but her eyes were hard.

"Am I right, Agent Logan?"

For a moment she thought she'd pushed him too far. His eyes were slits as he looked down at her, and the thumb that had been unconsciously circling on her wrist moved to the sensitive hollow in the palm of her hand. Without volition, her fingers curled lightly inward, and Logan started to pull her closer.

Then he took a deep, ragged breath. Any emotion that she'd thought she'd seen vanished from his features, to be replaced with his usual detached expression as he dropped her wrist and lifted his shoulders slightly, once again hiding any sight of the holster under his jacket.

Voices came from the hall and he nodded. "Kortachoff. Let's play nice in front of him, okay?" His voice was almost steady, she noted. Steadier than hers would have been if she'd had to speak right now, she thought shakily.

He took a few steps across the marble floor and then turned to her as the door began to open. "Oh. Yeah—you were right, Annie. But I'm not your type, am I?" He flashed her a tight grin and moved forward to greet the man who entered the room.

"Agent Logan, is it true? The Rubicon—it has been recovered?"

Standing a few feet away as Logan spoke with the Russian and the entourage of assistants and staff that had followed him in, Annie scrambled to collect her composure. The last thing she'd expected was that he would admit to the suspicion she'd put to him. And that was all it had been, she confessed to herself—a suspicion. It had been based as much on her reaction to him as anything that he'd ever revealed to her.

They'd only met twice, but both times there had been undercurrents in their dealings with each other. Right from the start they'd been natural antagonists, even though they were supposed to be working on the same side. Neither of them had wanted to admit the truth—that every confrontation had been edged with a dark, unacknowledged heat.

But she'd slept with his brother, for God's sake! She'd slept with Lucky just last night, and she still couldn't get him out of her mind, despite telling herself that he'd used her. She'd already made one stupid mistake that she knew she wouldn't get over for a long time—was she trying to convince herself she could assuage the pain by making another?

Maybe she *was* attracted to Matt, Annie thought grimly. That would be understandable—the two brothers were mirror images of each other, and obviously she was irrationally vulnerable to something about the Logan men's identical good looks. But if it had been foolish to let herself get involved with Lucky, it would be criminally stupid to do the same with Matt. He might look like his twin, but he wasn't a substitute for the man who'd walked away from her.

She'd be wise to remember that for the remaining time she was forced to deal with him.

"And this is Bail Enforcement Agent Ryan, who retrieved the Rubicon. Unfortunately, as you know, we haven't apprehended Lucky yet," Logan said smoothly, glossing over the uncomfortable reference to his brother. "We expect to have him back in custody soon."

"The Rubicon, Miss Ryan—you have it?"

Dmitri Kortachoff was suavely distinguished, his thick dark hair silvered at the temples, a heavy gold signet ring on his left hand. He wore an Italian suit and tasselled loafers, but although he gave an outward impression of confidence and success, he wasn't entirely able to mask his emotions as Annie handed over the twist-tied sandwich bag with its precious contents.

His dark eyes held hers. "The Russian government is forever in your debt, Miss Ryan. You have restored the Rubicon to its rightful owners."

He took her fingers and pressed his mouth to them gallantly. The extravagant gesture took her by surprise, and as she felt his lips on her skin she wanted to snatch her hand back. She restrained herself with difficulty. It would have been gauche and rude, she thought as he raised his head and smiled at her, but nevertheless for one moment she'd felt violated, as if she'd been forced into an intimacy with someone she disliked.

How provincial can you get, Ryan? A little continental smoothness and you're totally flustered, she told herself chidingly. She caught Logan's sharp glance on her and realized he'd guessed exactly what was going through her mind.

How infuriating, she thought in annoyance.

"Stand back," the Russian commanded the jostling crowd around them. "Natashya—my loupe." A slim blond woman, wearing oversized tortoise-shell glasses and with her hair scraped severely back, stepped up nervously and handed him a silver jeweler's loupe. Kortachoff took it from her and waved her away. Squinting, he positioned it over his eye. Withdrawing the Rubicon from the plastic bag and letting the bag drop to the marble floor, he frowned.

"Chamois," he barked, snapping his fingers impatiently. Natashya hurried forward and placed a small square of soft leather in his outstretched palm.

"That wouldn't have been a peanut butter sandwich, would it?" Logan said in an undertone. Annie shot him a quelling glare and then fixed her attention back on Dmitri Kortachoff.

The exhibit director wiped the sapphire clean and re-set the loupe in his eye. The room suddenly fell quiet as he held the stone up to the light of the brilliant chandelier and peered at it.

What a showman, she thought, amused. Still, this was his big moment. Let him milk it for all it was worth, but then she was out of here. She was going to insist that Cartwright take her statement when they got back to Logan's office—or maybe she'd simply say she had nothing more to add to what she'd already told him. With luck she'd be able to make him disappear from her life as fast as his brother had.

Then all she'd have to do was to forget she'd ever met either of them.

"We've got trouble."

Logan's murmur was almost inaudible. His eyes were fixed on the Russian. Annie craned her neck to see what was happening, but there were people in front of her. She had the sudden certainty that Mary Margaret had somehow damaged the pride of the Treasures of Imperial Russia exhibit yesterday in a hot game of marbles.

But it was worse than that.

"It's a *fake!*"

Dmitri Kortachoff tore the jeweler's loupe from his eye and swung around to face her. The crowd in front of her parted like magic and a sea of shocked faces turned her way. Kortachoff, no longer urbane, held the blue stone in one trembling hand, while with the other he pointed accusingly at her.

"It's a fake! She's replaced the Rubicon with a fake!"

She stared at the huge, apparently worthless rock that was being thrust in her face, but all she could see was a pair of lying green eyes and a roguish grin. It made sense now, she thought numbly, her stomach turning over in a sickening free fall. She felt Logan grasp her by the elbow as she swayed, her balance suddenly insecure. Everything made perfect sense now.

She shrugged off Logan's steadying hand and drew herself up to her full height, her face white with rage.

"Lucky, you *bastard,*" she hissed under her breath.

Chapter Nine

"I had to cuff you. It was the only way I was going to get you out of there without Kortachoff starting a riot."

She had a smudge of ink on her thumb from having her fingerprints taken. Annie scrubbed at it with a tissue, but it wouldn't come off.

"And once you had me cuffed, you just had to march me down to the police station and have me charged with stealing the Rubicon. It was the *logical* thing to do, wasn't it, Logan?"

She gave up on her thumb and hit the bell on the desk sergeant's counter in frustration, leaning over the partition in frustration and raising her voice. "Hey, Shaunessy! You find my stuff yet? I'd like to get my belt back on before my jeans fall down."

"Seemed weird to see you on the other side of the bars, Ryan." The sergeant ambled out of an adjoining office with a brown paper bag and set it in front of her. "Sign here. Pat know about this?"

"No, Pa *doesn't* know about this. And I don't intend for him to find out." She scrawled her signature and grabbed the bag, taking out her cell phone and belt. "So tell the other fellas to keep a lid on it, will you?" Her voice broke from gruffness to a plea, and she felt a stupid prickle of moisture behind her eyelids.

"Sure. The boys know this is all some kind of a screw-up, anyway."

He glowered significantly at Logan, who was leaning against a bulletin board with his arms crossed negligently, watching a hooker being booked with mild interest. Shaunessy turned back to Annie. "Saw Pat with Bridie down by Faneuil Hall the other day."

He pronounced it "*Fan*-yuhl," his accent even flatter than Annie's. He was making a point, she realized, touched. He was emphasizing that they were locals and Logan was the interfering outsider from the Bureau.

"Probably going to the Haymarket. Bridie likes to buy her vegetables there and Pa doesn't mind taking her—not when she makes her corned beef and cabbage for him." Annie forced a smile.

"I thought your pa was packing a few extra pounds. Home cooking'll do that to a man." Shaunessy leaned on the counter, obviously settling in for a chat. "Heard he turned down O'Neil and Russell on their offer. Their security company's taking off like a rocket, but hell—Pat's paid his dues. Why shouldn't he sit back and collect his disability?" He chuckled. "Bet he misses the excitement sometimes, though. He comes in and shoots the breeze with the fellas once in a while."

"Pa comes down here? To the station?" She'd been about to leave, but his last sentence stopped her. "I didn't know that."

"Once a cop, always a cop, I guess." His smile faded and he clenched a meaty hand around his pen. "And Paddy Ryan was one of the best. That punk who shot him took a lot more away from him than just the use of his left arm."

"But Pa didn't die, and that's the important thing," she

said flatly. "He's well out of it, Shaunessy. He not out there putting his life on the line every night, wondering if some creep who just did a hit of diesel is going to pull a gun on him again."

"Someone's got to do it, Annie." Mild blue eyes held hers for a moment and then softened. "But I expect you're right. He's well out of it. Tell him I was asking about him, will you?"

"I'll do that. And Shaunessy—" Annie paused, clutching her paper bag. Out of the corner of her eye she saw Logan moving away from the bulletin board toward her. "—thanks. For everything."

"This'll all get sorted out in no time, don't you worry." The sergeant shoved a piece of paper across the counter. "Badge number and signature, Agent Logan. We got to keep this all *official*, don't we?"

"Thanks." Logan sounded unruffled, despite the fact that the room was filled with hostile eyes. Coolly he snapped one handcuff around his left wrist and the other around Annie's, ignoring her stunned look. "Ready, Ryan?"

She'd never been so humiliated in her life, Annie thought miserably as they walked out of the station. Despite the fact that everyone had shown their support for her, the last hour had been gruelling. She was one of the good guys— she wasn't supposed to be dragged in here like one of her own skips. And for him to put the cuffs back on her now as if she was Public Enemy Number One was completely unnecessary.

But being printed had been the worst—having her fingers held, one by one, rolled on the pad, and then pressed onto a file-card. She'd stood there numbly, unable to respond to the awkward small-talk of the woman who was performing the unpleasant duty, feeling as if with each print a barrier was being erected between her and her old identity.

Lucky had done this to her. Lucky had set her up. He'd known the consequences of what he was doing, and he hadn't thought twice. He must have had a stone made for him on short notice—something capable of fooling a layman for just long enough so he could sell the real one and make arrangements to leave the country. When he hadn't heard any news yesterday about the Rubicon being handed back to its rightful owners, he'd figured out that either she hadn't found it yet, or she was holding on to it in the hopes that he'd show up to retrieve it. He'd known all the time that she was setting a trap for him, and had neatly turned it back on her.

And now she was shackled to his brother, not even knowing where he was taking her. All she knew was that there was no way she could make Matt Logan believe she'd had nothing to do with switching the Rubicon.

"Hold out your hand." They were standing beside his Taurus and he fished a key out of his pocket. The next minute the steel encircling her wrist was gone. "Get in."

For some reason he didn't think she was Dillinger anymore, Annie thought. But obviously she was still in his custody. She turned to him.

"Logan, we've got to talk. It looks bad, but I didn't—"

"Yeah, you didn't switch the Rubicon." He started the engine.

"I know what you're thinking, but it's true!" She heard the desperation in her voice and took a deep breath. "I swear I didn't take it."

"Annie." Logan switched the car off and looked at her steadily. "Shut up for once and listen to me. I *know* you didn't do it." He gestured at the glove box. "There's a first-aid kit in there. Get it out for me, will you?"

There was no expression on his face. She couldn't read the man at all, she thought, bewildered. If he believed her, why had he had her arrested? Why the charade with the handcuffs, even after they'd left the station? Wordlessly she handed him the first-aid kit, almost expecting him to pull the Rubicon out of it.

Instead, he tipped a small bottle of rubbing alcohol onto a cotton pad and reached for her hand. Slowly and methodically, he wiped away the last traces of ink from her thumb. He looked at the rest of her fingers, cradled lightly in his, and then curled them back into her palm. A smell of alcohol pervaded the interior of the car.

"Why?" Her one-word question was so quiet it hardly broke the silence between them. She held his eyes with her gaze.

He could have thought she was talking about the Rubicon, but he didn't. "I saw your face when they printed you—you felt like a criminal. And I feel responsible for that." His voice was low and calm but he was twisting the cap onto the bottle so hard that his knuckles whitened.

"Lucky's the one responsible for this. But you already knew that, didn't you?" she said, lowering her gaze and staring at her clean fingertips.

"I knew as soon as Kortachoff said the stone was a fake." He started the car again, and put it in gear. "We can't stay here. I'm taking you to my place."

"Your place? Your office, you mean?" She leaned back, suddenly exhausted, as they swung into traffic.

"My home." Smoothly he changed lanes, his movements unhurried and precise. "We'll talk there."

She knew him well enough now to note the small signs that betrayed his unruffled facade. He was gripping the steering wheel with one hand and the other went unconsciously to his suit lapel, adjusting his holster.

"Your home? Why not the office?" she demanded, sitting up straight.

"For God's sake, I'm not abducting you." His voice was clipped. "It's just more convenient this way."

"And it's a hell of a lot more irregular this way, too. That's not you—you *never* step out of line. You do everything by the book." Her eyes darkened. "What's going on, Logan?"

"I'm about to throw the damned book out the window, that's what's going on." They'd come to a stoplight and he turned to face her, his jaw tight. "Why the hell do you think I had you arrested like a common thief? Why parade you around down at the station where people knew who you were? Do you think I'm such a bastard that I'd have done that without a damn good reason?"

The light changed and he started driving again, his profile hard. "If I'm right, my brother's little shell game might have landed you in a world of trouble. Somebody's after the Rubicon—someone who wants it so badly they already tried to kill you and Lucky for it."

"The shooter on the motorcycle," Annie said faintly. "But he was after Lucky, not me."

"He was after the stone. The *real* one." He glanced over at her. "And with you trying to pass off the fake in front of Kortachoff and about twenty other people today, the general consensus is going to be that you must know where the genuine article is. Whoever the shooter was, you can bet he's looking for you right now."

She slumped back in her seat and stared out at the passing scenery with unseeing eyes. Everything about the man she'd spent last night with was false. She had to accept that. But would he knowingly have put her in danger? Or was Matt Logan's assessment of his brother so tainted that he could attribute any crime to him, no matter how heinous?

They were in the Beacon Hill area, and he slowed to turn onto Chestnut. She might have known he lived in an area like this, she thought dully, as the Taurus stopped in front of an elegant eighteenth-century brick town house. Lucky had said that their mother's side of the family had been old money. She just hadn't realized how old and how much money.

"You don't believe me," Logan said. He shot her an appraising glance as they got out of the car and approached the house, his mouth tightening grimly at her silence, but he didn't press the subject. Only after he'd unlocked the front door and stepped inside to disable the security system did he speak again, his words commonplace enough. "The living room's through there. I'll be with you in a minute."

The perfect host, she thought with a flash of frustration— next he'd be asking her if she wanted to freshen up after their journey. What did it take to ruffle him? Once or twice he'd come close to revealing the man inside, but he'd always made an immediate recovery, closing himself off behind that seamless exterior and sealing up any cracks that might have appeared so perfectly that a minute later they were invisible again.

She stepped into the living room and paused. It was perfect, like a room out of *Architectural Digest*. Filled with a balance of antiques and modern furnishings, the common denominator was that everything was tasteful, exquisite, and obviously valuable. Heavy silk draperies, caught back with thick tasselled cords, partially veiled a set of white-panelled French doors. Through the glass she glimpsed the gardens beyond. A small bronze statue of a girl sat on one of the antique mahogany tables that dotted the room, an enormous arrangement of fresh flowers in a crystal vase graced a sideboard, and several paintings hung at focal points on the pale green walls. She perched on the edge of a rose velvet sofa, almost afraid of marking it. Unclipping her cell phone from her belt she placed it gingerly on a nearby table.

Perfect, beautiful—and soulless. No, she corrected herself, gazing around once again. That was wrong. This room reflected someone's soul. But for some reason, she was pretty sure it wasn't Logan's.

"I need a drink. You could probably do with one too."

She hadn't heard him walk into the room. Shrugging off his jacket and tossing it onto a spindly gilt chair, he set a heavy crystal tumbler on the low table in front of her. He still wore his gun, she noticed. He sank into a nearby wing chair, his head tipped back and his eyes closed, his own glass carelessly held between two fingers over the edge of the chair's faded silk arm.

"You looked like a Scotch drinker." He didn't open his eyes.

"I'm not much of a drinker at all," she replied. "But when I do, it's Irish whiskey."

"I'll get some in for next time." He rubbed his cheek wearily and sighed. "God, I need a shave and about ten hours' sleep. And it doesn't look like I'm going to get either for a while."

Aside from the slight shadow on his jawline the man looked as perfectly groomed and unreal as ever. "Yeah, you look terrible," she said sarcastically. "Big date last night or something?"

"Or something," he agreed noncommittally. He took a healthy swallow of Scotch and paused, holding the wet crystal rim against his bottom lip. The single cube of ice clinked like a far-off bell. "You don't like me, do you, Annie?"

The question caught her off-guard and she looked away. Nervously she picked up her own glass, and then she put it down again, harder than she intended. "No, I don't," she said flatly.

"That's tough, honey." Setting his glass on the table, Logan gave her a brief cold smile. He started rolling up his shirtsleeves, focusing his attention on the task as if it were the most important thing on his agenda. "I'm not Lucky, but I'm all you've got right now."

The brief kindness he'd shown earlier in the car might never have happened, judging from his harsh tone. All of a sudden she needed that drink. Annie swallowed a mouthful of single malt scotch as if it were punch and then took another. It was time for both of them to lay all their cards on the table because if he was right, the stakes in this game had gotten too high to continue bluffing each other.

"You know about last night, Logan," she said as the liquor spread a slow heat in her stomach. "I know that you know...and you know *that* too. So, no more games. I slept with your brother. He's a bastard, but he's great between the sheets. We did it all night long, and then you got to watch him do it again to me today—big-time." She stood up jerkily, her eyes like amethysts in her white face. "Anything else, Agent Logan? Do you want more details?"

"God, no." He drained his glass and stood to face her. A strand of hair had fallen across his forehead, but he didn't seem to notice. "Except one. How the *hell* can you still be attracted to him? He's a crook, a thief—he's got the morals of an alleycat and if you read his file you had to have known that. Is that what you like?"

"I like that better than a man with no emotions at all," she countered swiftly, her words barbed. For some reason his question cut her and she felt the need to hit back. "I like that better than a man who probably has to pull out his calculator and his desk calendar before he decides to schedule in an hour of—''

''You're wrong. Lately my schedule's been shot to hell.'' He took two strides towards her and his hands were on her shoulders. ''Let's get down to basics. You know what I want. And even if you don't like admitting it, you feel the same way about me. What are we going to do about it?''

She stared at him for a long moment. She'd wanted to know what ruffled him, she thought shakily. It looked like she'd found out. *She* ruffled the imperturbable Agent Logan. And he was right—however unwanted the feeling was for both of them, it was mutual. He wasn't Lucky, she didn't like him, and she wasn't the type to make the same mistake twice, she told herself desperately. She'd acted way out of character with his brother, though at least with Lucky she'd been able to tell herself she was a little in love with the man.

But Logan and she both knew there was nothing between them except desire. They'd been that honest with each other.

''We're not going to do anything about it,'' she said hoarsely. ''We're going to pretend this conversation never happened. Face it, Logan—we can't even *stand* each other most of the time.''

''You're so damned inflexible, Annie.'' He spoke in a whisper, but there was a determined edge to his voice.

His mouth, that sensuous mouth that had fitted so well with Lucky's personality and on Matt was a startlingly erotic contrast to his normal remoteness, was close enough that he could have kissed her. But he wasn't going to, she thought with acute certainty. He wasn't going to let himself taste her, even though she knew he needed to.

Not yet, anyway. But the leash he kept his emotions on

was frayed and starting to break. All it would take was a word from her and he'd let it snap. And all it would take was for her to move away, and he'd let her go.

She could put a stop to this right now, just by taking one step backwards. She swayed towards him, a movement so infinitesimal that he shouldn't have even felt it.

His hands slid down her shoulders to her hips, and then to the curves filling out the seat of her faded jeans. His arms, brown against the white shirtsleeves, were corded with muscle but he didn't tighten his grip on her. If he was trying to prove to himself that he was under control, she thought faintly, he'd overlooked one sure giveaway. She shifted slightly and saw that hard gaze waver as she moved against him.

"I'm not inflexible," she said, unable to look away as his lashes dipped to his cheekbones and his breath caught in his throat. He couldn't know how blatantly sexual he looked, she thought distractedly. With an effort she continued her argument. "But you said it yourself, Logan—you're not my type. You're cold and tough and ambitious. And I'm a scrapper from Southie who hauls in bail-jumpers for a living and isn't looking for hearts and flowers anytime soon." She stared up at him, her eyes wide and challenging.

"That's a yes?" he asked tightly. His hand was under her chin, tipping her face back. He seemed to be devouring her with that glittering green gaze, and her lips, soft and full, parted involuntarily.

"Yeah, that's a yes," he muttered.

His mouth was on hers, hard and hot and immediate. *This was what he was like.* The thought tore through the part of her mind that was still coherent. On the outside he was cold and collected, but this fire must have always been there, raging under the ice.

It was like being swept away by some elemental force,

a tidal wave of sensuality that drowned her before she could even think of saving herself. She could barely hear the tiny voice deep inside her that was telling her that she was in danger, that she would regret this if she didn't end it now, that this was an even bigger mistake than last night had—

His arms were around her, and, without breaking off their kiss, he lifted her effortlessly up and deposited her on the polished edge of the low antique sideboard, and with that the voice inside her was overwhelmed by a flood of pure sensation. He was leaning over her, one knee on the sideboard, his arms braced at her sides. She could smell jasmine and roses, and as she moved beneath him she felt the cold crystal vase beside her.

"You knew I wanted this, didn't you?"

Logan's voice was a rasp, his breathing shallow. His mouth trailed from her lips to the side of her throat, and his eyes were closed, like a man who had reached the limit of his endurance. With one arm he swept the vase off the surface of the sideboard and continued kissing her as it fell to the floor. It shattered on a high, musical note, like glass bells in a storm.

She'd known, Annie thought, her throat thrown back, arching itself to his touch. And like a child with a box of matches, she hadn't been able to resist seeing what it would be like. But she hadn't counted on this searing molten heat spreading throughout her, this almost mindless obsession to have him take her farther and deeper.

She wanted more. She wanted to have everything he could give her. She wanted to feel his skin on hers, she wanted to see his hair falling into his eyes and she wanted to hear what he sounded like when he couldn't keep quiet any longer. She wanted all that with an intensity that frightened her, and she knew she'd never be able to live with herself if she didn't stop now.

With immense effort she brought her palms to his chest, almost faltering as she felt the trip-hammer beat of his heart. She held onto one last shred of sanity and spoke, her voice a thready gasp.

"I want it too. But I'm not going to let it happen, Logan."

He stopped, and beside her she saw his fingers tighten against the polished wood of the sideboard. Then he looked at her, his mouth tense as he met her eyes. What he saw in them brought a fleeting regret to his own.

"Good thing one of us is still thinking straight. I sure don't seem to be able to, lately." His voice was harshly reluctant, and his mouth moved slowly back to hers, as if in farewell. His words were pressed like promises against her parted lips. "I should have stayed the hell away from you until I got this straight between us. I lied to you, Annie."

He stood up, raking a defeated hand through his hair. It took a moment for her to grasp what he'd just said, but when she did the heat in her veins turned to ice. Unsteadily pushing herself off the sideboard, she felt something under her foot. There was a crushed rose on the floor. Shards of crystal lay on the Aubusson carpet.

"Someone could get hurt on that," she said, walking over to the sofa and inwardly marveling that her limbs still seemed to be obeying her brain. Her tone was flat and dangerous and she felt a ballooning sense of outrage filling her. She picked up her glass and drained it, carefully keeping her voice under control. "So you lied to me. How about we forget about everything else that's happened between us and concentrate on that, Logan? Just what have you been lying about?"

He walked over wearily and took the glass from her. "Lucky was working for us." He had his back to her as he dropped this bombshell, and she could hear the brittle clink of an ice cube in a glass. "He was working with us when you tailed him that day."

He came back to where she was sitting, stunned, on the sofa. He held out her drink and she took the squat cut-crystal tumbler in both hands, not trusting her grip.

"Lucky's working with the Bureau." She lifted the glass to her lips and took a tiny sip. The ice was numbingly cold. "Try again, Logan. Lucky's an international jewel thief— the FBI wants him behind bars, not drawing one of their paychecks."

He sat down in the chair across from her, leaning forward, his expression remote. "That's right. But he's an international jewel thief with a price on his head. He came to us when the police picked him up."

"And you took him in out of brotherly love?" She'd had enough of this, Annie thought with a searing flash of anger. "Damn you, Logan! Stop lying to me!"

"He came to us with something to sell—and we were in a buying mood," he continued as if she hadn't spoken. "He offered to give us the name of his client if we got him safely out of the country."

She sank back against the sofa, her head pounding. None of this made sense. If Lucky had been cooperating with the FBI, then why didn't they have the Rubicon? Why hadn't it been given back to the Russians in a blaze of publicity?

Across from her, Logan suddenly stood up and went to the French doors that overlooked the garden. He stared unseeingly out at the manicured lawn, the rose bushes. He kept his voice neutral, as if he was giving a report.

"Lucky stole the stone from the Treasures of Imperial Russia exhibit just like the newspapers said. He already had a buyer for it, and he'd been paid for the job."

"For a jewel that hadn't even been stolen yet?" She sat up in astonishment.

"Lucky's a legend. He can dictate his own terms," he said, rubbing the back of his neck and flexing his shoulders. "So he went ahead and pulled off another incredible heist, risking life and limb scrambling over rooftops, getting shot at, walking away without a scratch—and then, ironically enough, he got caught because of one of the few good deeds he's ever done in his life." He laughed shortly and humorlessly.

"I picked up a copy of the *Globe* and read that story in a donut shop a few days ago, while I was scoping out a bail-jumper's neighborhood," Annie said cuttingly. "That's last week's news, Logan. What I'm really interested in is how you could have made a deal with him without getting the Rubicon as collateral."

She pinned him with her gaze as she waited for his next lie.

"Oh, we had it, all right," he said abstractedly. He looked over at her. "We'd never have let him get sprung from jail without it."

It was pure Logan, she thought incredulously, as he turned away and gazed out at the gardens again. Two minutes ago he'd been ready to take her any way he could. Now he was the complete FBI agent again, giving her as little explanation as possible. All inconvenient emotions had been sealed over—covered up. *Eliminated.* And she was expected to go along with it.

"Right. Of course," she said tightly, rising from her seat and strolling over to where he stood. "The Bureau had it all the time, but now they don't."

He flicked a glance at her. "I can't give you all the details. This is strictly on a need-to-know basis."

It was the last straw. She grabbed a fistful of his shirtfront and pulled, her teeth gritted with frustration and her eyes blazing. "Get this, Logan—*I need to know*. Some bozo almost killed me two nights ago, and you're so worried he might try again that you dragged me down to the police station in cuffs an hour ago. So my guess is that I need to know *everything*."

Her voice had risen until she was nearly yelling at him, but now her words were emphasized with a deadly calm. "I want to hear *why* you lied, *how* you lied, and *what* you lied about. Got it?"

"Let go of the tie. It's Sulka silk," he said, looking down at her expressionlessly.

"The clock's running." Annie loosened her grip and crossed her arms to keep from revealing the fact that she was shaking with emotion. "It's time to play straight with me, Logan."

He held her gaze for a long minute, and then he nodded slowly, his mouth grimly straight. "Maybe you're right. You got pulled into the middle of this through no fault of your own."

A brief shadow crossed his features. He sighed and sat on the arm of the couch, his hands hanging loosely between his knees, his tone bleakly detached.

"Right from the start Lucky'd been the prime suspect in the Rubicon theft, but when he was arrested he insisted on using his one call to phone the FBI. Said he wouldn't talk until brother Matt came down to the station personally." He shrugged. "I went. We talked. What you didn't read in the newspapers was that he had the stone on him and he handed it over."

"But in return he wanted to make a deal?" Her eyes were narrow with suspicion.

"That's my kid brother all over," Logan said tiredly. He saw her confusion. "I'm the older by two minutes, though sometimes it feels like twenty years. Anyway, he figured he'd just dump the problem in my lap and I'd make it go away. He'd give us his buyer if we had the charges against him dropped and gave him a one-way ticket out of the country. It sounded good.'' His gaze hardened. ''So good I should have known the bastard was lying to me. But just for once I wanted to believe he was telling the truth.''

Lucky had betrayed both of them, Annie thought. But she'd only given him her body—and a corner of her heart. By turning on his own twin he'd ripped Matt's soul in two.

It was wrong, she thought suddenly. No matter what, they were still brothers—twins! There had to be a basic bond there that nothing could break. Lucky had tested that bond. He'd tested it way past the point it should have been stretched, and of all the crimes he'd committed in his life, that had been the worst.

But he'd acted impetuously, the way he did everything else. Matt's retaliation would be cold and emotionless. He'd approach it as a mathematical problem to be solved, one step at a time, until he logically, pitilessly, had his brother where he wanted him. It would be like setting a machine into motion.

And after he'd brought his brother down the machine would self-destruct, Annie thought. Maybe Logan wouldn't even realize what he'd done to himself, but something inside him would be damaged beyond repair if he allowed this icy vengefulness full rein.

''You never should have taken on this case,'' she said in a low voice. ''You're too close to him. I know you were brought up by different relatives when your parents died— but the bottom line is that once you were two halves of the same being. Let someone else handle him from now on, Logan.'' Her words came out in an intense rush. ''Can't you see that hating Lucky is like hating yourself?''

Slowly he turned his gaze from the garden to her. "He's irresistible, isn't he? A risk-taker, a rebel—the perpetual bad boy. And despite everything, you're still on his side."

Slowly he brought his hand up to her face and traced her mouth with his thumb, forestalling her attempt to interrupt him. He smiled faintly, the dangerous edge in his voice sheathed with velvet. "Hell, Annie—you've got it all wrong."

His palm slid to the back of her neck and he pulled her to him. For a second his mouth was on hers, hard and electrifying, and then he drew back. "The only thing I have in common with Lucky is that we both want the same woman."

Chapter Ten

Abruptly he released her. "Sit down. There's more you should know."

She wanted to hear it. But after she did, she wanted him to listen to her, Annie thought, dazed. Her lips felt full and moist where he'd kissed her and her mind wasn't tracking clearly, but for some reason it was vitally important to set him straight on one thing. She'd fallen for Lucky—Matt was right about that. But she'd allowed herself to have that one night with him precisely because she knew there was no commitment involved on either side—because she knew that Lucky could never become that important to her.

Bridie had been right, she thought. Annie Ryan, intrepid bounty hunter, was terrified of really falling in love. She sat down on the sofa, suddenly shaky.

"We should have given the Rubicon back to the Russians as soon as we got it from Lucky," Logan said brusquely. "If we had, his story would have been blown out of the water right away. But he said that he could give us his buyer too, if we let him go ahead with his original plan, and someone higher up at the Bureau thought it was worth the risk. Lucky didn't know his client's name," he added wryly. "He'd only ever dealt with him through a third party. But he said he could insist that he'd only hand the stone over to him in person.''

''And that was where I came in. He was about to meet his client on the bridge, wasn't he?''

''We'd arranged for it to look like he'd gotten out on bail like any normal perp,'' he said, nodding. ''We didn't want to spook his buyer. Lucky phoned a contact number and left a message telling his client that he still had the stone stashed safely away and was ready to make good on his end of the deal. He was contacted that same day and told to be at the bridge that night.''

Annie closed her eyes as a sudden thought struck her. ''My God—you were there, weren't you? That bridge was staked out to catch Lucky's client when he showed up, and instead—''

''Yeah. Instead of his client, his bondsman's bail agent pulled a gun on him and ordered him to give himself up.'' Logan's eyes gleamed and he rubbed his jaw thoughtfully. ''There were two dozen FBI agents hiding behind bushes having chest pains watching you flush their carefully planned sting down the tubes.''

''Why didn't somebody *tell* me!'' She'd had an *audience,* she thought in humiliated chagrin. She'd come charging into a delicate federal operation like a bull in a china shop, scaring off the criminal they'd been after and forcing the Bureau's informant to leap from a bridge. Her runaway thoughts came to a screeching halt.

''Just how long *were* we being watched, anyway?''

''Long enough,'' he said laconically. His gaze held hers unwaveringly, and she felt hot color creep under her cheekbones. ''I'm told there were a couple of minutes when the walkie-talkies fell completely silent,'' he went on blandly.

''All right, Logan,'' she snapped. ''I get the picture. When was the surveillance called off?''

"Too soon," he said, frowning. "You were last seen cuffing Lucky and heading to your car. You'd been identified by then, and it was obvious you were taking him in to the nearest police station, so we knew nothing about the shooter until you called the cops for help. And by then Lucky had disappeared. That's when everything hit the fan." His expression was grim. "We still don't know who the hell that biker was working for."

"And you weren't sure about me." She smoothed suddenly damp palms on her jeans. "I guess I don't blame you."

"Cartwright was on your side from the first," he said surprisingly. "After we left your house yesterday he kept telling me there was no way you could be involved. No one was watching your house last night, Annie."

"I wish someone had been," she said tonelessly. "When I woke up this morning and found Lucky gone I was sure he'd taken the Rubicon. When I saw it was still there, somehow it seemed as if what we'd had together might— just *might*—have meant something. But even the stone he left me was a fake."

"It was the same one he handed over to us," Logan said into the silence. "He conned us too."

He rubbed the back of his neck, his shoulder muscles tensely defined through the fabric of his shirt. "He must have had the duplicate made up to leave in the Fabergé egg, but he was discovered by the guards before he could make the switch. When he was slipping around on those roofs he wasn't carrying one Rubicon—"

"He had two," Annie breathed in understanding. Her mind was racing, putting the pieces together. "And he stashed the real one in a safe place before he went back to his hotel. When he was arrested, he decided to use the Bureau get the police off his back and double-cross his client at the same time. He planned to be well out of the country, courtesy of a grateful FBI, before you returned the stone to Kortachoff and found out he'd scammed you all the way down the line.''

"Except for a few minor adjustments, that's exactly how it worked out.'' Logan looked at his watch. "God knows what continent he's on by now, but wherever he is, I'm sure he's got the real Rubicon in his pocket.''

"And whoever tried to kill us two nights ago thinks it's in mine.'' Her throat felt dry. It was unnerving to think that someone might be stalking her. She'd always been the hunter. Now she was the prey.

"Having you arrested was just damage control. I had to get you out of there fast,'' he said. "While we were at the station I phoned the office and put an alert out for Lucky, but my guess is he's long gone. The Bureau will issue a news release tonight making it clear that you were nothing more than an innocent bystander, so by tomorrow morning the heat should be off.''

"Tomorrow?'' Her gaze flicked instinctively to the gardens outside, to the concealing rose bushes, the high brick wall surrounding them. "What about tonight?''

"A safe house is being arranged. I'm expecting a call any minute—'' Even as he spoke, a muted buzzing sound interrupted him. Logan nodded. "That's them now.''

He went to his jacket, reaching into the pocket, and then frowned. "Mine's not ringing. It must be yours.''

"Probably Lew Jacobs, wanting to know why I'm not working today.'' Annie grimaced. "What do I tell him?''

"Say you'll get back to him within the hour. I'll tell the Bureau to get moving on that safe house.'' Logan picked up his own phone and started punching in a number. He glanced over at her, his eyes narrowed to brilliant green. "I don't think it's a good idea to keep you here tonight.''

He wasn't talking about the security aspect. He was already distancing himself from her, she thought. Probably he was right to do so, but suddenly she felt as if a cold wind had blown through her, chilling her very soul. She picked up her phone abstractedly and hit the connect button.

The sound on the other end of the line was barely recognizable as a human voice at first. Then Annie caught part of a garbled sentence.

"—got her. They've *got* her!"

"Who is this?" she said sharply. Across the room Logan looked up, alerted by the tension in her abrupt question.

"Can't you understand what I'm telling you? They've *stolen* her, Annie! Mary Margaret's been *kidnapped!*"

It was Bridie, her words a keening wail punctuated by breathless sobs, and as Annie's legs gave way and she sank blindly onto the sofa, she felt as if her whole world was falling apart.

"I ORDERED protection for your entire family. First we bring her back—then I'm going to get the son-of-a-bitch who screwed up and take him into a back alley." Logan's voice was low and deadly. He swung the Taurus onto Annie's street and glanced over at her. "We *will* find her. That's a promise."

She didn't respond. She *couldn't* respond, Annie thought numbly. It was all she could do to hold on to the last vestige of self-control that was keeping her from breaking down completely.

Bridie had been practically incoherent on the phone, barely able to talk past the breathless sobs that had been wracking her. But when Pat Ryan had taken the phone from her his words had been sharp with pain.

"We got a call. Some bastard's got Mary Margaret and

he says he's holding her in exchange for that damned Russian stone that got stolen a while back. He said you'd know what it was all about.'' He sounded older than she'd ever heard him sound before. "Anne Maureen, get home as fast as you can. We need you.''

Logan had seen her stricken face and had grabbed the phone just before it had slipped from her hand, asking her father a few curt questions while he was steering Annie towards the door. Then he'd proceeded to break all speed limits on the way to her house.

There was a malignant irony in all this, she thought through a haze of fear. It was as if some evil fate was demonstrating to her that no matter how many precautions she took, no matter how high a wall she built around the ones she loved, they were never truly safe. They could be snatched away from her at any moment.

And as a final twist, she had brought this danger on her family herself. She never would have heard of the Rubicon if she hadn't been assigned to bring in Lucky.

"Has he called back?''

Logan's swift question as he opened the car door and Pat Ryan came out of the house was answered with a shake of the head.

"Not yet. Let's get inside. I don't want Bridie taking the call when it comes.'' Annie's father stuck out his hand. "Pat Ryan. Thanks for making it here so quickly, Agent Logan.''

"Matt'll do. A kidnapping's no time to stand on ceremony.'' Logan flashed a tight smile that disappeared almost immediately. "Fill me in on the details.''

His arm was around her as they hurried up the walk and into the house. Everything seemed strangely sharp and bright to her eyes—all the familiar homey objects were somehow wrong, as if she was looking at a garishly retouched photograph. Just for a second, the worn carpet in the hall, with its busy black-and-brown Oriental pattern, appeared to be slightly undulating. She had the crazy impression that it was no longer anchored to the floor, but hovered a hairbreadth above it, and that she would lose her balance if she put her foot down on it. A smell of spices and sugar filled the air, and she found herself recoiling from the overly pungent scent. Then her gaze fell on a small jacket hanging on the hook behind the front door. It was red corduroy—an almost glowing red. It looked too vibrant, like a rose in full bloom in the middle of a dead garden.

Mary Margaret's jacket.

This was *home*. This was the protected place, the sanctuary against the randomness of the outside world. And now something had invaded it, exposed it, changed it so that it would never be the same.

"Give them the stone." Bridie wheeled her chair around sharply as they entered the kitchen. "You have it, don't you? They said you had it, Annie!"

She propelled herself forward. Her eyes were almost colorless, only a faint wash of blue standing out from the staring white. She'd obviously been baking a short while before, and the smudge of flour on her cheek looked terribly like the ashes of a mourner.

"I don't have it." Annie's voice came out in a dry croak. "I never had it, Bridie."

Her sister stared a her a long moment, her fingers digging like claws into the padded armrests of her chair. When at last she spoke, her words seemed to come from some dark place deep inside her.

"*Get* it."

She didn't understand, Annie thought helplessly. What she was asking was impossible. "We're going to have to call in the police, the FBI—we'll have a trace put on the phone—''

"If you do they'll kill her. That's what they said and I believe them." Bridie's dry, stony gaze didn't waver. "You should have kept this from her. You didn't. Now you have to get the Rubicon and bring my daughter back."

Pat Ryan stepped forward, placing a big freckled hand on her stiff shoulder. "Your sister's going to do all she can. We all will, and we're going to find Mary Margaret and get her safely home, Bridget." His eyes were worried. "But Annie's not responsible for this happening. Don't lay that burden on her."

"I'll do whatever I have to for my baby." She moved away from his touch, still holding her sister with her eyes. "You took the burden on when Mom died, Annie. No one else could share it, no one could help you with it. *We* were the burden, weren't we? And when Sean died it just got worse."

"What are you talking about?" Annie whispered. "You were never a burden—you're the people I love!"

"We're not people—we're figures, frozen in place like that damned insect stuck in amber that Mary Margaret got at the Science Museum!" Bridie said in her harsh cracked voice. "And you run around making our world safe, fighting our battles for us, putting the bad guys away in some losing battle to atone for God knows what! Of *course* we're a burden—so much of a burden that you're unable to live a normal life or get a reasonable job. You won't even let yourself fall in love like the rest of us mere mortals—that would just be taking on one more worry, one more fear, *wouldn't* it?"

"That's not fair—" The back of Annie's hand was pressed against her mouth and she took a stumbling half step towards her sister.

"No, it's not fair." A fire seemed to die out in Bridie's wild gaze. She looked suddenly frail and trapped. "But it's the bargain you made with your life—with all our lives. And you broke it when your job put my child in danger. They let her speak to me for a second—did you know that?"

It felt as if she was being pierced and the knife had suddenly gone in deeper. "What—what did she say? Is she all right?"

"She said that it was scary but she knew Aunt Annie would be there soon. She said they'd be sorry when Aunt Annie showed up and kicked their butts." Bridie's normally soft mouth thinned to an implacable line. "I'm making cookies for my little girl. She's going to be here to eat them. Get the Rubicon and bring her home, Annie."

She spun her wheelchair around to face the low kitchen counter where a mixing bowl sat, half-full of dough. Her hand reached out for the wooden spoon propped in the middle of the sticky mass, and then her shoulders started to heave. In two strides Logan was in front of her, balancing lightly on the balls of his feet as he brought himself down to her eye level. He grabbed her hands and held them tightly in his own.

"Bridie, I'm Matt Logan. My brother stole the Rubicon. I'm going to be working with Annie to find Mary Margaret." His voice was steel. Slowly Bridie raised her head to look at him, her eyes flooded and her mouth anguished.

"They said they didn't want the FBI involved."

He fumbled in his pocket and drew out his leather ID wallet. He threw it on the floor without looking at it. "Then I'll make it personal."

Watching numbly, Annie saw the crippling hopelessness on her sister's pinched features change as a faint spark of spirit rekindled behind her fixed gaze. Bridie's hands, till now lying slack and unmoving in Logan's, tightened.

"Your *word*." The well-developed muscles in her arms, such a contrast to those pitifully thin legs, stood out like cords as she returned his grip. "Swear you'll bring her back safe." It wasn't a request. It was a command, her voice a compelling whisper.

No, Bridie! Annie cried silently. What her sister wanted was a guarantee, and no one could give her that. She flicked a pleading glance at her father and Pat Ryan shook his head at his older daughter.

"He can't promise you anything—"

"You've got my word." It was as if they were alone in the kitchen, just the woman in the wheelchair and the man in front of it, his answer flat and uncompromising. "We'll bring her back safe. *Both* of us will." He looked over at Annie and then back at her sister.

Bridie held his eyes for a long moment, as if she was looking into his very soul. Then she nodded slowly. "I believe you." She released her grip on him and let her hands drop into her lap, her mouth working as she held back her tears.

Logan stood up abruptly, turning to Pat Ryan. Lowering his voice, he drew the older man a few feet away while they talked and Annie heard him asking her father to repeat everything the kidnappers had said in their phone call. Beside her Bridie spoke, her voice rusty with pain.

"I can't ask you to forgive me. What I said was unforgivable."

Swiftly Annie knelt beside her. "No—you were right. I should have been more careful. I should have guessed something like this could happen."

"I needed someone to blame." Bridie's lips trembled.

"It made the situation more manageable, less random. But what I said was wrong."

"Let's go." Logan was beside them, leaning over to press Bridie's hand in farewell, and Annie caught a quick glimpse of the Sig Sauer in his well-worn shoulder holster. He looked as coldly urbane as if he was on his way to a board meeting.

Or on his way to a killing. She didn't know the man at all, she thought as she hurriedly collected her own weapon from the locked case in her bedroom and shrugged into a concealing windbreaker. But she was beginning to understand that the image he projected was a thin veneer for the real Matt Logan inside, and in the last few hours that veneer had worn dangerously thin.

"Be careful." As they moved to the front door her father stopped her, his hand on her arm. "If I didn't have to stay here in contact with those scum I'd go with you. I'll call your cell number as soon as I hear from them."

"And we'll let you know as soon as we get a lead on the Rubicon," Logan said. "We'll get her back, Pat."

"I'm beginning to think you just might." Her father's gaze rested briefly on the two of them, the grim-faced agent in the impeccable suit and Annie, her head barely reaching Logan's shoulder, but with the same cool competence about her. "You make a good team."

Not true. They didn't make a good team, she thought as she got into the Taurus and Logan started the car. She was the weak link. She had a healthy respect for the perps she chased down in her work, and she'd felt fear before, but she'd never been seized with the paralyzing terror she was feeling now. She wasn't going to be any help at all. She'd allowed herself to be hustled out of the house with no clear idea of what the plan of action was, and she couldn't even seem to care.

All she could think about was Mary Margaret. As hard as she tried, she couldn't blot out the images that kept running through her mind—worst-scenario images in which she got there too late to save her niece, or she got there in time but somehow panicked the kidnappers into reneging on their bargain. Most likely of all was the scenario where she and Logan never located the Rubicon.

In that scenario Mary Margaret was simply never heard of again. In that scenario a tough little girl who thought her Aunt Annie was the best bounty hunter around was just...*disposed* of.

In the dark interior of the car, Annie tasted blood. She'd bitten through her lip.

"While you were upstairs getting your gun I called Cartwright. I asked him to pull up some information on the computer."

Logan's voice barely penetrated the fog of foreboding that surrounded her. She forced herself to respond.

"What was he supposed to be looking for?" She felt as if someone else was talking.

"Lucky's bank accounts. They're still frozen."

When she said nothing he looked sharply over at her. The headlights of passing traffic cut deep shadows under his cheekbones and he went on a little impatiently.

"Don't you see what that means? I've been operating on the assumption that he could be anywhere in the world. In all likelihood he's still in Boston, trying to scrape up enough money for a plane ticket out of the country."

"The plane ticket he would have gotten from the Bureau if he hadn't double-crossed them. I understand," Annie said dully. "Well, that certainly narrows our search."

"I also requested a check on any jewel thefts reported in the last twenty-four hours," he said shortly. "Cartwright should be getting back to us with the information any time now and then we can plan our next move.''

Why was he going on about jewel thefts that had nothing to do with the Rubicon? She stared straight ahead at nothing with eyes that felt dry and burning. *Aunt Annie's not afraid. She'd just zap 'em with her Taser.* Yesterday at the Aquarium, Mary Margaret had been fascinated by the electric eels. It had only been in the last few months that she'd started acting like a regular seven-year-old instead of a politely stiff little statue. She and her friend Ranjeet had snickered in the back seat of the Buick all the way home. Mary Margaret had been giddy, slightly show-offy and more than a bit irritating at the dinner table. She'd spilled juice all over the floor, insisting petulantly that she was old enough to pour from the full carton, and at one point Bridie had had to threaten her with no dessert if she didn't sit down.

She'd behaved like a normal little girl—something her mother and her aunt had sometimes feared might never happen again. And now she was gone, Annie thought, her nails digging into her jean-clad thighs. She was gone and it was her beloved Aunt Annie's fault.

''You're blaming yourself. Don't.'' Logan adjusted the rear-view mirror and overtook the car in front of him.

She didn't want sympathy from him. It *was* her fault, and with a sudden certainty she knew that her worst-case scenario would turn out to be true. They wouldn't find the Rubicon. It was an impossible task, even if Lucky was still somewhere in the city. And they wouldn't get Mary Margaret back alive. She knew it, and she didn't think she could bear kindness right now.

''If you can't concentrate on the job you're going to screw up.'' His words cut harshly into her consciousness. ''I won't take that kind of chance with your niece's life.''

She felt as if he'd suddenly reached over and slapped her across the face. The attack was so unexpected that for the first time since she'd gotten the phone call from Bridie an hour ago, the numbing shell that she'd surrounded herself with cracked open slightly—just enough to allow a spark of anger in.

"I don't screw up, Logan," she said. Her voice shook a little and she controlled it with difficulty. "But I'm responsible for this. I'm a bail agent, for God's sake—I make enemies every time I slap the cuffs on someone and hand him back to the authorities! It was just a matter of time before the job endangered my family."

"So look for another line of work when this is all over," he said laconically. "But try real hard to shelve the guilt trip for tonight, Annie—because right now you're just going through the motions, and I need a partner."

He glanced over at her in swift assessment. "If you're not sure you can handle this, tell me."

"I can handle this, Logan." How had she ever thought he was capable of offering her sympathy, Annie thought with dull fury. She'd forgotten—human wasn't his style. "And I don't need your advice on my future career path, either. You don't know anything about me or my job, so back off."

For a moment he said nothing. She thought she saw a flash of regret pass over his features, but when he looked over at her again his face was expressionless.

"Your mother was killed in a convenience store hold-up when you were twelve, with you in the car outside watching the whole thing. She'd picked you up from ballet class and had stopped at the store on the way home. You never danced again—you started taking karate instead." His jaw tightened. "How am I doing so far?"

It was if there was a box of dynamite inside her, and he

had pried up the lid with a crowbar, splintering the wood and breaking the lock. Now he was striking a match and holding it to the fuse. Annie felt as if she couldn't breathe. Seemingly oblivious, he went on like an accountant reading a bleak year-end report.

"The perp who murdered your mother was out on bail at the time he killed her—just like the nineteen-year-old addict who shot your father during a pharmacy break-in. Pat Ryan nearly died in the line of duty, and when he got out of hospital his daughter had quit her secretarial job at a bail-bond company to become a bounty hunter."

"You said you'd run a check on me. I should have guessed it would have been thorough," she whispered, her face bloodless.

"It was," he said flatly. "The police report on your mother's murder was destroyed long ago, but the investigating officer at the time is still around. He never forgot the case—a young girl holding her mother's blood-soaked body on the floor, and telling them to arrest her because it was all her fault."

"She'd given me money to pick up a quart of milk on my way home from school, but I bought a ballet magazine instead." Annie's voice sounded small and far-away. Her eyes were glazed. "I didn't tell her until we were nearly home that night. She was annoyed and I was sulking when we stopped at the store…when she got out of the car I said I wished she wasn't my mother."

She looked over at Logan, her features very still. "A couple of minutes later, my wish came true."

Smoothly he pulled the Taurus over to the curb and turned to her. "I'm sorry."

"I don't think so." She looked away. "You're steel, Logan. You've got no emotions at all—and certainly no understanding of what I'm going through."

"I didn't mean I was sorry for you. I'm sorry for her." His voice hardened. "That twelve-year-old kid you handed a life sentence to."

His gaze was flatly accusing, and suddenly the fuse inside her flared into flame. "You just don't get it, do you?" she hissed at him. "I caused my mother's death—and now I'm going to end up being responsible for Mary Margaret's!"

"Come off it, Ryan!" For the first time since she'd known him, Logan raised his voice. "Your niece was supposed to be home this afternoon helping Bridie. She snuck out of the house to play ball down at the park. It's her own fault she got snatched—how the hell can you take the credit for that?"

Appalled, Annie stared at him. She felt curiously light-headed and it seemed as if she was seeing everything through the wrong end of a telescope. There was a painful pressure in her chest.

She exploded into action.

"You cold *bastard!*" she screamed at him, lunging for him across the car seat. She grabbed his shoulders and pulled him forward, feeling his muscles tense beneath the material of his jacket.

"She's only a *child,* for God's sake! How the *hell* can you blame this on her?" She shook him, tears suddenly blinding her vision. "She's just a little girl—it's not her fault. Damn you Logan—it's not her *fault!*"

She was screaming at the top of her lungs, her voice harsh and broken, and she was hitting him with a clenched fist. He didn't dodge the blows and Annie stared into the enveloping darkness of his eyes. The world seemed to be tilting crazily around her, falling on her, crushing her so she couldn't breathe. But she had to convince him. Pushing short blond strands of hair out of her streaming eyes, she grabbed his lapels and brought her face to his, her features tortured with effort.

"It's not her fault—it *wasn't* her fault, don't you understand? She saw her mother bleed to death in front of her eyes—don't you think that was punishment enough?" Her breath was coming in ragged gasps and her face was wet with tears. "It was never her fault, Logan, don't you see? But she's paid for it ever since."

Her voice dropped to a painfully hoarse whisper that seemed to echo in the stillness of the car. Her eyes, flooded with tears, widened in shock as she realized what she'd just said and the back of her hand went to her mouth as if to recall her words.

"I know, honey." He moved then, his arms going around her rigid body. "And it's time to let it go."

A dam that had been pent up for too many years suddenly gave way in her heart. With a terrible wrenching sob she let herself be drawn into the strong circle of his arms, her face pressed wetly against his shirtfront. She felt his hand on her hair.

"It's been so *hard,*" she said, her words low and barely audible. "No matter how I tried, I never could keep them all safe. If I could only protect the ones who were left I thought I could make up for what I'd done—make up for Mom dying like that. And then Pa got shot, and I tried harder. But when Sean was killed and Bridie came home in a wheelchair, I knew I'd failed them."

"Down at the jail they say you bring in more bail jumpers than any other bounty hunter," Logan said, tilting her head back and forcing her to meet his eyes. "You didn't fail anyone, Annie. And it's not your fault that Mary Margaret's been kidnapped. You can't cover every contingency, foresee every possible danger. No one can."

"But what if—" She closed her eyes, one last shuddering sob convulsing her. She swallowed dryly and forced herself to ask the question. "What if we don't get her back, Logan? What if we can't find Lucky and the Rubicon?"

"I gave my word," he said flatly. "I don't give a damn what I have to do to get her back—and finding my brother is the first step."

Something in his tone made her draw slightly away from him. "He might not have the stone. He might have sold it already. What then?"

"Then he's a dead man," Logan said in a voice as cold as ice. On the seat beside him his cell phone rang and he reached for it. "Or he'll wish he was."

Chapter Eleven

"Thanks, Jack. I'll get back to you." Logan tossed the phone onto the seat and started the Taurus. "We've got a lead," he said curtly, pulling into the stream of traffic.

"The jewel thefts you had Cartwright checking on?" Annie asked.

"Yeah. One of them had all the earmarks of a Lucky Logan heist." He turned into the lane that led to the expressway. "A diamond necklace, worth at least thirty grand. It was reported just a couple of hours ago, and the police figure the theft must have occurred early this afternoon. He'll have had time by now to have fenced it."

"So he still must have the Rubicon!" A note of excitement crept into her voice.

"I knew he wasn't about to sell that." He sounded mildly surprised. "He's going to have to find another private buyer for it—probably in Europe, where his main contacts are. That's why I wanted to know if anything had been stolen today. He needs traveling money."

"And now he has it." She saw the sign for the Callahan Tunnel flash by. "So the odds are he's standing in line at the airport right now."

"Cartwright checked on that for me too. There's an Air

France flight leaving for Paris in—'' he glanced at his watch ''—in forty minutes. We'll make it.''

''If Mary Margaret's kidnappers phone back before then, I hope Pa can stall them.'' Annie gnawed her lip nervously.

''Your father's an ex-cop. He can handle himself.'' As they entered the tunnel that led under the city's inner harbor to East Boston and the airport, he shot her a brief glance. ''What we should be trying to figure out is who the hell's behind all this. Someone wanted that damned sapphire bad enough to send a hit-man after you and Lucky the other night, and now they've resorted to kidnapping.''

''It doesn't make sense,'' she said, frowning. ''If the killer on the motorcycle was working for Lucky's buyer, I can see that he would have tried to stop me from getting your brother out of there before he could turn over the stone. When Lucky saved my life, the killer might even have thought there was a double-cross going down, and tried to take us both out.''

''But after that attempt failed, why assume that Lucky entrusted the Rubicon to the bounty hunter who was trying to bring him in, and target a member of her family?'' He rubbed his jaw. ''You're right. Either we're talking about two different factions—the shooter and the kidnappers—or we're on the wrong track altogether and Lucky's client isn't even involved.''

''For all we know, Lucky himself could have been working with the killer on the motorcycle to create a diversion. Except he had no way of knowing that I'd show up,'' she trailed off, her brows drawn together in thought.

''He wasn't working with the biker.'' Logan sounded positive. She looked over at him but he kept his gaze on the road. ''I don't have time to go into all the details right now, but that wasn't part of his plan that night.''

''You're holding something back,'' she said slowly.

"You said you'd told me everything, but there's something more I don't know, isn't there?"

"We're here." He turned onto the ramp that led to the departure terminal, his gaze hooded. He didn't look over at her. "You have to trust me on this, Annie. Right now we've got to concentrate on getting Mary Margaret back safely—and for that we have to work together as a team." He narrowed his eyes against the bright sodium lights that lined the curving drive in front of the terminal. For a second he looked immensely weary.

She suddenly knew that no matter what he said, he would have given almost anything not to have to confront his brother like this. It was tearing him apart. He was a master at concealing his emotions—at burying them so deep that he seemed to have none at all—but under that icy exterior he had to be feeling something for the man he was about to bring in. Or bring down, she thought, apprehensively. If Lucky tried to run...

"I've got questions, Matt. I don't like to work in the dark." She gave him a direct glance and saw his features tense. "But I'll save them for later. Let's go find your brother."

He drew the Taurus up to the curb, directly under one of the No Parking signs lining the drop-off lane. She saw the stiff line of his shoulders relax slightly, but the smile he gave her was brief and oddly remote. "Yeah. Let's get him."

They entered the terminal at a fast walk, Annie taking two strides to every one of his, both of them scanning the crowd for Lucky's familiar features. They hadn't had to bring a photo for identification, she thought with grim amusement. All they had to do was ask if anyone had seen Logan's double.

Passengers were shuffling along in line at the departure

gates, most of them with an air of pleasurable anticipation; some worriedly slapping pockets for passports or dubiously counting pieces of luggage. What if he was in some kind of disguise? she thought suddenly. A mustache and beard, or wearing glasses and a concealing hat?

You'd know the man anywhere, Ryan, she told herself dryly. *You know every inch of his gorgeous, lying hide— there's no way he could walk by you without you sensing his presence.*

As they headed towards the Air France departure gates, she kept her eyes on the passers-by, but even without looking at him she was aware of the man beside her. Another snap judgment that had proved wrong—she'd taken an instant dislike to him because he was everything that Lucky wasn't. Unconsciously she'd known from the first that Matt Logan could prove much more threatening to her peace of mind than his brother ever could and she'd done everything possible to keep him at arm's length.

But tonight he'd broken past the barriers she'd erected around herself—barriers that had been put up long ago by a grieving, pain-ridden girl. He'd looked past the tough image that she projected and seen a bereft child, so weighted down with crippling guilt that she was afraid to reveal herself to anyone—and he'd set her free.

She'd hated him at the time. He'd ripped open a scar that she'd hidden for years, and he hadn't been gentle about it. He'd done what he had to do, even knowing that she might turn on him in her pain. He never took the easy way out, Annie thought slowly. *That* was the basic difference between him and Lucky.

"Agent Logan, I thought you'd already boarded. They're about to disengage the ramp." A slim brunette in a tailored blue Air France uniform paused in front of them, a small frown between her perfectly groomed brows. "Is there a problem?"

Logan stood stock still, looking at the woman. His face was carefully blank, but Annie could see a cold fury growing behind his gaze. How had the woman known who he was? she thought in confusion. He'd kept his promise to Bridie, deliberately not identifying himself as FBI. He'd actually left his badge on the kitchen floor where he'd tossed it, she remembered. So how did this airline rep know immediately that he was with the Bureau?

"Yes, there is a problem." His voice was as controlled as ever. Eyes the color of arctic ice flicked a glance at the departure gate, now being closed. "Tell them to hold the ramp and delay the flight. I'm pulling one of your passengers off."

The exquisite brows lifted in consternation. Then the brunette's professionalism took over and she headed swiftly towards the gate, calling out to the attendant.

Suddenly Annie knew. "He's passing himself off as you!" Her gaze flew to Logan's icily enraged features.

"That's right," he said tightly. "If it gets confusing, just remember I'm the one with the gun and he'll be the one who's handcuffed. Wait here."

He walked away without looking back, broad shoulders stiff beneath the impeccably cut suit. Elegant, tough, and totally pissed-off, Annie thought as she watched him enter the boarding tunnel with long easy strides. If the situation wasn't so serious, she'd almost be tempted to smile at his outrage. Almost—but not quite. She found herself gnawing nervously at her lip as she waited for him to reappear with Lucky.

He *had* to have the Rubicon. If he didn't, the desperate hope that burned inside her would flicker and die—and so would her very spirit. Matt wouldn't be able to bring her to life a second time.

She heard a muffled thud from the enclosed departure ramp, and lifted her head, her eyes wide and staring. Beside her the brunette from the airline gasped.

Rounding the corner of the ramp and coming toward her were two men. They were exactly the same height and build, both tall and leanly muscled. Both of them moved with a kind of casual ease, an almost arrogantly lazy grace, except that one of them seemed to be favoring his right leg. The hard cheekbones in both tanned faces were identical, a similarly dense sweep of inky lashes set off two pairs of glittering emerald eyes, and a renegade strand of midnight-black hair fell across both men's straight dark brows. That erotic mouth, such a dead giveaway to the smouldering fire behind that coolly restrained facade, was exactly the same on both.

They were handcuffed to each other.

"I'm throwing a bash for a girlfriend who's getting married next week," the brunette breathed. "I don't suppose those two moonlight at parties, do they?"

Annie's mouth was suddenly too dry to speak. All she could do was stand there as if she were rooted to the spot, unable to take her gaze off the Logan brothers.

Lucky was wearing a duplicate of the suit that Matt had on, with the same plain white shirt and subdued tie. There was really no way to tell them apart, she thought in confusion. For all she knew either one of them could be the philandering thief, or the straight-arrow agent. It was the Rubicon all over again—one was the real thing and one was the counterfeit, and try as she might, she didn't have a clue as to who was who.

Or did she? She squinted as they came closer, forcing herself to look past the externals, studying both pairs of deep-green eyes as the two looked up at the same moment and held her gaze. There was a lurking wry humor behind the chiseled features of one of them, she was almost certain. And the other *had* to be Matt. In his hand he held a leather ID wallet that looked a lot like the one he'd left on her kitchen floor. Behind his eyes there was nothing but a barely controlled fury, carefully concealed but still discernible.

He *could* be Lucky, though, she thought dubiously. A man who'd just had his flight to freedom cancelled at the eleventh hour might be more than a little irate.

And then they were standing in front of her, one of them lifting a corner of his mouth in an ironic half smile.

"I'm the one you want, sweetheart," he said. His voice was dark velvet, with an undertone of amusement. The arm that wasn't cuffed to his brother pulled her unresistingly to him and that lying mouth came down on hers.

"You ever try anything like that again and I'll personally take you apart, limb by limb." The words were expressionless. Logan looked coldly at his brother as he unlocked the cuffs that shackled them together. "Ryan's with me— and she didn't come here to kiss you good-bye. You're in deep—"

"Shove it, Matt." There was an edge to that velvety voice and Lucky's mouth tightened. "I'll listen to whatever else you have to say, but back away from my personal life. That's between Annie and me."

The security lounge that airport personnel had provided for their use was bare and impersonal, with dull beige walls and only a few straight-backed chairs and a wooden table as furniture—which was good, Annie had thought at first. She'd hoped that the very blandness of their surroundings would remind the Logan men to keep this civilized, but it didn't seem to be working out that way.

"You're both out of line," she said, her tone icy and her eyes hard. "The next one who drags me into the conversation as if I'm a bone to be fought over better remember that I'm armed." She turned her gaze to Lucky. "The Rubicon—where is it?"

She was totally over him. Whatever insanity had gripped her that night, it had mercifully disappeared without a trace. She'd thought she would feel *something* when he kissed her, but she hadn't. He was sexy, handsome, and that roguish charm was as devastating as ever, but he was wrong— he *wasn't* the one she wanted anymore.

"That's a trick question, right?" he smiled. "You've got it, sweetheart. I'm not such a bastard that I'd pocket a lady's jewels as I'm leaving her bedroom."

"That's not what I've heard," she said shortly. "But we both know that the stone you left on my dresser was a fake, so stop stalling, Lucky. A child's life is at stake here."

He'd been about to sit down on one of the uncomfortable-looking chairs, but at her words he halted. "Run that by me again," he demanded. The easy-going grin had disappeared.

"Annie's niece has been kidnapped," Logan said, giving his brother a searching glance. "She'll be returned in exchange for the Rubicon—the *real* Rubicon. I hope to hell you didn't know anything about this, Liam."

The fact that he'd used Lucky's real name was a condemnation in itself, she thought. And his brother knew it.

"No, I didn't," he said flatly. "We're brothers, for God's sake—have we grown so far apart that you'd think that of me?" His expression was oddly bereft as he gazed steadily at the man facing him, his mirror image, and then he rubbed his jaw wearily. "Maybe we have." His voice was quiet, with a note of finality in it.

Looking down, he reached into the inner pocket of his jacket, his movements lacking their usual grace. "It's just a damned rock. Who the hell would think it was worth endangering a little girl's life for?"

He withdrew the Rubicon; huge, glittering and intensely blue, and set it carefully on the table in front of Annie. Reaching over, he brushed a stray strand of hair away from her eyes. "How do we arrange the handover, sweetheart?"

Annie averted her eyes from his and fixed them on the sapphire in front of her. It was blurry and out of focus all of a sudden, and she blinked, desperately trying to hold back the tears. That had been true, at least, she thought. That unexpected tenderness in his voice hadn't been calculated or contrived—it had come straight from the real Lucky Logan. She was almost positive it had.

"We wait for them to contact Bridie. As soon as they do, Pa phones us with the time and place," she said hoarsely. She cleared her throat and passed the back of her hand across her eyes. "It'll be sometime tonight—they were convinced I had the stone all the time."

"So we just sit and wait." Lucky raked his hair away from his forehead in a tense gesture. He pulled a chair up to the table and swung his leg over it, sitting down and using the back to support his folded arms.

"Not exactly—*we* just sit and listen," Logan said tightly. "You sit and talk. Do you have any idea who these kidnappers might be? Is there any chance they could be connected with that shooter on the motorcycle who tried to gun you and Annie down the night she jumped off the bridge after you?" He held his brother's gaze fixedly.

If anyone could judge whether Lucky was telling the

truth or not it was Logan, Annie thought. He was staring at his brother as if he was trying to see into his very soul.

"The biker who shot at us?" He shrugged. "I'm totally in the dark about him, too. All I can tell you is that if I'd known this damned stone was going to cause so much trouble, I might have thought twice before I stole it a couple of months ago."

"Yeah. We all wish you'd get an honest job, Lucky," Logan said abstractedly. Then his head jerked up and his eyes narrowed. "Okay. Once again, real slow and clear, Liam. You stole the Rubicon *when?*"

"You heard right. I stole it a couple of months ago, from the private safe of a collector in Argentina." He grinned ruefully. "I was there for a black diamond that had once belonged to Marie Antoinette. It disappeared from a museum a few years ago and I knew my mark had it."

Logan had been sitting on the other side of the table, but in a flash he was out of his seat, his chair crashing back onto the floor and his hand at Lucky's throat. "Little brother, if you don't stop jerking me around right now, you'll be picking up stones in a prison yard for the next twenty years, not lifting diamonds—black or otherwise." His voice was low and vehement. "That's a promise."

"Hands off the tie, Matt." Lucky looked supremely unconcerned. "It's Sulka silk."

Déjà vu all over again, Annie thought sardonically. They looked like two Bengal tigers after the same antelope haunch, and she had a sudden vision of what they must have been like as boys, before they both took such different and widely diverging paths. How did it feel to be so like another person that no one could tell you apart? Was it a quest for identity that had created such barriers between them, more than their separate upbringings?

Then, even as she watched, she saw a typical Lucky expression cross Matt's hard features—a flash of real amusement mixed with ironic self-mockery. They still had a little in common, she realized with a touch of amazement.

"Hell, Lucky—why was it the only thing you ever learned from me was how to dress?" Releasing his brother, Logan took a step back and held up his palms up in a hands-off gesture. "I'm asking you nicely, okay? Just fill us in on the Rubicon and leave everything else out for now." His voice dropped and he added quietly, "It's important, Liam."

Lucky shrugged his jacket back into position and met Matt's eyes. What he saw there made him sigh, and he shook his head slowly. "Yeah, I know it's important. I guess the only reason I'm stalling is because you're never going to believe my story—and for once it happens to be the truth."

"Try us," Annie said. "You said you stole the Rubicon from this collector in Argentina. But you're talking about the duplicate, right?"

"Wrong. I knew as soon as I saw it that it was the real McCoy." He looked up and saw her disbelief. "Annie, listen to me. I'm a lousy card player, women always eventually leave me to get married to someone else, and once in a while my big brother gets the better of me in a fight." His hand rested on the knee he'd been favoring earlier, and he gave an unconscious wince. "But nobody's better than me when it comes to jewels. The real Rubicon was the one I stole in Argentina. What I took from the Treasures of Imperial Russia exhibit was a fake."

"Why?" Logan sat on the edge of the table and crossed his arms casually. He sounded mildly interested, as if his brother was recounting some past exploit that had no bearing on the matter at hand. "Why would you steal something that you knew was counterfeit when you already had the real thing?''

''Because of the provenance,'' Lucky said with an edge of surprise in his voice, as if the answer was obvious. ''I knew what I had was the genuine article, but the value of the Rubicon isn't the fact that it's a big damn sapphire—it's the history of the thing that makes it unique. It's the fact that it belonged to tsars, that it's shown in the portrait of Peter the Great that's hanging in the Louvre, that it was hidden from the Nazis in the war by a Russian peasant in a sack of potatoes.'' He shrugged helplessly. ''That's the provenance, the documented history of it. Without that, all I had was a valuable jewel—with it I had a king's ransom.''

''Let me get this straight.'' She wasn't sure if she understood him. ''As far as everyone knew, the Rubicon was the property of the Russian government—in fact, it was on display in their exhibit. So for a buyer to be convinced that what you were selling was the real one, you had to steal the *fake?*''

''Right.'' He grinned wryly. ''Who would believe me if I tried to tell them that what the Russians were guarding under lock and key was just a big hunk of glass? It *had* to be stolen in a well-publicized theft. When it was, every crooked collector in the world would be standing in line to make me an offer.''

''I believe you.'' Logan was examining his knuckles thoughtfully, but as he spoke he raised his eyes to his brother. Lucky looked astonished, but before he could speak Logan went on. ''Not about the fake Rubicon, of course—that's just another one of your instant fairy tales. But I believe what you said earlier about us growing apart. I don't know you anymore.'' He stood up stiffly, looking suddenly exhausted. His eyes were shuttered and remote as he looked down at Lucky. "I don't even want to know you."

"I'm playing straight on this one, Matt." Lucky's voice was low and even, but Annie saw a muscle jump at the side of his jaw. "God knows I don't blame you for not believing me—hell, I know how crazy it sounds. But I swear I'm telling you the truth this time."

"No more, okay?" Logan gave his brother a swift humorless smile. "I asked airport security to notify the Bureau to come and pick you up, so we shouldn't have to spend much longer in each other's company. Till then, just keep your mouth shut or I'll shut it for you. I swear I will, Liam. This time you've gone too far."

"Annie hasn't said she doesn't believe me." With a hard assessing look at his brother, Lucky gave her a slow smile that didn't quite reach his eyes. "Is it possible you still feel *something* for me, sweetheart? After all, that night together was unforgettable—"

He never finished his sentence. Logan covered the distance between them with a single stride, and pulled him from his chair. Even before Annie could react, he'd slammed Lucky up against the nearest wall, his face only inches from his brother's.

"I warned you, Liam, but I guess that wasn't enough, was it?" His voice was a soft and deadly whisper. "Let's finish this, here and now."

"You've been warning me all my life, *brother.*" Lucky's words came out in a hoarse rasp as he tried to break Logan's hold on him. "I've had enough of your warnings and advice. You don't know how great it feels to know that you've finally screwed up big-time too!"

"Let's remember what we're here for," Annie cut in sharply. "You two obviously can't be in the same room without ripping each other apart so—"

Her cell phone rang.

She could feel the blood draining from her face. The Logan men looked over at her, their differences instantly forgotten. In the sudden silence, the phone trilled again, insistently.

"Answer it." Lucky's voice cracked with tension.

"I'll get it, Annie." Logan was halfway to her when she shook her head, her eyes wide and staring.

"No." She reached into her windbreaker pocket and took out her phone. She flipped it open and held it to her ear. "Pa?"

"You'd better have the stone, bitch."

The voice was a harsh, unfamiliar whisper and she felt her heart smashing against her ribs. Her fingers tightened around the phone.

"Who is this? Is Mary Margaret all right?" She barely had enough air to breathe, but miraculously her voice remained steady.

"The kid's fine, as long as you've got what we want. Same bridge as last time, midnight, and no one but you. That's how it's going down."

"Wait!" Her words came out in a rush. "The thief's coming with me."

"Lucky Logan? The one who stole it?" The voice sounded suspicious.

"We were working the scam together—he's willing to hand it over for the child but he doesn't trust me. He wants to be there himself to make sure I'm not ripping him off."

Annie closed her eyes and clung to the phone like a life line, praying that her impromptu lie had sounded convincing. She realized that the receiver on the other end had been muffled. Then the voice spoke again.

"What the hell—bring the thief. But any tricks and the kid dies. Right in front of your eyes, bitch."

The line disconnected.

Chapter Twelve

"Everything you do, warn them beforehand. Even if it's something totally innocuous, like bringing your hand up to your face."

It was raining lightly and they were tracing the same route through the park she'd taken—was it really only two nights ago? Annie thought in dull surprise. It seemed like a lifetime since she'd tracked Lucky half-way across Boston to end up here. Matt shortened his stride to accommodate hers.

"There's a textbook case of a mother making a handover of a suitcase full of cash for her young son. She kicked the suitcase across the parking garage floor, like she'd been told. They opened a car door and her child got out unharmed. Reflex action—she cried out in relief and her hands flew to her mouth." He cut his glance over to Annie. "The next minute the whole place turned into a shooting gallery. Someone was startled enough to let off a round and the rest of them followed suit. I'm not telling you this to scare you, Annie—but it's important that you know what you're up against."

"What happened to them—the mother and her son?" She kept her eyes on the still distant bridge, the dark arching silhouette pinpointed with the ornamental park lamps she remembered from the last time. When he didn't answer her she looked up at him.

"Double funeral for the family a few days later," Logan said curtly. "But that's not going to happen here. In a couple of hours Mary Margaret's going to be home with her mom and her grandfather."

There was enough Irish in her to wish he hadn't said it. It was like tempting fate, she thought apprehensively. So much could go wrong. There were so many bad ways this night could work out—and only one good way. The odds were stacked against them.

"Thanks for stepping in between me and Lucky," he said into the growing silence. "I shouldn't have let it go that far."

She looked up at him. "He was pushing all your buttons, trying to make you lose it. But I've got to admit, I'm surprised that you did."

"He pushed the right one," he said shortly.

Another cryptic answer from Agent Logan, Annie thought, shoving her hands in her pockets. The bridge was closer now, but they were half an hour early. The wait was going to be excruciating. She reined her skittering thoughts in, taking a deep breath and saying the first thing that came to her mind in an effort to keep her imagination at bay.

"Every time I think there's a real person somewhere inside you, Logan, you seal yourself off again. You know, you might actually be able to learn something from Lucky."

"Meaning what?" He didn't check his stride and his tone was even, but there was a slight edge of disbelief in his words that suddenly turned her anxiety to illogical anger.

"Meaning that despite all his faults, he's a lot more open than you are," she said cuttingly. "Don't you ever get tired of always doing the right thing? Always holding back, weighing your actions? Don't you ever want to let yourself off that leash you seem to keep yourself on all the time?''

''I'm not Lucky. I never will be,'' he said flatly.

And that was all the answer she was going to get from him, she realized as they continued on in silence. She'd caught glimpses of the man, but for some reason he was determined not to reveal the whole of himself to her.

But, whatever the personal barriers between them, there was no one else she'd rather have beside her right now, she thought. They were almost at the bridge and the rain had stopped. The slight mist coming off the river gave the old-fashioned park lamps diffuse halos, and, as before, she was struck by the fairy-tale quality of the scene. It looked enchanted and other-worldly, with the delicately etched lines of the bridge curving in a half-moon across the silvered water.

But appearances were deceptive. This wasn't going to be the setting for a lovers' meeting, a romantic rendezvous. In a short while they would be bargaining for a child's life here. Reflexively Annie's hand touched the reassuring bulk of the Glock under her windbreaker, trying desperately to shut off the part of her mind that held the image of Mary Margaret. She could see her as clearly as if she were in front of her this very minute—awestruck in front of the eel tank at the Aquarium; winning at marbles with all the intensity of a Vegas gambler; sneaking scraps of her dinner outside to the stray mutt that slunk around waiting for her.

I should have let her bring the darn dog in, she thought in sudden contrition. *Why didn't I let her have him?* She was stricken with guilt, and her throat felt tight with tears. *Tomorrow,* she thought. Tomorrow she'd personally scour the neighborhood for him and deliver him to Mary Margaret. Maybe even tonight. If he was hanging around the house tonight when they got home she'd let him in herself. He could sleep on the bed, she vowed fiercely to herself—anything, as long as it meant she heard Mary Margaret's laugh, saw her face again.

"Dear Christ." Logan stopped, his body rigid and his hand gripping her wrist. With a terrible sense of foreboding, Annie looked past the last small stand of trees that partially obscured the bridge. She saw what he was looking at, and her knees buckled. A strong arm went swiftly around her, holding her up.

"My *God,* Matt!" The harsh cry was ripped from her throat. "They're going to kill her!"

The delicate iron and masonry bridge no longer looked like something out of a fairy tale. It looked like something out of a nightmare. At the center of the span, high above the broken waters of the river rushing below, was the small figure of Mary Margaret, precariously balanced on the narrow stone railing.

"Let me *go!*" Annie twisted in Matt's grip, her breath coming in sobs. "Dammit, Logan, let go of me!"

"No." His voice was low and intense, his fingers like a vice around her wrist. "You charge onto that bridge and you'll get her killed, Annie. We're going to walk there together, calmly and slowly, and give them the Rubicon just like we planned." He forced her head up to meet his gaze. "We can't afford emotion right now. These people aren't professionals, or they wouldn't be playing a sadistic game like this and jeopardizing the handover. If you let them know what you're going through, they're liable to push her off just for kicks."

His words were blunt and uncompromising, and for a moment she felt a rush of anger at him. Everything he said was true. But how could he stand there so coldly, as if this was just a problem in logistics to be worked out as dispassionately as possible?

"I won't let them harm her, Annie. My life for hers, if that's what it takes, but I won't let them harm her." Again the same blunt tone, but this time there was a raw edge to his voice. "Trust me."

Those dark emerald eyes held hers, direct and compelling, and suddenly she saw past the controlled exterior to the agonized compassion he couldn't afford to display. He was just as stricken as she was, she realized slowly. But right now he only had one priority, and nothing would be allowed to interfere with that.

He would keep Mary Margaret safe. He'd given his word. She felt the choking panic inside release its crippling hold on her and she took a deep breath. She was ready to go through with this. Resolutely she straightened her spine and looked past the trees again.

"I'm okay now. I won't do anything stupid, I promise." She saw the waiting figures, one of them holding onto Mary Margaret's legs as she stood on the railing. "Let's go."

They were only a couple of hundred yards from the sinister tableau on the bridge, but it seemed like the longest walk she'd ever taken. In the park on the other side of the river a car was running, its headlights on and its doors open. There wasn't anyone in it, the bounty hunter in her noted. She could disregard it as a possible threat. As they got closer she could see that there were three men on the bridge, and she felt a spurt of icy disgust break through the professionalism she was attempting to maintain. Three of them—*three,* to stand guard over a defenseless little girl. If any one of the bastards had so much as touched her, Annie vowed silently, she would personally dedicate the rest of her life to hunting them down. And Logan would probably be right beside her when she did.

She felt like she was crossing a tightrope as they started across the bridge, but he gave an impression of relaxed calm. She tried to keep her movements just as slow and easy, but as she saw the small figure swaying on the bridge parapet it was almost impossible not to rush to her.

"Hi, Aunt Annie." Mary Margaret's voice quavered, but it was full of heavy scorn as she went on. "I told these jerks you'd come and kick their butts."

She still had her beloved Red Sox cap on, turned backwards on her head. Her jeans had a tear in the knee and she was wearing the T-shirt they'd bought yesterday at the Aquarium. She looked like a little street tough, with one of her high-top running shoes unlaced over a grubby sock.

She was scared to death. And she wasn't going to show it, Annie knew.

"Hi, Champ." She could barely get the words past the thickness in her throat. "We're not here to kick butt tonight. We're just here to take you home, okay? Don't look down."

"Where is it?" The man who spoke was the one who was hanging onto the back of Mary Margaret's jeans. He looked like the losers she brought in every day, Annie thought, not like the mastermind of a kidnapping operation. Knocking off gas stations seemed more his style than dealing with one of the world's most fabled gems.

He was working for someone. They all had to be. They were low-lifes, hired for the job by someone who didn't want to appear in person.

"I've got it," Logan said evenly. "How do you want to do this?"

He was keeping his hands slightly away from his body, and the gesture seemed oddly familiar to her. Then she remembered. It was how Lucky had stood on this bridge two nights ago, before she'd apprehended him. The same stance by both brothers—and it meant the same thing, she realized. He was trying to appear as non-threatening as possible, so as not to goad these thugs into a fatal reaction.

"Hand it over to your girlfriend, Lucky. Then she brings it over to me and I'll let her have the kid." The one who was holding Mary Margaret had red hair cut so short it looked like hog's bristles.

The second man was painfully thin, with a badly acne-scarred face. He kept scratching at his neck compulsively, and Annie wondered if he was on something. She didn't take her eyes off him as he spoke to Matt.

"You're like this James Bond kind of jewel thief, and then you let yourself get screwed over by some woman. Man, you must be pissed about this." He laughed and scratched his neck vacantly. A gun was shoved down the front of his jeans, and she wondered briefly if the safety was off.

"Shut up and let's get this over with."

Of the three of them, this one was the most normal-looking. He was more neatly dressed than the others, with a gleaming leather jacket and shoes instead of sneakers. But when Annie looked more closely at him, she felt suddenly chilled to the bone. His eyes were almost black, with about as much humanity in them as a snake's. They were dead-looking. She thought she could detect a faint accent in his voice when he spoke.

"While you're taking the Rubicon out and giving it to the woman, I'm going to be aiming straight for the kid's head." He looked over at Annie. "You must have something that's worth a lot more to him than money. You better hope he wants you bad enough not to be a hero at the last minute."

"I'm taking the stone out now," Logan said in an un-hurried voice. He reached into his pocket slowly and cautiously, his eyes on the man in the leather jacket. Annie watched him out of the corner of her vision, but she kept her gaze fixed on Mary Margaret. The little girl had fallen silent after her initial outburst and her face was as white as chalk as she stared down at her aunt.

"Take it from him and bring it over to Terry." Leather-jacket was addressing her, and as he spoke he moved closer to the redhead clutching Mary Margaret. His gun was still aimed at her.

Annie's legs felt like they were encased in concrete as she took a step towards Logan and felt him press the Rubicon into her palm. He reached for her other hand and laid it on top of the jewel, as if he was afraid she'd drop it.

"Do what the man says. This'll all be over in a few minutes," he said in a clear voice.

As she turned and headed at an even pace to the two men by the railing, the redhead was confronting the man in the leather jacket.

"Hey, I thought we said no *names*. That was the plan—no freakin' names!"

Carefully keeping all emotion from her features, she held out the stone, expecting the redhead to take it from her. Instead, the other man grasped it. He gave it a hard look and then shoved it deep into the inner pocket of his coat as he looked over at his irate partner.

"Sorry, I forgot. But it doesn't matter now anyway, Terry." His tone was casual. "The plan's been changed."

His arm had been extended while he'd been aiming at Mary Margaret, but in a blur of movement he brought it down and fired point-blank at the redhead.

Everything happened at once. Even as the redhead slammed back against the railing with the force of the bullet, Annie was frantically grabbing for Mary Margaret. She saw the muzzle of the leather-jacketed shooter's gun swing past her to the third kidnapper, who had finally stopped scratching his neck and was belatedly reaching for his own weapon, and she heard it fire again.

Her hand grabbed the back of Mary Margaret's jeans just as the little girl started to topple over the stone parapet, but before she could pull her to safety the gun swung back in her direction. In a moment of perfect visual clarity, her gaze focused on the trigger as his finger tightened on it.

And then Logan's Sig Sauer came up as he stepped in front of her, and both guns fired simultaneously.

Those black snake's eyes held a faint hint of astonishment as they looked at Logan, still standing with his gun in his hand but with his arm now hanging at his side. Then what little life had ever been in them vanished, and the man in the leather jacket dropped abruptly to the ground like a puppet whose strings had been cut.

But by then Annie's attention was on Mary Margaret, as she swung her down from the treacherous stone railing and crushed her to her. She felt the little body trembling against hers and the cold face pressed into the hollow of her shoulder.

"Are you okay, Champ? Did they hurt you?" She held her at arm's-length suddenly, needing to reassure herself that she was unharmed.

"They didn't hurt me. They just put a cloth on my face and I went to sleep." The little girl's voice was thready. "It made me feel sick."

"We'll get you to a hospital where they can check you over, baby," Annie said, setting her gently on the ground and keeping one arm tightly around her shoulders. "I'll phone for an ambulance right now, and then we're going to call your mom and tell her to meet us there. She's going to want to hear your voice, sweetie." She turned to Logan.

"She's all right?" he asked. He swayed slightly and put

his hand out to the stone railing. He looked drained, Annie thought. She probably did too.

"She seems fine." Still clutching Mary Margaret protectively, she held his eyes with hers. "You kept your promise, Logan—you got her out safe. I thought we weren't going to make it for a moment there. How did he miss you at such close range?"

He looked mildly amused, and then a spasm of pain crossed his features. "Honey, he didn't. I think he got my shoulder."

Chapter Thirteen

"Thank God she doesn't appear to have anything the matter with her—except shock, of course. The doctors want to keep her under observation so we'll stay overnight and bring her home in the morning." Pat Ryan handed his daughter a plastic cup of something that vaguely resembled coffee. "Vending-machine stuff," he apologized. "It probably tastes like old crankcase oil."

"You're sure they didn't hurt her? They didn't—they didn't do *anything* to her, Pa? You're not holding back on me, are you?" It had been a hidden fear that she hadn't dared express, and Annie needed to have it laid to rest.

"Nothing like that," her father said forcefully. "They were scum, but not that kind of scum." He sat down beside her and took one of her hands in his. "When they snatched her they knocked her out with chloroform, and then they seem to have kept her sedated right up until the time they were on their way to meet you. She can't tell us much." He sighed heavily. "Maybe it's good that she doesn't remember anything."

"I thought I was going to die when I saw her up there on that bridge. I thought *she* was going to die," she said tonelessly. "Have they identified the bodies yet?"

''All but one. They were punks. Small-time perps.'' He met her eyes, his blue gaze direct.

She fixed her gaze on the metal wastebasket on the other side of the small waiting room. It was overflowing with used tissues, mute evidence of other vigils, other pain. She suddenly wanted to get out of there. ''I have to give a more detailed statement to the police tomorrow, but right now I think I'll go home and try to get some sleep. Will you tell Bridie I'll see her in the morning?''

''You're sure you don't want me to drive you home?'' When she shook her head her father took the untouched coffee cup from her and drained it. He stood up to toss the container in the garbage. ''When will they release Matt?''

''Not for a day or two at least, depending on how bad his shoulder is. One of the nurses said he might have to have surgery.'' She looked over at her father, her eyes dark with memory. ''He stepped right in front of me, Pa. He deliberately took the bullet that was meant for me.''

Pat Ryan pulled his daughter to him with sudden fierceness, enfolding her in a bear-like hug. ''In the name of all the saints, darlin', I'm glad he did. He's a fine man, Anne Maureen—and a brave one, too.''

He squeezed her tightly and then let her go, fishing in his pants pocket for a handkerchief and blowing his nose loudly. ''He'd have to be, to keep up with you. You'll never know how it felt, watching you walk out the door. I wondered if I'd ever see you again, and I knew I had no right to stop you from doing what you had to do.''

He wasn't just talking about tonight, Annie realized. He felt like this every day that she went to work, and yet he'd swallowed that fear, allowing her to live her own life, make her own decisions. It hadn't been easy for him, but he had loved her enough to set her free.

She owed him that same freedom. It was time she

stopped letting the ghosts of the past rule all their lives, time to stop being afraid to live, to take chances. Being a bounty hunter hadn't taught her that. Matt Logan had.

She suddenly wished that he was with her. She *needed* him, she thought with a touch of surprise. She needed to have him beside her, to talk to him, to watch those amazing green eyes narrow with hidden amusement. She wanted to look at him. She wanted to be with him.

Oh, hell, Ryan—you've gone and fallen in love with the man.

A few minutes later she was walking across the hospital lobby, her head down in thought. There had to be some other explanation for the way she was feeling, she told herself. How could she have fallen in love with the same Agent Logan who had driven her crazy with his darned notebook and his silver pen and his freezingly polite disbelief the first time they'd met? Although now she came to think of it, she mused, his notebook had been nowhere in evidence today. Maybe he'd realized just how much it had annoyed her.

But that didn't matter. She couldn't be in love with a man she barely knew, even if they *had* gone through fire together and he'd risked his life for hers. She felt like she'd lived a lifetime in the last few hours. Her emotions were still off-balance. She was tired and shaky and probably in a slight state of shock.

It didn't have to be love.

"What the hell were you doing in there for so long?" He strode across the lobby from behind an unattractive arrangement of ficus trees and ferns and opened the door for her, looking irritated and impeccably elegant at the same time. He flicked an apprehensive glance at an orderly walking by them. "Come on, there's a head nurse built like a line-backer who's looking for me. I had to get Cartwright to bring me something to wear just to sneak out of here.''

It just might be love, Annie thought in defeat, letting her gaze linger on him and then glaring over his shoulder at a couple of candy stripers who were doing the same thing. But that didn't mean she had to give in to it.

''You snuck out of hospital. Smart move,'' she said crushingly. ''Are you trying to prove you're a superman or something, Logan?''

''I'm not trying to prove anything, I just can't stand hospitals. Besides, the bone was only nicked. The doctor taped it up and—''

He stopped so suddenly that she nearly ran into him. He was looking down at his chest, his face stricken.

''What is it?'' She was getting him back into the hospital right now, she thought fearfully. The man was obviously in pain.

''I can't believe he gave me a brown tie with a gray suit,'' Logan muttered. ''What the hell was he thinking?''

He looked up, catching her furious expression. One corner of that fabulous mouth lifted in a wickedly teasing half smile. ''Dammit, Annie—I've been skulking around behind a potted plant for the last half hour waiting for you to appear.'' His gaze sought and held hers. The light note in his voice sobered to compassion and a sudden shadow passed over his features. ''How're you holding up?''

He wasn't supposed to be like this, she thought, panicking. Logan was supposed to be tough. Caustic. She could deal with him that way, but not like this. Not tender and caring and gentle—that wasn't *fair*. She'd held back the tears through the ambulance ride to the hospital with Mary Margaret's cold little hand clutching hers, she'd held them back at the sight of her father and Bridie, and she'd managed to keep herself under control while the police had questioned her about what had happened on the bridge.

But his simple question disarmed her. Her eyes overflowed.

She'd have her family to support her through this. Who could Logan turn to? Not his brother, certainly. No—he would go back to that beautiful house that seemed to have nothing of him in it, and he'd be completely alone.

Tonight, so would she.

"Come on, I'll take you home." He was watching her with an unidentifiable expression in his eyes. In any other man she might have called it regret, she thought, briefly puzzled, but even as she looked at him he turned away and nodded at the parking lot. "Cartwright dropped the Taurus off for me. He wasn't happy about it, but I pulled rank."

"Aiding and abetting a hospital breakout." She tried to match his determinedly light tone. "Poor guy. It must have been the last thing he expected from his by-the-book partner." She paused, momentarily diverted. "That reminds me—where's your notebook? And the silver pen? Did you have them surgically removed or something?"

They'd reached his car and he was unlocking the door for her. He dropped his keys and swore under his breath as he picked them up. "I felt it was possible I was beginning to use them as a crutch. They were a habit I decided to discard," he said coldly. He opened the passenger door and paused, a reluctant smile at the corner of his mouth. "Besides, you made it obvious that if you saw them one more time there was a damn good chance I *was* going to have to get them surgically removed."

Annie laughed as she got in and he walked around to his own door. A moment later she realized what she'd done. She'd actually *laughed*. An hour ago she'd thought that nothing could possibly lighten the trauma of this terrible night, but for a few seconds Logan had shown her that life could be normal again, despite everything that had happened.

Suddenly she couldn't bear the thought of him taking her home to an empty house, and watching him drive away to an empty one of his own. The last few hours were too fresh, too vivid in her mind to deal with on her own. Even if they hadn't been, she admitted to herself with a flash of honesty, she still would have wanted to be with him. As he got into the car she spoke. Her words tumbled out swiftly, before she could change her mind.

"I don't want to be alone tonight, Matt."

She didn't look at him but she knew he was looking at her, and she could feel the color mounting her cheekbones. She was grateful that the interior of the car was dark.

"Neither do I," he said finally. His smile was rueful. "God, Annie, you shoot my good intentions all to hell. This probably isn't a smart idea."

Her eyes widened in understanding. Her face had been warm before; now it felt like it was on fire. "I—no, I just meant—" She floundered to a stop and took a deep breath. "I'm not saying we should sleep together. I just don't want to be alone—not tonight. I need to be with someone."

Not just someone—she needed to be with *him*, she thought, biting her lower lip in consternation. But she didn't seem to be able to express herself clearly right now.

"I knew what you meant the first time." He started the ignition and looked over at her. "We'll toss a coin for the sofa bed. There's one thing I have to ask you, though."

She raised her eyes to his, wondering if she'd ever really fathom what went on behind that lambent green gaze. Just when she thought she knew him, he turned out to be a totally different man. Right now something was definitely worrying him.

"Yes?" She tried to keep the concern from her voice.

"Stop looking at me like that, okay?" He put the Taurus in Reverse and backed out of the parking space, almost clipping the car beside them. "Because biting your lip is one of those little things you do that play hell with my good intentions."

As they drove out of the hospital lot and onto the street she was unable to think of a single thing to say to him in reply, but he didn't seem to expect further conversation.

Well, now you know, she told herself helplessly. *He's definitely the one.*

She wanted *everything* from him. She wanted him to fall in love with her. She wanted it to be forever. She wanted to be able to hand him her heart and soul and receive his in return. She wanted a lot from him, she knew—maybe she wanted more than he was willing to give.

This afternoon they'd proved that they could create a four-alarm fire just by being in the same room together, and even the memory of his mouth on her skin could make her feel weak. But as all-consuming as that fire between them was, there had to be a steady flame behind it—one strong enough so that nothing could ever extinguish it.

The city night slid smoothly by outside, the slim mirrored shape of the soaring John Hancock Tower throwing back the reflection of Trinity Church in graceful deference. Annie remained lost in her own thoughts. How did he feel about her? He wasn't one to reveal his deeper emotions easily—was she ever going to get past that seamlessly perfect exterior to the real man within?

There was one question she hadn't dared to ask herself, but she knew she would have to face it eventually. How high a price was she going to have to pay for that night she'd spent with his brother? Would it prove to be the final insurmountable barrier between them that nothing could tear down?

Had she thrown away her chance at the real thing for a counterfeit—a counterfeit that had glowed with a reckless beauty in the hours between dusk and dawn, but that had proven false in the light of day? She leaned her head against the cool glass of the car window and closed her eyes in sudden pain, thrusting the thought aside.

"When I spoke to Cartwright he told me that the Bureau had finally delivered the Rubicon to Kortachoff." As Logan spoke he pulled the Taurus over to the curb, and with a start she realized that they'd reached their destination. "He'd apparently been at some arts gala earlier, and no one could reach him. I gather there were a few tense moments while he examined it."

Despite herself, she smiled. "No one got hustled out in handcuffs this time?" She looked over at him as they entered the house.

"No, thank God. The stone Lucky gave us at the airport was the genuine article. He's still sticking to that story about the real Rubicon being stolen in Argentina, though."

He walked ahead of her into a gleamingly modern kitchen. Another sterile room, Annie thought, contrasting it with Bridie's domain. No plants, no touches of color, no dishtowel left on the counter. All the appliances were brushed stainless steel. A massive double-door refrigerator flanked a restaurant-style gas stove. A free-standing maple butcher's block stood over by the far wall, under a hanging rack of copper pans. Her curiosity got the better of her.

"Is the whole house like this?"

"Like what?" He shed his jacket with some difficulty. Through his shirt she could see the bulk of the dressing on his shoulder. "Red or white wine? Nurse Ratchett pumped me full of drugs before I escaped, so I guess I'd better stick to coffee.''

"Coffee's fine." She gestured around her. "Like this— like a magazine spread. It doesn't look like anyone really lives here. Everything's so…perfect." Her voice trailed off dubiously.

He flipped a switch on the coffee-maker. "This was my grandparents' town house. They had a place on the Vineyard that they left me too, but I haven't found the time to get out there this year." He shrugged and then gave a slight wince. "I just never got around to changing anything."

"So this is where you grew up?" It explained a lot. She had a vision of a small boy, suddenly orphaned and separated from his twin, being deposited in this beautiful, flawless house.

"Yeah. While Lucky was hitting the high spots of Europe with Sam and Yvonne, my father's parents, and learning the finer points of scaling walls and disabling alarm systems, I was being packed off to Miss Braithwaite's Dancing School every Saturday morning and shuffling around the floor with white-gloved little girls who traced their lineage back to the Mayflower and never let anyone forget it."

He didn't sound particularly bothered by the inequality. His attention was focused on pouring coffee into two bone-china mugs that looked nothing like the thick chipped ones she was used to at home. He handed one to her, and led the way into the living room.

A silk-shaded lamp created a warm glow of light near the sofa, but the corners of the room melted into shadow, softening the remote formality that had overwhelmed her earlier. Annie's gaze went automatically to the spot where the crystal vase had shattered. There was no trace of it now.

A different arrangement of pink lilies and out-of-season white lilac stood on the sideboard.

He followed her glance. ''I have someone who comes in to clean,'' he said dryly.

This life-style had certain advantages, she thought. But it hadn't turned him into the man he was today. The elegant facade was just that—a facade. It was the contradiction between it and the toughness it masked that confused her.

''Boarding school, summers on the Vineyard—why didn't you take the conventional route and go into something safe like banking?'' she asked, taking a seat on the velvet sofa. ''You don't exactly fit the mold that your grandparents must have had in mind.''

He didn't sit. Instead he walked over to the sideboard and touched one of the lilies with his finger, stroking it thoughtfully. ''They died within a few months of each other when I was sixteen,'' he said. ''I'd never really felt I'd known them, and after their deaths I realized I didn't know myself either. So I gave my trustees heart attacks and dropped out of sight for a while to see if I could make it on my own without the money or the name always backing me up.''

He tipped some pollen from the lily onto the polished surface of the sideboard and looked over at her, those sinfully thick lashes turning his eyes to green slits. ''I came back three years later with an extensive education in dirty fighting, thinking fast and getting back on my feet after the other guy thought I was down for good. I learned how to survive, and I figured I could put that knowledge to better use working on the side of law and order.'' He gave her a quick smile. ''I'm still hell on waltzes though.''

She believed him, Annie thought in sharp frustration. Right now he was demonstrating just how deftly he could move—away from any subject that concerned him by summing up his life in a few sparse sentences and considering the matter closed. She knew more about most of her skips from reading their files than she did about the man she'd gone and fallen in love with. It was almost as if he had some deep dark secret that made him so vulnerable that he couldn't allow her anywhere near the real Matt Logan.

She suddenly knew she'd hit on the truth.

He *was* hiding something from her—he had been from the start. There had always been a wary edge to their relationship, as if he couldn't trust her with the knowledge of who he really was. It was as if even while they'd been coming closer to being lovers there had still been an equal possibility that they could one day be enemies.

He wanted her. But he was holding something back. And if there was going to be any chance at all for this relationship she was going to have to discover what it was.

She already had a pretty good idea though, she thought heavily.

"Now I know everything about you," she said softly. She set her mug on the low table and leaned back on the velvet cushions, looking up at him. There was a faint hint of challenge in her eyes. "All that's missing from that exhaustive autobiography is the fact that you have a brother who happens to be your twin—a brother who's sitting in jail right now because you put him there."

She'd been right—Lucky was definitely the key. She saw the quick tightening of his jaw before he schooled his features back to their usual impassivity. A petal snapped from the lily onto the sideboard and Logan looked at it for a moment. He turned away from the flowers and walked casually towards the sofa.

She was close to the truth. If she pushed him further she'd know for sure, but suddenly she wondered if she really wanted to confirm the suspicion that was rapidly becoming a certainty. She caught her lower lip between her teeth and hesitated.

"Hell, Annie." Logan looked away, and then his gaze swung back to her as if he couldn't help himself. "We had a deal and he tried to get out of his end of it. All my life I've given him second chances, but not this time."

The moment to back away had come and gone. She met his eyes and realized that he was coldly furious, although he'd been able to keep any hint of anger out of his words, and for some reason this indication of the distance he still kept between them was the final straw.

"I *know* he doesn't get a second chance, Logan. That would violate your rigid code of ethics, wouldn't it? He reneged on a deal, and even though he made up for it in the end, you can't forgive him for that." She took a shallow breath, her voice an intense whisper. "Except that doesn't make sense. You said it yourself—you've always given him second chances in the past. What did he do this time that was so different?"

"You're all wrong." He leaned closer, his expression grim. "I didn't want it to come out like this but—"

"It's the same reason why you keep shutting down on me, isn't it?" In the lamplight her eyes were dark with pain. "You let me get just so close and no closer. Even tonight after everything that we went through together, you still make sure I don't cross the boundary line."

"I couldn't let you know me that well," he said flatly. "Not until now, anyway."

"Not ever. You look at me and all you can see is that Lucky got here first." She felt the anger seep out of her. It was replaced with hopelessness, and her throat was tight with tears. "That's never going to change, no matter how much you think you want me. If I spent tonight in your bed you'd still remember that the brother you're so hostile towards, the brother who stands for everything you fight against, made love to me before I even met you. And you don't ever come in second against Lucky, do you?''

"Not if I can help it," he said tightly. "But Lucky got nowhere with you, Annie."

"No, he didn't," she admitted dully. "When he kissed me today I knew there was nothing there. But you'll always—"

"There's no easy way to tell you, is there? He was right about one thing—I screwed up big-time." There was a harsh bitterness in his tone that set off a distant warning bell somewhere at the back of her mind.

"Annie." His voice was softly compelling. She looked at him.

He reached over and pulled gently at a strand of her hair. Bringing it around to her mouth, he let it lie there, curving in towards her lips. His hand traced the line of her jaw and trailed slowly down her neck to the hollow between her collarbones. The light turned his eyes to a brilliant gold-green and shadowed the hard lines of his face as he held her gaze.

She definitely shouldn't have let him touch her, she thought despairingly. Now she really was in trouble.

He was big, gorgeous and he belonged in bed, making love to her right now and all night long. She wanted to see those green eyes close in ecstasy, see those strong fingers gripping her, run the tip of her tongue along that incredible mouth even while he was gasping her name out. She was about to make the same reckless mistake that she'd made before.

She was incapable of walking away from the man. All she could do was make him walk away from her.

"I slept with your brother." She forced the brutal words out. They were a last-ditch defense, the barrier that had always been between them. This time she was using them to save her from herself and she went on, her voice shaking. "I *slept* with him, Logan—think about it! Everything that you want, he had before you. He had me first, in every way you can imagine, and you'll always know that. You'll always know you got here second, after him."

She stopped, her eyes blind with tears. She'd grabbed the front of his shirt while she'd been choking out the damning words at him, and now she released her hold, spreading her fingers slowly against his chest. She could feel his heart beating, hard and fast, under her palm. She blinked and his face came into focus.

He looked like a man who'd just lost the most valuable treasure he'd ever had.

"Kiss me, Annie," he said. His voice was raw and hoarse. "I want it one last time."

He brought his mouth to hers and his arms wrapped around her tightly, crushing her to him almost desperately. This was it, she thought as she tasted her own tears against his skin. He knew what she'd said was the ultimate truth, and this was his way of saying goodbye to what they might have had. She felt as if her soul was being left behind as she opened her lips to him and felt him inside her.

And then he drew back, bringing his palms to the sides of her face, his thumbs at her temples.

"*I* got there first, Annie." The green eyes were glazed with pain. "Do you understand what I'm trying to tell you? It wasn't Lucky that night—it was me."

Chapter Fourteen

Even as she stared at him, her pale face framed between the palms of his hands, she felt as if ice crystals were forming on her skin, inch by inch, overlapping and packing together faster and faster. Her lips were still warm from his, but she felt her body stiffening with the deadly cold that was winding around her like a shroud. The frost encased her heart, solidified in her throat, and then even the taste of him was gone from her mouth. It was almost impossible to speak.

"Tell me you're lying." Her voice cracked. Her eyes looked like violets under ice.

"Not this time. Not anymore." There were deep grooves at the sides of his mouth that she had never seen before. Her temples pounded from his touch.

"You bastard, Logan." She slanted her eyes up at him, feeling the skin pull tight where he held her, her words low and uninflected. "You absolute bastard. Get your hands off me."

She sat, small and with her spine ramrod-straight, on the edge of the exquisite velvet sofa and finally she felt his grip loosen. His hands dropped to his sides and slowly he stood up, looking down at her.

"I knew the longer it went on, the more you'd end up

hating me. I wanted to tell you before now, but I couldn't.'' He stopped, one corner of his mouth lifting in a sudden expression of disgust. ''That sounds like an excuse, and there isn't one for what I've done to you, Annie.''

''No, there isn't,'' she said tightly. Then her control snapped and she stood to confront him. ''Why didn't you *tell* me? What was this—some kind of twisted game you were playing?'' Her eyes widened, and her hand went to her mouth as a thought struck her. ''Does Lucky know everything we did together?'' Her voice sank to an appalled whisper. ''He *does,* doesn't he? He had to keep up the pretence when I saw him at the airport so you filled him in and he backed you up! What was the next part of the plan, Logan—was *he* going to pretend to be *you?*''

''He only knew he was supposed to have spent the night with you. My whole cover would have been blown as soon as you saw him, otherwise.'' He met her eyes steadily. ''I hated myself for having to tell him that much.''

She stared at him as the full force of his words seared itself into her consciousness. A terrible sense of betrayal spilled through her and without volition, her hand flew up and struck him abruptly across his left cheekbone. The sharp sound of the slap was out of place in the perfect room.

''I've never done that before. It always seemed such a girly way to hit,'' she said distantly. Under the pain a growing anger lent her the strength to continue. ''But it felt like the right thing to do in this situation.''

The imprint of her hand was still visible on his tanned skin. He hadn't moved a muscle as she'd struck him, but the expression in his eyes was wryly ironic. He touched his cheek cautiously.

''Hell, that didn't feel girly to me, Annie,'' he said evenly. ''But you had every right to do it. You're probably going to feel like taking a few more shots at me before I'm finished."

"Probably," she agreed shortly. "But don't let that stop you. What were you doing on the bridge that night, posing as Lucky?"

"We made the switch as soon as the bail bond was sworn out and he was released from jail." Logan raked an unconscious hand through his hair. "Like I said, the Bureau thought it would be a great idea to lay a trap for his buyer and they wanted everything to look as normal as possible—even to taking out a real bond with a real bail agency. It was just our bad luck we chose the one you work for." He sighed. "I couldn't believe it when you walked onto that bridge and identified yourself. Later on when we learned of your reputation, we realized we'd picked the wrong damn bounty hunter to skip out on."

"You should have asked around, Logan. Any of those losers down at the jail could have told you that." She placed her hands on her hips. "Which brings us to our little moonlight swim. Tell me, was what happened on the riverbank part of the job too? Or were you just improvising by then?"

Her stance was confrontational and her voice was mockingly skeptical, but the sarcasm didn't completely mask the anguish in her question. Hearing it, he took a swift step toward her but checked himself when she pinned him with her gaze.

"Don't touch me. Just tell me." Her voice was under control again. "I need to know why you did it."

A brief shadow passed across the hard planes of his features. The muscle at the side of his jaw flinched. "Because when I pulled you from the river I thought I'd lost you," he said simply. "Then you opened your eyes and looked up at me and I knew I'd found you."

Annie took a reflexive step backward, grasping the sofa for support. She felt as if she'd just had the breath knocked out of her. "You must really think I'm a fool," she said slowly, the corners of her mouth white with shock. "Love at first sight—I'm supposed to *believe* that? The perfect, controlled Agent Logan?"

"That's what I told myself." He smiled tightly at her. "But for the first time in my life I didn't give a damn about doing the right thing. All I knew was that there was this tough, loud-mouthed little blonde waving a gun at me and for some reason there was no way in hell I could bring myself to walk away from her."

"That was lust, not love," she said flatly. Abruptly she turned away from him, walking over to the French windows and looking out into the black night.

"I wanted it to be lust," he said softly to her back. "I wasn't looking for anything more complicated."

"Neither was I." Her words were bitter and nearly inaudible. Still staring unseeingly into the darkness, she continued in the same low tone, as if she was talking to herself. "Love scared the hell out of me. Falling in love meant handing fate one more hostage, and I was having a hard enough time worrying about the ones I had. It was easier to tell myself that it was just an overwhelming physical attraction that I felt—an irresistible compulsion that I had to give in to, just this once."

"Did you convince yourself?" Logan asked tersely.

"No. *You* convinced me." She turned from the window and faced him, her face a mask. "You convinced me when you left me the way you did, letting me think you'd just seen me as a one-night stand. You must have come straight here, changed, and then raced to the office so that I could deliver what I thought was the Rubicon to you—the very stone that you'd stashed in my car for safe-keeping when we were getting shot at by that biker. No wonder when you showed up earlier that day in your Agent Logan persona with Cartwright you were so sure I had it.''

''Yeah, I knew you had to have it.'' He smiled humorlessly. ''I also knew that I was the last man on earth you'd hand it over to.''

''I didn't find it until after you'd left.'' She looked up with renewed anger. ''I told you later on that night.''

''You told me when you thought I was my *brother*,'' he exploded. ''But whenever you had dealings with me as myself you made it damn clear you couldn't stand Matt Logan. The only time there seemed to be a chance that a relationship might develop between us was when I showed up as Lucky, a notorious thief who breaks every law I'm sworn to uphold.''

The steely control that was so much a part of him, that had been tempered and tested over the years, suddenly showed strain. ''I was caught between a rock and a hard place as it was, Annie—no one was to be told about the impersonation. The police, other agents…hell, even Cartwright wasn't in the loop. If Dmitri Kortachoff even *guessed* that we'd had the Rubicon and hadn't returned it right away, this whole thing would have escalated into a matter for the State Department—as it was, he seemed to suspect that we were holding out on him. But that wasn't all. After that biker tried to kill us, I couldn't let you become any more involved in this than you were. I'd diverted him once but there was no guarantee he wouldn't come after you again.''

''He won't be gunning for anyone anymore.'' She met his eyes. ''He was the kidnapper wearing the leather jacket.''

He paused, and then a corner of his mouth lifted in a

rueful half smile. He shook his head in defeat. "I keep trying to guard you from all the wrong things, don't I?"

"That's right, Logan." The anger had drained out of her in the last few minutes. Now all she felt was an aching sadness. "He was left-handed, which caught my attention, and then I saw that his pants were damp from the knees down. That's where a biker gets splashed when the road's wet. If I didn't notice details like that I wouldn't have lasted for two days as a bounty hunter."

She turned to the sofa and picked up her windbreaker, suddenly weary. "I wear a bullet-proof vest most of the time on the job. I just never thought to protect my heart from the man I was falling in love with."

His eyes were more topaz than emerald in the soft light and as she started to turn away a spark behind them flickered like a dying flame. "Lucky was right. I've lost you, haven't I?"

"Maybe you thought your reasons were good enough at the time, Logan." Annie's gaze was dull with a aching grief that she hoped she could contain for as long as it took her to leave him. "But you didn't trust me in the one situation where that's the most important thing that two people can share with each other. You *had* me. Whatever name you were going under, it was you all the time. And now it's you who's lost me."

She turned and walked away from him, her head up, her back straight and her heart cracking in two.

"HERE'S MY card if you need to call me." Looking more like a tired bloodhound than ever, Jack Cartwright heaved a sigh and pushed back his chair from the Ryans' kitchen table, his concerned gaze on Bridie's wan face. "Like I said, we'll keep the surveillance on for another week, but my guess is whoever masterminded this operation has left the country already. There's no reason they'd attempt another snatch on Mary Margaret.''

It had been five days since that terrible ordeal on the bridge, but as Annie walked outside with Cartwright to his car, she knew that it would be months before the memories began to fade. Pa and Bridie were trying their best to settle the household back to its normal routine, and Mary Margaret was due to start back at school on Monday, but the knowledge that the FBI still had no leads on who had commissioned the kidnapping was daunting.

Her heart felt like a lump of lead in her chest, but she knew that the investigation's dead-end wasn't the only cause of her depression. It just was the only cause she allowed herself to think about.

''The Rubicon was the key, Annie.'' Cartwright paused at the door of his car. Awkwardly he reached over and patted her shoulder. ''Now that it's back in Kortachoff's exhibit your niece is safe. If there was a chance she could identify anyone but the three thugs who did the dirty work it might be a different story, but seemingly whoever was behind this never revealed himself to her. He knows she's no threat.''

She attempted a smile, but it didn't reach her eyes. ''I'll feel a whole lot better when you catch him. What about the motorcycle shooter—any information yet on who he was?''

''Zilch,'' he said disgustedly. ''He was the only one of the three who wasn't carrying ID We ran his prints through the system and came up empty—which doesn't mean he was a fine, upstanding citizen, just that he didn't have a record. Not in this country, anyway.''

''What do you mean, not in this country?'' She looked over at him sharply, remembering the slight accent she thought she'd detected that night on the bridge. ''How would you know he wasn't an American without ID?''

"The leather jacket he was wearing," Cartwright said. "He'd cut all the labels out of his clothes, but there are people in the garment trade who can practically pinpoint the individual cow a piece of leather came from—differences in breeds, diet, and even the country of origin. Our guy guessed that this jacket was made in Czechoslovakia. We're still checking on manufacturers over there."

"And Czechoslovakia is a trading partner with Russia," Annie said slowly.

"It's a slim connection, but coupled with the fact that the Rubicon is a Russian jewel we're taking it seriously. I just hope their mob isn't somehow involved." He looked grim. "If they are then their next target might be Dmitri Kortachoff. We've already warned him, but he refuses protection."

She frowned. "Why doesn't he cut the show short and get the stone back home where it's safer?"

He shrugged. "Not an easy man to deal with, as you know. He plans to put the Rubicon back on display for the final night of the Treasures of Imperial Russia exhibit tomorrow. Apparently he's arranging a massive gala—a kind of farewell showing, with caviar, fireworks and for all I know the Bolshoi Ballet and the Moscow Circus. Plus the usual collection of diplomats and society types." He sounded morose.

"A security nightmare," Annie said sympathetically. "That kind of event always is. Are you going?"

For the first time in their conversation he dropped his gaze. Studying the ground at his feet with intense interest, he cleared his throat uncomfortably. "Actually that's one of the reasons why I'm here. *You've* been invited, and the message from our government is that they would be grateful if you'd accept. You're to be somewhat of an honored guest, from what I gather, and if you turn Kortachoff down it could be construed as a snub.'' He looked pleadingly at her. ''It'll only be for a couple of hours, but he wants to thank you in public for your help in returning the Rubicon.''

''Great.'' She ran her fingers through her bangs impatiently. ''The last time I saw the man he accused me of being a thief, and now he wants to give me the royal treatment in front of a bunch of photographers because it'll be good publicity. I guess I don't really have a choice, do I?''

''Not really.'' Cartwright grinned in relief and opened his car door. ''Bring me back a doggy-bag of Beluga caviar, will you?''

She'd been half-expecting him to mention Matt, but she was relieved that he hadn't. She wouldn't have known how to react. She hadn't even been able to confide in Bridie about what had happened, and she was afraid that just hearing his name would be too much for her shaky self-control right now.

She still could see his face every time she closed her eyes. She still felt the pain of his betrayal as sharply as she had the night he'd confessed to her. She wasn't over him, and maybe she never would be, Annie told herself wearily.

She watched as Cartwright got into his car and backed out of the driveway, but just as he was about to pull onto the street he rolled down his window and called out to her.

''I almost forgot to tell you—Matt's your official escort for tomorrow night. He'll pick you up at eight.''

He ignored her suddenly outraged expression with a sketchy wave and pulled away from the curb, his tires giving a little squawk as he drove off.

Good old honest Jack Cartwright, Annie fumed. He'd blindsided her. Whether he had guessed any of the details or not, he knew that *something* had happened between her and Logan. Just the fact that he'd been unaccompanied by his partner the few times that he'd come by to talk to her and Bridie this last week was proof of that. He must have known that she would never have accepted Kortachoff's invitation if he'd told her up front what it entailed.

She'd realized that there was a chance she'd come face to face with Logan again at some time during the investigation, but to be forced into a social situation with him was asking too much. There had to be some way she could get out of this, she told herself.

A moment later she sighed in frustration. Short of shooting herself in the foot, she didn't have a hope of dodging the invitation. It was a request from the State Department. However unofficially they might have phrased it, she had no trouble imagining the bureaucratic displeasure her refusal would incur.

She had to go through with it. She just didn't know how.

How was she going to be able to look at him without reliving that terrible moment when she'd realized that everything between them had been based on a lie? How was she supposed to forget, even for an evening, that what he'd done had completely violated her trust?

Most importantly, how was she going to pretend that she wasn't in love with the man anymore, Annie thought hopelessly. To pull *that* deception off, her acting skills would have to be on a par with his.

Her head jerked up and her eyes narrowed. For the first time in days she felt a tiny spark of spirit stirring below the despondency.

If she could persuade him that he hadn't broken her heart, at least she'd be able to walk away from the situation with some dignity. Maybe she wouldn't ever be able to think of Matt Logan without an aching sense of loss, but she might not feel such grinding betrayal and humiliation if she was able to encounter him without falling to pieces.

"You've got a nasty glint in your eye, sis." Bridie looked up as Annie strode into the kitchen. "What's the matter?" Her face suddenly paled. "Did Agent Cartwright tell you something that you're hiding from me?"

"Nothing like that." Annie shot her sister a reassuring smile. It felt forced. "I'm supposed to go to a gala at the Treasures of Imperial Russia tomorrow night. There's no way I can get out of it. Where's Mary Margaret?"

It was an automatic question these days. Whenever the little girl was out of sight the whole family felt uneasy. She wondered how long it would take before the fear subsided.

"She's in her room drawing. Why don't you go in and keep her company until dinner's ready?" Bridie wheeled over to the fridge distractedly. "I'm worried about her."

"Me too." Annie took a carrot from the colander on the counter and bit off the end. She looked down at the lump of brown fur curled up morosely under the kitchen table. "She won't even let Mutt in with her. Before this happened she seemed to love that dog, but now she refuses to look at him. Are the nightmares still continuing?"

"Every night." Bridie paused, her blue eyes clouded. "The counsellor at the clinic says not to expect too much too soon and I know it'll take time for her to get over the trauma, but I can't help thinking there's something else there—something she's keeping locked up inside."

Her blood ran cold. "But she was checked out at the hospital. She hadn't been—"

"Not *that*." Bridie's voice shook. "Thank God, not that. But I always could tell when she was trying to keep a secret, and that's the feeling I'm getting now."

Her sister was right, Annie thought as she knocked at Mary Margaret's door a minute later. There *was* something secretive about the little girl's behavior that seemed even more concrete than the after-effects of a kidnapping ordeal, as hard as that naturally would be for a child to deal with. And it tied in with the dog somehow. Her reaction to the stray was completely opposite to her former adoration of him. She seemed almost…almost *afraid* of him. But that was ridiculous. A week ago she'd been begging for permission to let him into the house.

"Hi, Champ. Can I come in?" Her niece was sitting at the play table that Pat Ryan had built for her, her small blond head bent in concentration over a sheet of paper. Colored pencils were spilled on the floor beside her.

"Sure." Mary Margaret looked past her aunt and her eyes widened. "But not him, okay?"

Annie shut the door behind her, ignoring the pleading look in Mutt's soulful gaze. She heard him settle down outside the room as she walked over to Mary Margaret.

"No problem. What are you drawing?"

"Nothing. I'm just doodling." The child closed the pad of paper firmly. "Just stupid stuff."

Her apathetic attitude was only to be expected, the counsellor had told them. But again Annie was struck by the secretiveness Mary Margaret was exhibiting, so far removed from her former open and confiding personality. Something was badly wrong.

Outside the door Mutt gave a little whine. Mary Margaret looked fearfully at the door.

"Don't worry, he can't get in." She looked over at her niece's white face and her heart turned over in pity. "Come and sit on the bed with me. Let's cuddle."

Stiffly Mary Margaret sat on the edge of the bed. As Annie put her arms around the little shoulders she felt a tremble running through them. The child was *terrified*, she thought, shocked. She was scared to death of the dog on the other side of the door. It made no sense, but logic wasn't the issue here.

"You know what I'm going to do?" She squeezed Mary Margaret to her tightly. "I'm going to take Mutt down to the animal shelter so that he can be adopted by another family. I only let him into the house because I thought you wanted him, Champ, but I was wrong, wasn't I?"

"I used to like him." Mary Margaret's voice was barely audible. "But that's when I thought he was a dog."

Annie felt a chill run through her at the strange pronouncement, but she was careful to keep her tone low and steady and her arms reassuringly around the little girl. "He looks like a dog to me. What is he really?"

Instead of answering, Mary Margaret nodded towards her sketch pad on the desk. Her shoulders shook.

"Can I look? Did you draw a picture of him?" She was feeling her way in the dark here, she thought in trepidation. She wasn't a professional, but this was the first time Mary Margaret had revealed even a glimpse of the fear she'd kept locked inside her, and the moment might not come again. Very carefully she reached over for the pad, one arm still around the trembling shoulders. She flipped open the first page, and then the second and the third.

The pictures were all the same. They were crudely drawn—a child's depiction of terror—but their very ineptness made them all the more frightening. Over and over again Mary Margaret had outlined a wolf's head, fangs bared, tongue lolling past the razor-sharp teeth, ears flat to the head. In each the wolf's eyes were bloodred and glittering.

"It comes at night." She had her head averted from the pictures, and she was staring at the floor. Her words were whispered. "It comes into my dreams, looking for me."

Annie felt like she was on the edge of a precipice. One false step and not only would she fall, but she could take Mary Margaret down with her. It was crucial she gave the right response—but how could she arm a terror-stricken child against the demons in her mind? Obviously the wolf stood for the ordeal she'd been put through, and she was reliving it in her nightmares, but adult platitudes were no weapon against the strength of a child's imagination.

Only fire could fight fire, she thought slowly. A symbolic enemy could only be vanquished by a symbolic ally. She reached over for one of Mary Margaret's colored pencils and began drawing.

"In the olden days there used to be wolves in some countries," she said in a low tone, her hand moving rapidly over the page. Mary Margaret's shoulders were still tense, but out of the corner of her eye Annie saw that she was darting glances at the sketch pad. "In cold countries, like Russia. People were afraid of them, just like you are. Wolves are pretty scary, aren't they?"

"Yeah," Mary Margaret breathed. Now her attention was fully fixed on the drawing that was emerging under her aunt's hand. "They run faster than people can."

"They do. But you know what runs just as fast or faster than a wolf?" Annie asked casually. "Dogs. And so the people in those countries bred a special kind of dog—a dog that would fight the wolves and protect them. They called them wolfhounds. And wherever they went, their wolfhounds went with them to guard them and keep the wolves away."

She angled the page so that Mary Margaret could see what she'd drawn, wondering suddenly if she was doing the right thing. Her picture was lurid and melodramatic, but no more so than the original wolf's head in the corner of the page. Now, however, there was another sketch spreading over the rest of the paper. It showed two dog-like creatures—she'd never said she was an artist, Annie thought defensively—who had obviously been engaged in a fight to the end. Lying on the ground, eyes closed in death, was the frightening animal that Mary Margaret had drawn compulsively so many times. But now he looked shrunken and small, and standing over him was another animal—a small brown dog, battered and torn, but lifting his muzzle in a victory howl.

Mary Margaret took the sketch pad from her and moved out of the circle of her arm. Her little body was stiff, her gaze intensely blue as she stared at it.

Oh, God, she'd probably done completely the wrong thing, Annie thought in consternation. Maybe she should have just explained that nightmares weren't real, that the wolf was only in Mary Margaret's mind. She held her breath, waiting for a reaction.

"I gave you that dog key-chain to protect you when I was a little kid. I told you he'd keep the bad guys away, remember?" The small blond head was still bent over the picture.

"I'm still here, aren't I? I guess it worked," Annie said shakily. "But maybe I should give him back to you for a while."

"This one would be better. He looks like Mutt." Mary Margaret sounded thoughtful. "He's got the same kind of brown eyes."

"Let's see." Annie peered over her niece's shoulder and nodded. "I think he does, a bit. That's how you can tell that he's strong at heart. His eyes are clear and true."

"If he stayed with me at night I guess that wolf might not even show up, huh?" Mary Margaret looked up at her with a flash of her old spirit. "He'd kick that wolf's butt right out of town."

"Out of town? Right up to the moon, more like," Annie laughed weakly, feeling a sudden spurt of moisture behind her eyes. She wrapped her arms around Mary Margaret and pulled her close. "What do you say, Champ?"

In the hallway Mutt let out a gusty sigh, still keeping vigil. Mary Margaret wriggled out of her aunt's grasp and ran to the door. She opened it and looked down at the small dog staring hopefully up at her. She dropped to her knees and put her arms around him, staring solemnly into his nondescript face.

"Clear and true. That's what my Aunt Annie said, and she's right. But your name's not Mutt anymore." She glanced over at Annie. "From now on we have to call him Buddy—the same name as Dad's dog. Do you think Dad would mind, Aunt Annie?"

"No, Champ." Annie swallowed, her eyes dwelling on the tough little figure in the ripped jeans and the mongrel gazing up at her adoringly. "No, I think your Dad would like that just fine. Let's go tell your Mom we've got us a guard dog."

The healing wasn't complete—not by a long shot, she thought as she followed them down the hall to the kitchen. She heard Bridie's surprised exclamation and her father's lower tones, and suddenly she felt weak with gratitude. No, the healing wasn't complete, but it had started. They'd come close to losing Mary Margaret altogether, and nothing would have been worse than that. Despite everything else he'd done, if it hadn't been for Logan the child could have been lost to them forever.

She owed him for that, and it was a debt she could never repay, Annie told herself. What had happened between the two of them couldn't erase what he'd done for her and her family.

But it still would have been easier if she didn't have to

see the man again. From now on Buddy would protect Mary Margaret against her own imagination, she thought wryly. Too bad there wasn't anything on earth that could protect someone against her own heart.

Chapter Fifteen

"Wicked lethal, sis. The man doesn't stand a chance." Bridie let her wheelchair roll back a foot to get a better view of her sister. "I bet the old credit card took a whaling today, but it was worth it."

Annie looked at her reflection in the mirror on the back of the bedroom door. Her credit card hadn't just taken a whaling, it was out for the count, but it *had* been worth it. The mocha silk slip-dress was bias-cut and skimmed her body like lingerie. The spaghetti-straps kept slipping over her shoulders, and in the boutique where she'd bought it she'd kept pushing them back into place until the salesgirl had dryly told her that they were meant to look sexy.

"Yeah, we Ryan girls clean up good, don't we? But the only man I'm out to impress tonight is Dmitri Kortachoff. As long as he and the State Department are happy, then I've done my duty."

"Right. And Matt Logan has nothing to do with this," Bridie said innocently. "Are you wearing a bra under that thing?"

"Jeez, Bridie!" Annie said, her face flooding with color. "I'm buck naked under it, what do you think?"

"So that's how you bounty hunters get your man. I always wondered."

Last night while they'd been washing up the supper dishes together, she'd told Bridie a little of what had happened between her and Logan, but her sister's reaction hadn't been what Annie had expected. In fact, she'd defended Logan.

"He could have handled the situation better, sure. But the man's an FBI agent, for God's sake—posing as his brother was his cover. He told you as soon as he could, right?" she'd argued.

She'd been operating on the misconception that all they'd shared had been a few heated kisses. Her attitude might have been different if she'd known the whole story, Annie thought, but not even with Bridie was she willing to share every intimate detail of what had occurred.

Still, there was some truth in what her sister was saying now. The dress, flimsy as it was, was armor. She was going to look good tonight if it killed her, she thought grimly as she slipped into a pair of strappy high heels that looked capable of doing just that. They added height. Height was an asset. She needed all the assets she could muster just to survive this night.

She hadn't wanted this last encounter with Logan, but since it had been forced on her, she was going to carry it off with style, grace and dignity.

She took a tentative step towards the mirror and nearly turned her ankle.

"You gotta get out more often, sis," Bridie clucked sympathetically. "Or at least wear something with a higher heel than Keds sometimes. It's been a while, but if I remember rightly you have to let your hips do the work."

"You *are* talking about walking, aren't you?" Annie ground out. She took another cautious step. It wasn't that hard, she thought in relief. She could do this. Maybe she couldn't run down Benny Lopez in these things, but she could certainly pose for a few photographs, stand around nibbling caviar and sipping champagne for an hour, and ensure that Matt Logan's final impression of her was tinged with regret at his own loss rather than pity for her.

Giving him a few sweat-soaked, sleepless nights wouldn't be a bad idea either, she thought, narrowing her eyes at her reflection. She let a spaghetti-strap slide off one shoulder....

"Aunt Annie looks different," Mary Margaret announced seriously from the doorway, Buddy at her side like a shadow. "Is that underwear?"

"No, it's a dress. Just barely," her mother said with a gleam in her eye. "Aunt Annie's a babe out for revenge tonight, sweetie."

"I get it. She's like Arnold in the *Terminator* movies, right?" Mary Margaret nodded wisely and turned to go. "Oh, yeah. Matt's here." She imparted this last scrap of information casually as she sauntered back down the hall.

Not exactly the cool and sophisticated meeting she'd planned, Annie thought a moment later as she entered the kitchen and found him leaning against the counter, surrounded by a sea of Ryans and one small brown dog. It looked more like a Norman Rockwell painting. *Sis Lands a Date* might be an appropriate title, she thought in chagrin. All she needed was a big pink corsage pinned to her dress.

But in the split-second before he lifted his gaze to hers, she realized that as hokey as the family scene was, he was enjoying it. She saw him grin at something her father had said, while ruffling the top of Mary Margaret's hair absently. He wouldn't have had this, growing up, she realized in sudden comprehension. The close-knit support and unconditional trust that was so much a part of her life was something he'd never experienced.

Hold it right there, Ryan, she told herself brutally. The

last thing she needed was to start making excuses for the man, especially when just the sight of him was already making her feel ridiculously vulnerable.

And then he looked across the room at her, and vulnerable didn't come anywhere close to how she felt. For a moment it was as if everything and everyone around them had melted away, leaving only her and Logan.

He looked...*perfect,* she thought helplessly. It wasn't fair, dammit! He was wearing a dark suit with a dark shirt and tie, and the lack of contrast was elegantly and devastatingly attractive.

"Aunt Annie's a babe, huh?" Mary Margaret said proudly, breaking into the sudden lull in the conversation.

Okay, let me die now, Annie thought in furious embarrassment. *Or at least sink through the floor before my darling niece delivers any more cute one-liners here.*

"We should be going—" she started to say briskly, but Logan interrupted her.

"Yeah, your Aunt Annie's a babe, all right. But this isn't the first time I noticed it." He gave Mary Margaret's hair a last ruffle, and pushed himself away from the counter, his eyes still on Annie. "Ready?"

It seemed an eternity before they were in the car and out of the driveway, but it probably only seemed that long because she remembered that Mary Margaret had heard Bridie's revenge remark, and she was suddenly positive that it was fated to be shared with Logan too. It wasn't until they were a few blocks away from her house that she felt safe.

"What are the rules tonight?" His voice was velvet-smooth, and immediately any illusion of safety fled.

"What do you mean?" she asked suspiciously.

"I know you got shanghaied into attending this damned function—if it makes you feel any better, I wasn't given a choice either." He glanced over at her. "I realize I'm the last man on earth you want to be with."

She gave him a cool look. "You're my official escort for the evening, Logan, because we both had a hand in returning the Rubicon to the Russians. I see this as good public relations, not a date."

"Okay." His hands tightened on the steering wheel, but his tone was even. They drove in silence for a few minutes before he spoke again. "So the rules are I can't tell you that when you walked out on me the other night, I knew I'd just lost the only woman I'd ever want?"

With an immense effort of will, Annie looked casually out the window at the passing cars. He was good, she thought. He didn't waste time in sparring, he went for the jugular straight away. But it wasn't going to work. Where Logan was concerned, she was ready for anything.

"Right. If you told me that you'd be breaking the rules." She didn't look over at him.

"Asking you if there's any way you could give me another chance—that's out of line too," he said after another silence.

"Good guess, Logan."

Her words were clipped. She saw with relief that they were almost at the museum, the sidewalk outside it thronged with arriving guests. Tiny lights twinkled in the ornamental bushes that flanked the entrance, giving the sedate street a formally festive atmosphere. A few more minutes and she'd be surrounded by strangers, Annie thought. There was safety in numbers—she'd be able to regain her self-control as soon as she got away from the forced intimacy of sitting here alone with the man.

"Hell, I'm breaking the damn rules anyway. What have I got to lose?" Logan said tersely. He pulled the car into a parking spot and switched off the engine in one swift movement. He turned to her, and suddenly she could see the lines of strain etched on his features. "Annie, I knew I'd only get one opportunity to say this and I wanted to give you more time. Tonight's too soon—I wasn't sure you'd even be speaking to me. But we're here together now and just being close to you is tearing me apart." His voice was rough with emotion. "If I could relive the last week and a half I'd do it all differently, believe me."

"But you didn't. You didn't trust me with the truth, and now I'm finding it hard to trust you, Logan," she said in a low voice. "I might want you. I might even love you. But the trust is gone, and without that everything else is worthless."

She raised her gaze to his, and saw the shuttered look come down behind his eyes. "That's pretty clear, then," he said softly. "But if you're ever looking for a man who's stupid enough to have messed up the one good thing in his life, who's terrified of heights, and who'll always be in love with you, just say the word. I'll be there." He smiled tightly at her, his eyes dark green and unreadable. "Let's get this over with, Annie."

Without another word he got out of the car and walked around to her door. As they entered the Danninger Museum's opulent foyer, with its crush of perfumed guests, she wanted nothing more than to turn tail and run—straight back to her own home, her own bedroom, her own pillow that she could soak with her own tears. Had she just made the biggest mistake of her life?

Later, she told herself, pasting a social smile on her face. Later she'd ask herself that question. But right now she had a duty to perform.

The next hour passed in a blur of sound and color. Vaguely, she realized that they were being introduced to people as the heroes who had recovered the Rubicon, and, as if she was in a daze, she accepted the thanks of a group of dignitaries from the Russian government who kissed her hand and paid her flowery compliments in strongly accented English. But nothing seemed real. She still felt as if she was back in the car with Logan, hearing the raw honesty in his voice and seeing the pain on his features.

Surely they weren't expected to stay for the whole party, she thought wretchedly, looking around at the laughing, chattering throng that crowded the exhibit room. The glittering chandelier overhead and the spotlights focused on the display cases were harshly brilliant, the room uncomfortably warm. And Logan was no longer at her side.

During the numerous introductions he'd become separated from her. She could see him across the room talking to Dmitri Kortachoff, a politely bored smile on his face and those incredible green eyes half-veiled by his lashes. The hard planes of his cheekbones and the broad shoulders under his jacket were a marked contrast with Kortachoff's sleekly distinguished good looks. Annie saw his hand reach unconsciously to his lapel and then stop. She knew instantly that he'd been checking his gun out of habit, forgetting that he wasn't wearing it tonight.

Their eyes met across the room as he saw that she'd noticed the gesture, and he smiled wryly at her before he turned his attention back to Kortachoff.

The tiny, unspoken exchange hadn't lasted a second. But in it was the answer to the question she'd been asking herself for the last hour. She turned blindly towards the brocade-hung windows behind her and fumbled behind the thick draperies.

When she'd been here previously she'd seen that they led out onto a small balcony, and as her hand found the latch she slipped behind the heavy curtains and stepped outside into the cool night air. She closed the window behind her and took a deep breath.

What had just passed between them hadn't needed words. Each of them had known what the other was thinking, as if they were two halves of a temporarily separated whole. It was the way she'd felt the first time she'd met him, Annie remembered. No matter that he'd been going under another name, when she'd looked at him she'd felt as if he was seeing right into her soul, past the defenses and the shields, to the person she was inside. And she'd seen the man she'd been looking for all her life—the same man who'd just held her gaze across a crowded room a few seconds ago.

Logan had held on to his defenses a little longer than she had. But if she needed any proof that they were down for good, he'd given it to her in his ironically self-deprecating assessment an hour ago.

A man who's stupid enough to have messed up the one good thing in his life, who's terrified of heights, and who'll always be in love with you.

She'd wanted trust from him. With those few words he'd entrusted her with his whole heart, and in that moment nothing else had mattered anymore.

She had to find him. She had to tell him how she felt, Annie thought suddenly, before she spent one more lonely second away from him. Swiftly she turned from the balcony railing.

Her heart gave a frightened lunge in her chest.

In the shadows between the glass and the heavy draperies inside was the figure of a man. Even as she watched, the window opened and Dmitri Kortachoff stepped out onto the balcony with her, closing the massive glass pane behind him.

"Miss Ryan?" He sounded concerned. "Forgive me for

startling you. It is a great success, the gala, but I also found the room a little stifling.''

He cleared his throat nervously, his former suavity apparently having deserted him. The lights from the courtyard below were the only illumination cutting through the shadows on the balcony, and she saw him fumble in his pocket for something. He held out a cigarette package toward her.

''Do you smoke?''

''No. No thanks, I don't,'' she said awkwardly. She knew what was coming, she thought in resignation. As much as she wanted to find Logan right now, Dmitri Kortachoff obviously was steeling himself for an apology for the last time they'd met. If the condemnation he'd rained down on her head when he'd accused her of stealing the Rubicon was any indication, she was in for a verbose ten minutes, at least. She leaned back against the railing and fixed a polite smile on her face.

''I owe you a debt of gratitude that all the jewels on display in there could not wipe out,'' he said, extracting a cigarette and waving his hand towards the curtained window. ''But how did I repay you? By hurling a false accusation at you—by jumping to the conclusion that you had stolen the Rubicon. All I can say in my own defense is that the loss of the gem had completely devastated me. Can you accept my humble thanks—and my apologies?''

The man was sincerely troubled, she realized with a twinge of compassion. His hand was trembling slightly, and his voice shook with real emotion. It had been an unsettling episode in his life, too, she told herself. She injected a note of warmth into her response.

''Please, Mr. Kortachoff—the sapphire is back where it belongs, and the incident is over as far as I'm concerned. It was gracious of you to invite me tonight to see the Rubicon one last time.''

"If not for you and the FBI agent, there would have been no reason for this celebration," he said somberly. He tapped his cigarette thoughtfully on the package and shot her a keen glance. "But you also have something to be thankful for, yes? I am glad that your niece was returned safely—I would have felt somehow responsible if the Rubicon had brought tragedy to your family."

The kidnapping had been kept out of the media, but he would have been informed of it, Annie knew. She nodded in reply.

"Mary Margaret was badly frightened, but thank goodness she wasn't physically hurt. It'll take a while for her to get over it, though."

"No clues as to who did this to her?" When she shook her head he exhaled sharply. "Scum. I heard that the accomplices were killed, but I could not find it in my heart to feel sorry for their deaths. Men like that are expendable."

She saw the gleam of his teeth in the dark as he smiled apologetically. "Forgive me again. This cannot be a pleasant subject for you, and tonight we must only think of pleasant things. The Rubicon flies back to Russia with me tomorrow and it may be some time before I return to America again. So we shall join the party and celebrate, yes?"

He wasn't so bad, she thought as he moved forward to open the heavy window for her. He still didn't seem totally at ease with her, but he had sounded sincerely troubled by the kidnapping.

She smiled at him as he lifted the latch with one hand and with the other flicked an expensive-looking lighter to the cigarette in his mouth.

"I hope your last night in Boston leaves you with happier memories than the rest of your stay here—" She broke off, staring numbly at the lighter in his hand.

She'd seen it *dozens* of times. She'd seen that boldly enamelled wolf's head, with its lolling tongue and snarling jaws just yesterday—on page after page of Mary Margaret's sketchbook. The bloodred eyes were rubies, glinting in the flare of the flame.

She had to tell Logan. And most importantly, she couldn't let Kortachoff know that she'd guessed his deadly secret. Even as the frantic thought ran through her mind, she saw him pull the window closed again.

"I too had hoped that my last night in Boston would bring only good memories," he said slowly. "But the child saw something, didn't she? What was it? This?"

He stood against the exit from the balcony, barring her way, and looked at the lighter in his hand. He shrugged in resignation and slipped it into his pocket, and when his hand came back out Annie saw the snub-nosed shape of a gun in his hand.

"An indulgence of mine that I now must pay for," he said regretfully. "The head of the wolf used to be on the crest of my family in tsarist Russia, and I thought it would be amusing to have it on certain of my personal possessions. There was a brief period when the sedation was wearing off and I wondered if the child had seen anything. Tell me, Miss Ryan—what else does she know?"

"Nothing," Annie said through frozen lips. "She doesn't even have a real memory of that. She's just had nightmares about wolves chasing her, Kortachoff, but she's no threat to you."

"I believe you." He smiled at her in the shadows, the silver at his temples catching what little light there was from the courtyard below. "If she'd known anything more, I would have already been detained by your Agent Logan. No, Miss Ryan, the only threat to my leaving the country tomorrow is you. And so we must resolve our problem."

"I get the feeling the immediate problem is more mine than yours, Kortachoff." She looked over her shoulder at the drop to the cobbled courtyard far below. "After all, you've got the gun and I've only got a few seconds to live. That *is* the plan, isn't it?"

Keep the guy talking, Ryan. Buy time, and figure out what to do with it as you go along.

It was sound advice, especially since she didn't have any other options, she thought. And while she was at it, she'd try to slip out of these damn high heels, just in case.

"That's the plan. But you have more than a few seconds, Miss Ryan."

"Why the bonus?" Annie asked skeptically.

"In three minutes, at nine o'clock exactly, there will be a fireworks display set off at the front of the building and everyone will be watching it from the windows on the other side of the room." He tapped his cigarette ash carelessly. "Symbolic, you understand—all the colors of the Treasures of Imperial Russia jewels. We were given special permission by the city, and it should be very beautiful. Very distracting, too," he added. "Any gunshot will be assumed to be part of the bursting of the rockets. That is how you say it, am I right? Rockets?"

"If I've only got three minutes left, I'm not spending them teaching you the finer points of the English language." Annie edged closer to the window, but he waved her back impatiently with the gun. "Why don't you satisfy my curiosity and tell me how you got involved in the kidnapping of a little girl?"

She couldn't keep the anger from her voice, but he merely shrugged. "Why not? It will pass the time. At the time I had your niece kidnapped, I still thought that you were working together somehow with the thief."

"Lucky Logan?" She slipped her left foot surreptitiously

out of her shoe and braced herself on the railing behind her. He still didn't realize that Matt had been impersonating his brother, she realized. "You had him followed the same day I tailed him. The biker saw us on the bridge together and thought we had the jewel, didn't he? That's why he tried to kill us—because you wanted the Rubicon back right from the start."

"Exactly. Vladimir Solsky was a young Russian I knew here in Boston who had some unsavory connections. I hired him for the job." Kortachoff drew on his cigarette and glanced at the gold Rolex on his wrist before continuing. "Of course, now I know that your involvement was totally innocent, but you gave me the leverage I needed in the end. I had to return the true Rubicon to a South American client of mine who was threatening to expose me."

Her right foot was almost bare, but at the Russian's casual confession she froze. Her thoughts were chaotic, but suddenly all the pieces fell into place and her eyes widened incredulously.

"I don't believe it. For once Lucky was telling the truth," she breathed. "The stone in the exhibit *was* the fake, wasn't it? You'd sold the real one long ago."

"Not only the Rubicon, but that was the most lucrative sale, yes," Kortachoff smiled thinly. "However, when the theft of the substitute from the exhibit was made known to my Argentinean client, he thought that I had arranged both thefts in order to re-sell the stone."

"Because of the provenance." She recalled what Lucky had told them. "As soon as the fake was stolen, your client knew that the one stolen from him could be sold at its true value."

"He was correct, except for believing that I was involved. But there was no way to convince the man I wasn't trying to double-cross him." Dmitri Kortachoff sighed, and tossed his cigarette over the railing in a shower of sparks. "That's when I had to promise that I would get the real Rubicon back to him to stop him from informing my government that for years I had been selling the jewels, one by one. And so I contacted Vladimir once more, and he and the other two took the child. I only saw her once, you know. It's just your bad luck that she gave you a clue to my identity."

Lucky Logan had done it, Annie thought desperately. He'd scrambled over these rooftops, climbing around the crazily pitched angles and running across the slippery slate tiles. The day she'd returned the substitute Rubicon she'd stood on the sidewalk and wondered how he'd ever had the nerve to take such an insane risk.

Now she was going to find out for herself. Cold fear trickled through her as she darted a furtive glance at the drop from the balcony. If she jumped to the left, she had a good chance of making the adjoining roof four feet away, and from there she could take cover behind one of the old brick chimneys. A good enough plan, as far as it went, but she didn't have a clue what she was going to do after that.

Of course, if her jump fell short by even a couple of inches, she'd be freefalling through space for a few seconds and then she'd hit the cobblestones of the courtyard. At that point she wouldn't need a part two for her escape plan. She swallowed past the lump in her throat and tried to still the sudden trembling in her knees. She didn't *want* to die.

And she wasn't going to let it happen, she thought with a flash of anger. Iron determination replaced the fear that had gripped her and a calm strength flowed through her. She was going to see Logan again. She was going to walk into his arms and feel them around her, and then she was going to ask him if he still wanted a woman who'd come close to messing up the one good thing in *her* life.

That was the plan. And no perp with a gun was going to screw it up for her.

"How are you going to explain away a dead body, Kortachoff?" Both her feet were bare now and she was watching him intently, waiting for him to make his move. "Logan's not going to leave without me and somebody's bound to check out this balcony eventually."

He cocked his head to one side, obviously listening for something, then frowned and glanced at his watch again. "They're late," he said abstractedly. He smiled at her. "I only need to conceal your death until my flight leaves. I'll tell Agent Logan that I saw you departing with someone else and by the time he learns that you never returned home, I'll be out of his reach."

"Wrong—you'll be extradited and brought back for questioning. You'll never get away with it," Annie said quellingly. Then her eyes widened in understanding. "Except you're not planning to go back to Russia. This was your 'retirement' party, wasn't it?"

He chuckled with real amusement, his teeth gleaming white in the dark. "I like that. Yes, I'm retiring. In fact, Dmitri Kortachoff will cease to exist only a few hours after Annie Ryan ceases to exist. I, however, will merely be exchanging one name for another—one lifestyle for a much more luxurious one. It's what I've been working for all these years—and as much as I'm enjoying your company, I really couldn't let you ruin it all for me at the last moment."

Behind him from the other side of the building, high in the night sky, a thin glowing light sizzled upwards. As it reached the apex of its trajectory, it exploded into a dazzling burst of sapphire blue. Kortachoff lifted the gun.

"*Dos svedanya*, Annie," he said pleasantly.

She uncoiled like a spring. Even as the phrase was leaving his lips, she was moving, her actions all one fluidly agile motion; hoisting herself swiftly onto the fragile iron railing, swinging her legs over to the outside edge of the balcony and, without pausing for balance, leaping across the shadowy abyss towards the neighboring roof. She heard the side seam of her dress rip, the darkness was suddenly tinged with a luminous ruby light as another rocket burst into mosaic-like pieces in the sky above and Kortachoff fired.

She slammed jarringly onto the sharp tiles of the roof, falling to her hands and knees and scrabbling for a handhold. There wasn't one.

"Perfect!" From the balcony behind her came the Russian's low laughter. "A young woman falls to her death— a tragic accident, and much better than my original plan. It seems I'm always thanking you, Miss Ryan."

The sky lit up with a topaz glow. As she slid towards the edge of the roof Annie's desperately searching fingers grasped and held tight on the corner of a partially broken tile. Using every ounce of strength she had and praying the tile would hold, she used the leverage to stop her downward fall and regain her balance. She brought one trembling leg up under her and heaved herself to her feet.

It was like running up a forty-five-degree rock-face. Behind her she heard Kortachoff's annoyed exclamation, and he fired again. She felt something sting her cheek.

He missed, she thought in panicky relief. She'd been cut by a ricocheting piece of tile, but if she could make it to the massive brick chimney-stack just ahead, she'd be safe. Only a couple more steps.

He fired again just as she dodged behind the chimney, holding onto it with both hands to keep from falling down the other side of the roof.

"Now you begin to annoy me, Annie." His voice had

hardened, the spurious charm that he'd displayed earlier no longer in evidence. "But only briefly. Do you know what my hobby is in Russia? Can you guess where I spent my last vacation?"

What was the man talking about? Biting her lip nervously in the dark, she wondered if his mind had snapped. Who cared about his damned vacation, and why would he bring it up now, for heaven's sakes?

She heard a heavy thud and realized that he'd just made the same jump she had. *He was only a few feet away!*

"Rock-climbing in the Ural Mountains." He sounded slightly out of breath, but totally relaxed. "I've done it since I was a boy."

She was on her feet and running along the roofline, looking for another hiding place, but this time her movements felt leaden and futile. The man was an expert, her mind screamed at her. What was the use? She was going to die, whether from one of his bullets or from taking a wrong step in the dark and falling to the stones below. The method didn't really matter.

All that mattered was that she was never going to see Logan again. She was never going to feel his touch, she was never going to hear his voice. Panting, she sank down behind an oddly angled projection. She was out of sight for the moment, but how long it would take before Kortachoff discovered this hiding place and flushed her from it?

A figure melted from the shadows beside her and a hand wrapped around her mouth before she could scream.

"Annie, it's me." He took his hand away and as the sky lit up with an explosion of emerald sparks, the familiar green eyes narrowed in concern. "Are you all right?"

"*Logan!*" She stared at him wildly. "How—what are you—" She felt her lips tremble and her voice came out in a broken whisper. "I thought I'd never see you again. How did you get here?"

"I was looking for you downstairs. When I went out into the courtyard I looked up just in time to see you jump," he said in a low tone, his eyes closing briefly at the memory. "When my damn heart started beating again I broke into this building and found an opening onto the roof. Listen—when I give you the word, start heading toward that chimney. Just beyond it is a flat area with an open trapdoor. You'll be safe once you reach it."

"Kortachoff's an expert climber," Annie said vehemently. "What exactly are you planning to do while I'm running away?"

"I'm going to take him down, one way or another," Logan said. His tone was flat. He slipped out of his jacket and quickly removed his tie. "I don't want to give the bastard anything to grab hold of."

"Logan, I'm not leaving—"

"You don't stand a chance, Miss Ryan. Please, let us put an end to this foolishness before it gets tedious." Kortachoff's accent was thicker, his words laced with impatience. The sound of his sure footsteps came closer. "Why keep fighting the inevitable—"

Brilliant diamond starbursts pierced the black velvet of the night as his bulky silhouette came around the corner, and at the same moment Logan rose from his crouching position like a tiger springing towards its prey.

"*Run*, Annie! Run like hell—*now!*"

He knocked Kortachoff's arm upwards as the Russian fired, and she saw the blue-and-orange muzzle-flash of the shot just miss him. As he recognized his opponent, a swift look of surprise crossed Kortachoff's features, but then he lunged.

Matt Logan still didn't know the first thing about her if

he thought she was going to run out on him, Annie thought grimly, edging her way towards them. If she could grab Kortachoff's leg and destroy, even for a moment, that highly proficient climber's balance of his, Logan could make a move for the gun. But as the rudimentary plan formed in her mind, she saw that he'd moved in on the Russian, the two of them grappling each other in a desperate battle for control.

If Kortachoff went down, the man she loved would fall with him.

And then it happened. Wrenching himself away in a powerful bid for freedom, Dmitri Kortachoff broke out of Logan's hold and took a lightning-fast step backward as he aimed his gun straight at his adversary.

"Matt!"

Annie threw herself at Kortachoff, but even as the scream was ripped from her throat, she saw the Russian's eyes widen in horror as the slate tile he'd stepped onto pulled free. With mountain-goat agility, he tried to regain his footing, but the surface was too treacherous even for him. Arms windmilling wildly, he fell heavily onto his back and started sliding down the steep incline of the roof.

"No, Matt!"

As the Treasures of Imperial Russia fireworks display burst into a flurry of multi-colored explosions, Logan instinctively tried to halt Kortachoff's fatal plunge, but he was too late. His hand closed on thin air as the screaming Russian shot past the edge of the roof into space. Annie caught a glimpse of Kortachoff's distorted features and bulging eyes as he disappeared from view and a split-second later she heard a sickening thud far below.

And then she heard the thin scrabbling sound as another tile slid free, and she saw Logan begin the long slide to destruction that his enemy had just taken. His gaze, desperate and strained, was fixed on her, and his fingers were clutching at the edges of the tiles as he slowly slid farther down.

"Annie, stay back," he whispered hoarsely. His legs were over the edge of the roof as she frantically reached out for him. "Don't come any closer, sweetheart."

Even as he spoke his torso slipped half-way over the edge of the tiles, and then he stopped. As the sky rained down a confetti of scintillating sparks, Annie could see that somehow he had found a precarious handhold.

The slate could snap at any minute. She would watch as the only man she'd ever wanted, the only man she would ever love, fell to his death.

"No damn way!" she hissed in coldly furious denial.

As swiftly as she dared, she made her way back to the projection that they'd hidden behind, and found what she was looking for. There was a sturdy iron bar mortared into the brickwork. With shaking hands she knotted one end of Logan's tie to it as securely as she could.

"You're a bounty hunter, Ryan—you *always* get your man," she muttered ridiculously to herself. "Don't you *dare* lose him this time!"

She made a tight loop in the other end of the tie and slipped it over her wrist. If it held, they had a chance. If it didn't, she thought calmly, she'd die with the man she loved.

"Logan!" On her hands and knees, she maneuvered gingerly back over the roofline and saw his eyes focus on her. Where his shirt had ripped, she could see the muscles in his arms corded with the effort to hold on. She felt the tie pull taut on her wrist and halted. "Grab hold of the jacket. When you're ready, tell me!"

He looked incredulously at the garment she was letting slide towards him, and then one corner of that fabulous mouth lifted in the ghost of a grin. "Mouthy blonde, always barking commands," he said in a cracked voice. "What the hell do I have to do to shut you up, Ryan?"

"Grab the jacket, hold on and I'll show you in a minute, Logan," Annie ordered, her tone peremptory and her eyes blurring with sudden tears. "I said grab the jacket, Mister!"

With one last, loving look at her, he let go of the slate tile. Even as he began to fall, his hand shot out and gripped the sleeve of the jacket a few inches away from him, and immediately Annie felt as if she was being pulled in two different directions.

She couldn't do it—she wasn't anywhere *near* strong enough, she thought in paralyzed fear. She met his eyes again.

In them was complete and total trust.

Slowly, excruciatingly and feeling like her arms were about to give way any second, she pulled with all her strength, praying that the tie would hold, the jacket wouldn't rip, and the iron bar wouldn't give way. She saw him move forward slightly onto the roof, then a little more, and all of a sudden he was bringing his leg up under him and the strain in her muscles eased.

She'd done it. A shrimpy blonde with a tie of Sulka silk, Annie thought lightheadedly, feeling a bubble of ragged laughter rise in her throat. She'd *done* it. All of a sudden a choking sob tore through her and her eyes were filled with tears of relief.

"Hold on to me, sweetheart," Logan said hoarsely. "Let go of the jacket and let me get your other hand free."

He unbound the tie from her wrist and propelled her forward a few feet. Behind the second chimney was a step down onto a flat cinder-strewn roof with an open trap-door leading down into the building.

Her arms felt like spaghetti. She looked down at her

bloody knees, her shredded dress, her bare feet, and then she looked up into Logan's face.

He was smiling down at her, and behind the emerald eyes she saw the man she'd *always* known was there—tough, honest and loving. Gently he pushed back a strand of hair from her scratched cheek and traced the line of her lips with his thumb.

"I thought you were the Logan brother who hated heights," she said unsteadily. "How come you always end up with me on a ledge somewhere?"

"Sweetheart, I was scared spitless up there." He gave a slow grin and pulled her closer. "But if you're wondering whether I'm Lucky, I can show you some proof."

His mouth came down on hers lingeringly and sweetly, and his arms held her with sudden urgency. Then he raised his head and held her gaze with his.

"I'm the Logan brother who hates heights," he said simply. "But I'm also the Logan brother who loves you, Annie. Can't you tell by now?"

His emerald eyes widened slightly as the final rocket burst in the sky overhead, lighting up a little corner of Boston with golden stars. The amethyst eyes staring up at him smiled in total certainty.

"I can tell," Annie whispered, pulling him back down. "But show me again, Logan."

Epilogue

Lucky Logan caught his brother's eye from across the room and raised his glass in a silent salute that included the radiant blonde in white satin and lace standing beside him. Matt looked like a different man, he thought pensively. He looked younger and more relaxed than he'd ever seen him. Hell, big brother was actually *laughing*.

He took a sip of champagne and scanned the crowd. The angel with the red-gold hair sitting at a table with Jack Cartwright was out-of-bounds, he told himself glumly, watching Bridie rise to her feet with the help of a cane and Jack's ready arm. She obviously wasn't interested in anyone but the man she was with. Another wedding looming, he thought, draining his glass. At least he wouldn't be expected to be Cartwright's best man, even if he *had* been working with him these last couple of months.

How Matt had swung the deal for him he'd never know, but his brother had not only saved his sorry butt from a jail sentence, he'd also finessed a new career for him. Special Consultant Lucky Logan, assigned to liaison duty between insurance operatives and the FBI on major jewel heists. Right now he was still on probation with the Bureau, and they were watching his every move. He couldn't even pause to tie his shoe outside a jewelry store without being questioned about it the next day.

He sighed. Turning over a new leaf was proving to be even harder than he'd figured, but he'd stick it out. Somehow after that Rubicon caper he hadn't wanted to continue in the profession anyway. His glance lighted on the towheaded little girl a few tables away and his expression softened.

Mary Margaret. Cute kid—and she'd nearly lost her life over that damned stone. His green eyes clouded with memory for a second, and then he saw what she was doing and he grinned. Her flower-girl garland discarded on the floor beside her, she was cutting a pack of cards like a pro for the group of kids around the table. Even as he watched, she palmed a card and stuck it under the collar of the brown mutt lying by her feet.

Now he knew how she'd beaten him in six straight games of Go Fish last week when he'd been at the Ryan house.

On the other side of the room Matt was looking down into Annie's eyes, and then he suddenly bent his head and kissed her, long and hard. This was it, Lucky thought curiously. This was the real thing between his brother and the woman he'd just married. He hadn't really believed in it before, but here it was, right in front of him.

True love. It actually existed, and his brother had found it.

"Gorgeous couple, aren't they?" The brunette drifted up beside him in a cloud of Opium perfume, gesturing with her champagne glass at Matt and Annie. Then her glance turned towards Lucky and she gave a little astonished giggle. "Oh, my God—twins! That's right, someone told me you two were brothers."

She was a looker, Lucky thought. Big blue eyes, long

·legs, and an extremely kissable mouth. And she didn't seem to have an escort. He wished she'd lose the giggle, but what the heck. He let a slow, one-sided grin lift the corner of his mouth.

"That's right, darlin'. We're brothers. He's taken, but I'm still available."

She giggled again and swayed against him. "Okay, so let me guess. If he's Matt Logan, then you must be Lucky, right?"

He raised his eyes to the sight of his brother lifting his mouth from Annie's. It was as if the two of them were in a world of their own, he thought. They didn't even know there was a roomful of people around them.

Lifting a couple of glasses of champagne from the tray of a passing waiter, he nodded towards Matt and Annie. "You got us mixed up, darlin'. I'm Liam Logan." His smile was tinged with a sudden wry regret. "*He's* the lucky one."

Looking For More Romance?

Visit Romance.net

Look us up on-line at: http://www.romance.net

Check in daily for these and other exciting features:

Hot off the press

View all current titles, and purchase them on-line.

What do the stars have in store for you?

Horoscope

Hot deals

Exclusive offers available only at Romance.net

Plus, don't miss our interactive quizzes, contests and bonus gifts.

PWEB

Come escape with Harlequin's new

Series Sampler

Four great full-length Harlequin novels bound together in one fabulous volume and at an unbelievable price.

Be transported back in time with a Harlequin Historical® novel, get caught up in a mystery with Intrigue®, be tempted by a hot, sizzling romance with Harlequin Temptation®, or just enjoy a down-home all-American read with American Romance®.

You won't be able to put this collection down!

On sale February 2000 at your favorite retail outlet.

◆ HARLEQUIN®
Makes any time special ™

Visit us at www.romance.net

PHESC

*Amnesia…an unknown danger…
a burning desire.*

With

HARLEQUIN®

I N T R I G U E®

you're just

A MEMORY AWAY

from passion, danger…and love!

**Look for all the books in this
exciting miniseries:**

**THE BABY SECRET (#546)
by Joyce Sullivan**
On sale December 1999

**A NIGHT WITHOUT END (#552)
by Susan Kearney**
On sale January 2000

**FORGOTTEN LULLABY (#556)
by Rita Herron**
On sale February 2000

A MEMORY AWAY…—where
remembering the truth becomes
a matter of life, death…and love!

Available at your favorite retail outlet.

HARLEQUIN®
Makes any time special ™

Visit us at www.romance.net

HIAMA3